The Hostage

Greece, 1107 BC

Fiction by Kathryn Berck

The Hostage

Kathryn Berck

Peryton, Part One

Cover photo Shutterstock.com
Author photo Bil Sullivan Photography

ISBN-13: 978-1544641393
ISBN-10: 1544641397

kathrynberck.com

For Mel Gilden, Michael Davis and Monique High, each for a very different reason. For my known accomplice, editor emeritus Michael Carr. And for Cecelia Holland, who led the way.

The Peryton has a deer's head and forelegs, but the body, wings and feathers of a huge bird. When flying, it always casts the shadow of a man, because it carries the spirit of one who died far from home and who cannot rest in alien soil. The peryton is a fierce hunter, preying on men who travel alone. When a peryton slaughters a man, the spirit it carries can finally rest in the tomb that was meant for the man it killed. And that man's spirit is, in turn, condemned to roam.

– after Jorge Luis Borges, The Book of Imaginary Beings

You will learn; you will all learn. But not from me.[i]
— John Gardner

*I will deliver them to be . . . a curse, and an astonishment,
and a hissing and a reproach, among all the nations whither I
have driven them.*[ii]

—*Jeremiah 29:18*

The young man crouched down on one heel in the frozen straw and
slime, at eye level with the thing in the corner. He asked, "Who are
you?"

Behind him, the Regent of Arne buried his nose and mouth in
the crook of his arm. Maybe to block the smell. Voice muffled, he
said, "It can't talk."

"Can't? Or won't?" The fog of the young man's breath blurred
his face for a moment, then cleared. "Will you talk to me?"

Talk? Talk required words. Useless phantasms. No, not
useless. Freaks. Monsters. All of them lies.

The Regent said, "It's never talked all the time it's been here.
But it seems to understand."

"So, 'won't,' not 'can't.' I wonder why."

Brightness sat on the Regent's other, open hand. Not by
magic, since there was no such thing. Its parts had names, of
course, but even those were not innocent. *Fire. Lamp. Hand.* When
the Regent moved, light flowed up and around and down the grimy
stone walls.

With the Regent stood two other men. One, black-bearded and
wearing sleek leather with a gold-wire emblem on the breast, had
cast a disapproving glance as he entered, then stepped aside. The

other, clean-shaven, wore plain linen and an air of peeved humility. The three of them—Regent, officer, servant—crowded this space uneasily, each clearly keeping something from the others. The worst of the lot was this young one, holding no secrets at all. Too close. Too unwary to survive.

The young man said, "I am Tisamenus Oresteides, King of Lacedaemon, son of the High King Orestes. Who are you?"

Maybe truly a king, with such bright hair and clear eyes, gold on his hands and collar, all those names. All that guiltlessness. All those words.

Then Tisamenus reached out as if to stroke an animal's head.

It recoiled, the chain clattering. The three men jerked forward, tardily protective. Tisamenus withdrew his hand and they settled again, the Regent farther away, the officer and the servant nearer.

"Sorry," Tisamenus said without turning. "Do you feed him?"

"Of course we do," the Regent answered, still through his sleeve.

The officer exhaled a warning, and the Regent uncovered his mouth. "Porridge, my lord. And meat."

More words. A moldy brew of husks and shells. *Porridge.* Scraps of bone glittering with tendon, the marrow gone to slime. *Meat.*

"Bread?" Tisamenus asked.

Bread.

"My lord, my own people don't have bread. Isn't that why you're here?"

The officer breathed out again.

The Regent lowered his arm. "While my people starve, I can't give bread to . . ." He stopped, and the flame on his other hand wavered.

Tisamenus rose. "The stink makes my eyes water. Do you change the straw?"

"Change it? If you can't convince Thymoetes to lift this siege, the cattle and even the goats will be *eating* it soon enough. Men, too, likely."

Tisamenus opened his mouth, but it was the officer who spoke. "If you don't know who he is, you should treat him better."

"I did treat it better. I thought it . . ." The Regent's jaw tightened. ". . . thought he was Athenian, so they'd give ransom. Treated him like a guest. And look." He pushed the sleeve up the arm that held the lamp. A jagged bite, caked with ash and ointment, wept pus. Both the officer and the servant glanced down with new interest.

They had beaten him for that, but he had made his point. *Don't touch me.* Like an adder, from stillness to ferocity in less than a blink.

Tisamenus asked, "Is that when you cut out his eye?"

"We didn't! We found him like that."

"With a head full of rot?" Such roughness in that soft mouth. "Is he blind?"

"He can see," the Regent said. "It's only the color. Like your eyes are blue."

"And you found him outside somewhere. Wearing that . . . what is it?"

"Some decayed trash. How can anyone tell?"

"Thymoetes makes his Athenians keep clean," the officer said. The statement carried another reprimand.

"Where else could he have come from, Baron Hawmai?" the Regent asked, "If he's not one of them, who could he be? From where? Not even madmen go wandering around in winter."

"Not any other time, either," the servant murmured, then looked away from the baron's sharp glance.

"When my men found him they were careful, in case he might be valuable."

They had set dogs on him, beaten him, dumped him on the

stone floor in a tinkling hail of his own frozen blood. Then had come fawning, favors, food, but nothing about Athens or value—ransom?—until now.

"Then he bit you. Then this," Tisamenus said, as if accepting the logic of it all. "Always chained?"

Between the curled toes of Tisamenus's gilded shoes, the twisted links ran over a tangle of frozen rotted straw, its other end buried.

"Otherwise, he could get out anytime." The Regent indicated the door, beautifully finished but loose in its sockets, held only by broken staples and a bar. "And bound, as you see. No one would come to feed him if he weren't."

"You don't bind and chain the other hostages. Their doors aren't in any better repair."

"How could they get down Arne's walls? And they couldn't blend in with my people. We'd catch them again. They know. This one couldn't get away, either, but what damage would he do, trying?" The light dimmed as the Regent rubbed his bitten arm.

Flick the chain up, rip Tisamenus's foot from under him, tear that perfect throat. Then, in the outer corridor, the Regent, fleeing like a panicked mantis, sliding on ice, throwing a hand against a wall, himself racing after, low, fast, spiderlike, no motion wasted, claw up that scrawny back, twist the neck around, bite . . . He breathed out.

"Wanax Tisamenus, if you don't know him, it doesn't matter. Come back to my megaron hall. The lamps are lit and my damos members are waiting to give you their hands. Dinner must be ready."

Tisamenus stood nearly as tall as the others, slender and erect, fair hair draping his shoulders. He gleamed in the dark like a new foal, incapable of guile.

"Give him to me."

The baron Hawmai snapped, "No!"

By rights, it was Tisamenus who should hold fire on his palm.

Baby Prometheus, wielding deadly light. "Why not? No ransom, and I can spare your having to feed him."

The Regent's face stiffened, hiding a smile.

"With that dog and Oxylus," Hawmai said, "you have enough pets."

The servant twitched. The Regent's face relaxed into satisfied blandness.

Tisamenus went down again on his heel. "Who are you? Tell me."

He closed his eye. Waited. Finally felt Tisamenus rise, turn, and go.

* * *

When the guard elbowed the door open, the chain whipped over his head and crushed his throat so quickly that his astonished spirit rattled through his bones like a bee in a bottle. Only when the killer laid the corpse all the way down could the spirit flee out the mouth, over the floor and under the straw to safety.

The bowl had dropped from the guard's hands and smashed, the stuff it carried now too fouled by feces to eat. *Porridge.*

Horsehair bonds wound up the killer's forearms to the elbows, bending his shoulders into a stoop, leaving only his hands free. Still, it was freedom enough. He gathered the chain in his fingers and stepped over the corpse and out between the warped leaves of the door.

To his monocular view, the corridor of stone and mud—hung with cobwebs, lit faintly from the Athenian hostages's rooms all down its length—was blindingly complex. The only sound not his was the hiss of rain above. Maybe the other hostages had heard the guard's single bleat, took its meaning, and feared calling attention to themselves. He himself feared nothing but that valiant, idiot child.

Roaches on the walls bolted into cracks and holes, only the trembling tips of antennae showing. At every doorway, the men inside touched their foreheads in wary respect as he passed.

* * *

No one could escape Arne, the Regent had said. Maybe everyone believed that, so it didn't have to be true. He looked out into a yard bare of any hut or shed or animals. No cart, laden or empty, or even a colonnade for cover—just a vast space of dark, sleety rain, occupied by this long building and its twin opposite and surrounded by an unscalable wall.

At the lower end of the yard was a closed gate, also too high to climb even if he could climb, the bar as thick as his thigh and impossible to lift with bound arms. All the barriers around here, he remembered, led to occupied spaces, then more barriers. But in the upper cross-wall, a gate stood open. Traps and snares worked by hope and temptation—yet more dangerous words recalled.

He shuffled down the ramp in air so clean it burned his throat. The ground was spotted with dead weeds and running with water. He bent to touch his fingertips to the wet ground, thanking it for bearing him. Then he followed the face of this structure, staying under the eaves not for shelter but for the deeper shadow. Tisamenus must have come this way, stepping in the places he now stepped. They might still be warm from the boy's gilded shoes.

No one guarded the open gate. *Hope. Temptation.* He looked in.

That space held a double-winged palace in the angle of the far walls, one of those walls so tall that it must be the outer rim of the entire citadel. Lamps marked the palace's two entries. Carts stood under the eaves, leaning on their shafts. Beneath them, dogs raised their heads to stare, but none ventured out from its dry nest to challenge him as he entered the Regent's domain.

Water ran here, too, melting into a dense swamp against the wall. There should be a stone stairway somewhere, to climb that outer barrier. Following to this wall, he turned and then turned again, thigh deep in grass and thistles, ankle deep in a sludge of mud, excrement, pot shards, and bones even the dogs were done with.

Here were the stairs, steep and narrow as a ladder, half the stones fallen. He crawled and climbed, digging the chain into rotted ice, the decrepit leather of his boots and leggings clinging and sliding. The sharp air felt like swallowing thistles. Could one bleed to death on the inside? He had to cough—a weird sound in this inhuman place. He crept onto the top of the great wall itself, and finally rose to his full height.

There were planks and a handrail, but no living guard. No way to descend the outside. The Regent's enemies could not come at him this way, and at night there was nothing to see—not the Athenian siege camp, not the plain or the nearby hills, the distant mountains, moon, stars.

If he turned, he would see, outside the Regent's compound but within the great wall, a bedlam of people, light, and noise. Another stair somewhere would lead down into that chaos. But the Regent was right: if anyone saw him as he must look now, they would run screaming, bringing crowds. And then they would slaughter him, revere him, or give him back—all equally intolerable. *Fate.* Another word.

There was, also, the Regent himself, fretting over a surprise invasion: how to counter it, whether to counter it at all or just let it wear itself out, the Athenians giving up before their own people starved. What was that tool the Asian traders used? A balance. The thing desired in one pan, the offer in the other. Grain for grain, pebble for pebble, horse for horse, severed head for head, it was never a question of which side would quit, but which would quit first.

No matter. Not his business. He had only one piece of work to complete, and that had nothing to do with this place and these people.

He could not look up. If this were the night of changeover—the old moon burned away in the birth of the new—he might falter and retreat to some cover, where they would dig him out in the morning, like a rat from a drain.

Standing on the edge of the void, he felt the spit and bite of the blowing sleet. With two eyes or a hundred, he would see the same black emptiness below him as he did now. Above might fly all the winged horrors of the night. Below might be sharp stones, monstrous prowling nymphs, a bottomless sea, the land of the dead, or nothing at all.

He would not meet the murdered guard in the land of the dead. Outlaws such as he weren't allowed there. Their corpses were dog meat, and their spirits roamed without rest. This did not disturb him, except that he was tired of walking.

He had thanked the earth for bearing him, but had never asked its permission. If it expected him to pay now for every moment it had borne his weight, so be it. He once had sought the edge of the world. Perhaps this was it at last.

Since he couldn't stay here, he stepped off the wall, to find out what would happen next.

* * *

Swimming again. He hadn't forgotten how to do it, or how he loathed it. It wasn't so much fear of drowning, but fear that something followed below, matching his course with patient flicks of the tail. He thought of dolphins, but dolphins did not lurk. No seaman, he still knew this. No swimmer, he still swam.

Air erupted between his arms, in a huge exhalation of foam and stench. Immense, cylindrical, glossy, with a monstrous slanted eye, it reared up, curved over him, and drove him under.

Though long expected, it still caught him not believing the long shadow that wound between him and light. The shadow spiraled under; then he was splayed across it as it bucked and twisted like a fractious horse, in a wild gyration that no rider could follow. Cold, hard, and yielding all at once, bellowing, blowing the stench not of fish, but of rotting human meat. If this was death, so be it.

With a spin no horse could devise, it heaved him into the slipstream. He rolled and rolled faster and faster until the sea slapped him flat, dragged him back, then rattled off him and hissed away.

He gulped for air and got pebbles and foam. Surf churned over him again, sucking and pulling. He clawed up to where the rocks were larger, slimy yet sharp-edged, crusted with salt and frost. There he lay, just breathing for a moment. Then he turned and sat, back bowed, legs draggling in the wrack as he vomited brine. A mask of seaweed covered his face. When he tried to pull it away, it was his own snarled hair.

Rock, water, weeds, hair: *things with names, true to their kind. He slowed his breath, counting one, two, three, as when drawing a bow. He looked up.*

He had started crossing in daylight. It was evening now, dark sky over dark water, where lurked mysteries no man might believe. An early waning moon—Dark Moon they called it here, Thieves's Moon where he had come from—pierced a thick net of cloud. A few gulls blew sideways.

He would not swim again.

He twisted to look up behind him. The fortress wall was closer than he had expected, and he felt a shudder Perhaps the sea had risen or the land sunk since he first passed here. Perhaps he misremembered. There was no reason for fear. The place seemed empty now, rid of man and his leavings, barren as a skull.

On knees and hands, he scaled the slope. Vines looped his arms and dripped dry petals onto his hair. He staggered the last steps upright.

The bare log palings were now silver with age, the arrow slits cobwebbed. He laid his hands on them, watched the long, scarred fingers spread and settle.

Oh, *the wall said.* You again.

He woke to a boot caressing his face.

* * *

"Oxylus, stop!" Sigewas Teller pleaded.

But the runaway had come alive in an instant, ripped the servant's legs from under him and scaled his body like a spider up a rope. Only Oxylus's instinctive thrust of his own head back into the soaked, stinking litter under Arne's wall had foiled the flick of the chain around his throat. Only his superior weight had let him heave the lean body away. Only luck and balance had let him regain his feet quickly enough to thrust home a kick that drove the breath from that body and stopped it for the moment.

Another kick, and the runaway hunched over his bound arms, gagging.

"The king wants him." Oxylus, balanced on two separate rocks, was breathing hard himself. "If I have to bring him in a bucket, I will."

Sigewas climbed over other rocks protruding from the carpet of rubbish and the great mound of rotten straw the runaway had landed on. He squatted on the shriveled remains of what may once have been a dog, said, "You don't have to hurt him," and laid a palm on the bent shoulder.

The shaggy head whipped around and snapped at his hand.

"Shit!" Recoiling, he sat down with a squish. The lamp spun

away and flamed out.

The rain had paused, and the moon now gave a watery light by which he inspected his hand. Finding it unmarked, he clapped a fist to his own forehead. "What I said? Never mind."

The runaway was moving again, as if he might glide away like a snake and slither down a hole. If he was a power in disguise, they would know soon enough: he would tire of this game and come at them in a murderous flurry of teeth and wings. Or his night-flying kin would swoop down.

In the meantime, Oxylus kicked again. The runaway rolled aside, retching. Oxylus pulled loose a big stone and raised it above his head with both hands.

The hacking wheeze stopped, and the pale eye moved to Oxylus's face, to the stone. To the face again.

Then the runaway whispered, in the language everyone knew, "Don't."

* * *

The gate was closed at the bottom, but the tops of the leaves leaned apart. He stepped through, into stale air and calm antipathy. Thistles raked his leggings. Paving stones had risen and tilted, heaved into new patterns by root and ice.

An open doorway beckoned. Something waited inside, as real as a knife in a fist. His hand found the axe at his hip. He walked in.

Weeds lived here, too, crawling over one another, clammy and white in the dark. He heard the rustle of their noisome growth, their whispered greeting. There were no men now to bellow and eat and spit alien speech at the starving young stranger who crouched in a corner, calculating his chances of flight. Maybe some of those men still lived, old by now, unwelcome, too, if they had no other place to claim, the bond between man and place so vital, the fracturing of that bond so absolute. Here now was only a nest of vines, luxuriant and sterile, swarming and still. The megaron of the dead.

* * *

And now, in Arne, he crouched in yet another corner, arms still bound, every breath a stab, another crowd of men spitting words. There was a clay firepot for warmth, lamps for light, but his clothes and hair clung heavy and cold as seaweed.

After dumping him onto the floor, Oxylus had gone out again. Sigewas Teller dragged off his own shirt and leg wraps, toweled himself, then wound dry clothes around a body as hairy and sinewy as a monkey's. While he did that, the rest of these men— ten, twenty, however many—talked.

Talk. What was it about men, that they could never shut up? Their strings of yap ran over one another, even over Sigewas's, in their eagerness to declare what they thought they knew. The mesh of noise raked his awakened nerves.

A rush of cold passed as the door opened. The talk cut off. Someone dropped a stool in front of him, opened a cloak whose tails dripped rainwater, and sat down with a grunt. This close, in better light, the baron Hawmai's face resembled a boar's: heavy jowls, graying whiskers, pouches under small, intelligent eyes. The emblem on his breast was a pair of wasps, facing each other. He stank of cooked meat.

"Who are you?"

That again. He settled back against the wall, sipping air against the pain.

"I am Hawmai Aquileides. I am the Lawagetas of Mycenae, leader of the High King's armies, second-highest baron to the High King. Tisamenus's guardian. Leader of his Companions—these men here, his age-mates and equals. Well, the age-mates of his brothers who went to their dead. Sons of kings who rule under the High King." Hawmai waved a hand, shooing complications away. "Every one of them is more important than whatever you are, and I expect my no-name rubbish hostages to cooperate—like talking when I tell them to."

His? Fine.

Hawmai added, "I know what you did."

The jolt was instant. But Hawmai could mean only the guard. Just that.

Hawmai nested one fist in the other. "The Regent seems to think you're somebody important to me—us. I can't imagine why, but I need to know. So tell me who you are."

More cold gusted between the men's legs. In came Tisamenus, with Oxylus and a tall white hound.

Hawmai thudded to his feet and turned. "My lord, don't trouble yourself."

"I started it. I went to see him in the cells." But Tisamenus stopped and stood still.

"You went because the Regent asked you to. Why did he ask, do you think?"

"I don't know. I sent Oxylus to find him when he escaped."

"I went, too," Sigewas said happily. His voice was deep for one so slight. "The Boeotians were searching in the fields, but Oxylus said that since he couldn't leave by any gate, he must have gone over the wall."

Hawmai raised an eyebrow at Oxylus, who looked away.

Sigewas was suddenly thoughtful. "But if nobody knows who he is, why does the Regent even want him back?"

"You all had no business . . ." Hawmai exhaled. "I'll handle this now."

The hound's ears lay back on its neck as it raised its muzzle to Tisamenus. Without looking down, Tisamenus stroked its head. Its tail waved, slowed, stopped.

"Sigewas is right to ask," Tisamenus said. "If the Regent just wanted to know if I know him, and I don't, why bother to go looking for him? Oh, right, he killed the guard."

"Never mind." Hawmai's glance made Sigewas look away. "It's nothing you can manage."

Even with bound arms, if the hostage wanted a weapon, the stool would serve. Or he could let Hawmai do whatever he wanted. That would take him away from Tisamenus—to what, he didn't care. But Tisamenus stood, his luminescence fading as colors fade from a dying trout, while his Companions waited for the wrong man's—Hawmai's—lead.

He coughed, tasted blood, swallowed, and whispered, "Akhaïdes."

His voice hitched and croaked, barely audible. Still, everyone turned to stare. Sigewas's deep-set eyes seemed to protrude from his head. Even the hound raised its ears.

Hawmai snapped, "What was that?"

He waited until shuffling legs made a moment's gap, a line of sight to Tisamenus. Then he said, to the king alone, "Me. I. Akhaïdes."

Tisamenus strode between men. Not expecting this, they stepped aside, and he crouched down beside the stool.

"Greetings, Akhaïdes."

"That doesn't mean anything," Hawmai said, cool again. "It's not a name."

"Yes, it is," Tisamenus answered.

"Is," Akhaïdes said at the same time. And for that moment, they were accomplices.

"What is your patronymic?" Tisamenus asked.

"Don't . . ." Akhaïdes cleared his throat. "No . . . have." He heard his own accent: the crude gutturals and silky foreign vowels. The forgotten grammar.

Yet Tisamenus seemed to understand. "Even a bastard has a power to protect him, and uses that name. Everyone claims a father somehow."

"Not outlaws," Hawmai reminded him. "Outlaws don't. Can't." He turned. "Sigewas, stop bobbing around. This is not your business."

The white hound came, head and tail down, to sit beside Tisamenus. It put out its nose to Akhaïdes, then drew back.

"Are you outlaw, Akhaïdes?" Tisamenus asked.

Akhaïdes raised his chin, seeking words. "Long. Forever. Don't touch."

"There aren't any living first-degree outlaws," Hawmai said. "I would know."

"So would I!" from Sigewas.

Hawmai ignored him. "It's my responsibility."

"Yes, it is." Tisamenus rose. "So you'll soon know everything about him. For now, we'll free his hands so he can eat."

"What? No!" It was a chorus of protests. Sigewas added, with relish, "He murdered a man. And he didn't have to. He just did it anyway."

"Maybe he thought he had to," Tisamenus said.

"And if he thinks he has to murder *you*?" Hawmai answered. "Us? My—your—Companions need to sleep, not guard each other. We're not freeing his hands."

"An outlaw kills again," Tisamenus said. "What's the law in a case like that?"

"There isn't any case like that. It's never happened before."

"No outlawed killer ever killed twice?"

"And was taken in by . . ." Hawmai stopped on the edge of something. "It's never happened. And you don't know why he was outlawed. It might be something worse."

"What crime is worse than killing?" Sigewas asked, all innocence.

Still by the door, Oxylus cleared his throat.

"What?" Hawmai snapped without turning, but Oxylus waited until Tisamenus looked at him. Then he said, "An outlaw can ask for refuge, whatever he did. You can keep him three nights and two days. Like you kept me when I first came to Mycenae."

"You're only third-degree outlaw." Hawmai's jowls hardened. "And he spoke without permission. He's lawless."

"You asked his name before," Sigewas said. "He was just answering."

A glare from Hawmai silenced but did not appear to discourage him.

Tisamenus went down to eye level again. "Come with me, Akhaïdes Outlaw. We're going to the Athenian camp, then to Delphi. We'll ask the priests about absolution."

All the men in the room fell silent, even Hawmai. The hound also waited.

Without turning, Tisamenus called quietly, "Elawon."

"My lord?"

"Go to the kitchen, please. Bring my . . . bring something to eat. In a dish that can be broken after."

Akhaïdes knew without looking that Elawon silently checked with Hawmai before answering, "Yes, my lord," and going out. He also knew that he himself had shown no visible response to that name, although his heart had twitched sharply enough to make him catch his breath.

"Ask," Tisamenus said. "Just ask me. Three nights and two days of safety."

Hawmai snapped, "If he won't ask for refuge, you can't keep him. It's not forbidden to live as an unprotected outlaw. It's just impossible." He paused, maybe waiting for some further stir of impertinence from someone. "Feed him if you want, but then put him back outside—tonight, before they know he's here."

"They'll kill him," Tisamenus said. "Or he'll go to his dead all alone."

"Outlaws' spirits can't go there. They fly around stealing decent men's places."

Akhaïdes lowered his head and murmured, "Help me."

Response came swiftly: Hawmai's exasperated grunt, Sigewas's hoot of delight, Tisamenus's formal, "You are welcome, Akhaïdes Outlaw."

Tisamenus reached out both hands. "Do you know how to do this?" Then he added, "You can't pollute a king." So Akhaïdes had to lay his own long, grimy hands, still bound together, palms joined, between Tisamenus's. When he snatched them away again, Tisamenus smiled. Smiled.

Had his hands been free, Akhaïdes would have ripped Tisamenus's throat out. Had his hands been free, he would have caressed the boy's shoes in abject surrender. Had his hands been free, he would have held his own head and wept.

Instead, he was snared like any other stupid animal: tempted, hoping, strangled. All he'd had to do was sit here. Instead, he had slipped his own head into the noose. Like any smarter animal, he should have chewed one arm off to free himself. He should have found a way to do that.

18

$$| |$$

I accept chaos. I am not sure whether it accepts me.[iii]
—Bob Dylan

Makhawis Herakleidou stood over her half-brother the king. *"Please* don't go to Delphi," she said. "Don't go there." Her black hair, sparked with white and done up in loops and braids, tilted and swayed with her vehemence.

Temenus Herakleides looked up from the wooden platform where he sat, one sock on, the other in his hand.

Makhawis added, "Your wife is afraid for you."

Temenus's lip kinked. "My wife is afraid *of* me, except when she needs to get pregnant every year or so. That doesn't mean much." He pulled off the second sock and folded both together.

Makhawis's skirt ballooned around her as she knelt and laid her hands on his knees. "And *I'm* afraid for you. Everything the priests tell you ends up meaning something else, and they say it's your own fault that you misunderstood." She reached up to touch his scarred, bearded cheek. "Delphi ruined Herakles. It killed Hyllus. What will it do to you?"

"It will name me High King." He caught her plump, beringed hand.

She closed her eyes briefly. "Give me your socks. I'll darn them again."

"Yes, fix my socks, and thank you. But who will fix Nafpaktos?" He drew her closer until they were almost nose to nose. "There's no relief here even now, in the heart of winter. Beautiful green grass—inedible. Sickness of all kinds. Houses sliding into the sea. A palace that no one else would stable goats in."

He didn't let her go. "My supposed friends give me only words. Some tell me secrets, but who else do they tell? The few gifts I receive go straight to repay ancient debts." He released her hand. "Herakles was robbed, and so was his son, and then my father, and now me. I need Delphi to endorse me. Us."

Makhawis drew away. "If you still had your mother's dowry, it would be easier."

"Or maybe the thieves did me a favor. Would I have tried to trade for the High Kingship rather than work for it?"

"It wouldn't be the first empire won that way." She took the socks from him, examined the holes, and folded them together again. "You know you can use my own wealth: jewelry, animals, women—anything."

"No. It's your dowry. And you'll be needing it again soon."

"Am I going to divorce Hippotes?" she asked, suddenly playful.

He smiled. "You only married him to chasten me. Well, I'm duly chastened."

"It was time I finally had a husband who knew when to be plotting together with you, and when to be in bed with his wife."

He spread his hands. "But he was already mine by blood. My cousin."

"Everyone's your cousin."

"And he had nowhere else to go. I prefer to use you as a lure for men I can't get otherwise."

"You could have slept late that morning. If you missed us coming out together at dawn, you could have claimed we weren't really married."

His smile vanished. "You know that sleeping with a man you aren't marrying isn't possible."

She lowered her head.

"You trapped me," he said. "I had no choice. Please don't do that again."

She didn't answer.

He breathed out, his temper lightening. "We'll make the divorce before I go. And I'll take him to Delphi with me so he won't bother you while I'm away."

She looked up, smiling again. "And then you'll find my next husband. Do you have anyone in mind?"

His eyes glittered. "Someone rich, with forts full of warriors. And fields that grow actual grain instead of snakes and spurge."

"I don't know that man, but I think I'd like to." She tilted her head the way he always did. "Your boy is crying."

"Who? My foster son? He should be happy. He's going home. He'll learn all the rest that he needs to know from his family's old men, unlike . . ." He stopped.

"Unlike you, who had to make it up as you went along, what with all our old men gone to their dead Still, he's only fourteen. Give him some extra attention."

"Not if he's going to cry." Temenus made a sour face. "You know how I despise emotional fuss."

"He'll be a fine man and an ally, because of all you taught him. I was sorry I couldn't help you in your own fostering. The Dorians were so harsh with you. But then you seduced them And their wives."

Temenus finally laughed. "I could hardly fight them all, could I?"

She smiled with him, then touched his face again. "So be good to the boy. Remember, your sons will start going out to foster soon. You'll want them treated kindly."

"Yes, of course. Yes."

"You'll need a woman for your travel to Delphi. Shall I lend you a slave?"

"One woman in that crowd of men? They'll all be in love before the oars are wet."

"You need someone to sleep with. And to cook for you. Maybe Deione."

"The boat will barely hold the men that are going, along with all the things I need to trade with. The clerks can cook."

"Clerks will make that same disgusting gruel every day."

"All the easier for you to spoil me when I return." The creases at the ends of Temenus's mouth deepened. "As for sleeping, I wonder if I can find something more . . ." He breathed out, then looked at her and smiled.

"More substantial? A real lover instead of one-night visitors, your wife, slaves, the boy, who all bore you so? Maybe love?"

"Love?" He laughed again. "Certainly not. Just—what is it— engagement."

"Emotional fuss, which you claim to despise." Then she stopped smiling. "I have to tell you. A dream came to me last night."

He was suddenly alert.

"I saw . . ." She fumbled. ". . . I saw a wind move through a night forest, silent. All the trees—every trunk, every branch— leaned down and rose again. Just one time."

He touched his lips with the tip of his tongue. "That's powerful."

"I felt it here." She laid her hand on her chest. Then she pressed the hand to her abdomen. "And here. There was just Hippotes, the baby, my children, my women, in the room. I didn't dare look out through the shutters."

"Of course not."

"All I could think was, 'Why are such beautiful hands so cold?'"

They gazed at each other. Then she lowered her head. "Go to Delphi, my love. Leave me to do what I do best: worry about you." She looked up. "And if you find a wonderful new familiar, bring him back."

"Will you give him one of your famous baths? Soften him so I can unravel his secrets?" His mouth quirked with amusement while his eyes remained shadowed.

"I always do." Makhawis tucked the socks into her pocket and kissed his forehead. Since she was his elder by so few years, she also kissed his hand. She did not say, "Remember my dream." She just returned to her rooms and her work.

* * *

In the morning, it was Hawmai who wanted Akhaïdes' hands freed. And with Tisamenus and Oxylus absent, it was he who had to do it when even Sigewas backed away from the knife on his open palm.

"Last night, you preferred him tied," Elawon said primly. "So do we." Behind him, the other Companions mumbled agreement. "We send outlaws away to protect ourselves from reprisal. At least, if he's tied, revenge will know he's the one it wants, when it comes hunting."

"What about Oxylus?" someone asked.

Before Elawon could start up again, Hawmai said, "That's why Oxylus has no beard. This one has only that—what?—mustache. So it will still be clear that he's the one to aim for."

Elawon began, "All the more reason—"

Hawmai cut in. "You all know this already."

The wary faces told Hawmai otherwise.

"Who fostered you?" he growled. "Marmots?"

Sigewas murmured, "There were the Herakleid wars."

"That's no excuse for men not doing their duty. If they didn't teach you the oldest law, how can you know if someone violates it? Everything falls apart. Bah!"

Before Hawmai could organize a lecture, Sigewas told them, "Any king can outlaw a man for three years, like Oxylus, but only

Delphi can condemn him forever. And only Delphi can lift first-degree outlawry—although it never does, because the compensation is a kingdom's worth. The outlaw himself can't give it. Someone else has to. In the meantime, anyone can touch an outlaw, but an outlaw can touch only a slave, a king, or someone a shaman has prepared. Anything an outlaw touches, except an animal or a wall, is polluted and contagious. They can't open doors. They can't speak before we do."

"When I brought him food last night," Elawon reminded them, "after he ate, I made sure to break the dish with a stick and then shoved it down the drain."

"First-degree outlaws should sit by some roadside and wait to be killed," Sigewas continued in his tale-telling voice. "The priests at Delphi tell them so. The only first-degree outlaw ever absolved was our High King Orestes. One of the reasons Delphi's rich now is the compensation his supporters—our grandfathers and great-grandfathers—gave to have him back, all that time ago."

"That's right." Hawmai took over again. "I know that Tisa—um, the king—said something last night about absolution, but that will *not* happen. Anyway, we won't—"

"He killed again last night," Elawon interrupted. "What happens when an outlaw deliberately lays hands on someone?"

From his corner, Akhaïdes said unexpectedly, "Didn't lay hands."

The Companions goggled. Sigewas demanded, "How can you kill a man without touching him?"

Hawmai tightened his hand on the knife. "All of you, get ready to leave here. And where are the drivers?"

He turned back and glared down at Akhaïdes. "Don't speak if you aren't spoken to. You at least know the law. And call your betters 'my lord' if you have to talk at all."

The Companions hurried to dress, roll bedding, find shoes, tie bundles, urinate down the drain in the floor. Light shone through a well in the roof, whose limed stalactites still dripped with last night's rain.

Hawmai sat down heavily on the stool near Akhaïdes. "I'm going to cut you loose. I don't care if it's bad luck to cut a cord—I'd have to touch it to untie it. Then you're going to walk out with the rest of us."

Akhaïdes did not respond.

"I won't have a scene of any kind. I won't take you like a hostage. These people in Arne are all Boeotians. If they see us do that, they'll accuse us of kidnapping someone's favorite uncle."

"You don't want. Leave here."

"Their king is mad." Hawmai's eyes narrowed. "They keep him in the tower of Orchomenos. He has no sons, no brothers, so the High King put a regent here. He chose a Cadmean since the Cadmean city, Thebes, is so near and is still in ruins. Maybe Orestes never understood how the Boeotians and Cadmeans despise each other. I don't know. Anyway, he did that."

Hawmai paused, studying Akhaïdes' silent face.

"I—Tisamenus is the Regent's guest, so the Boeotians don't trust him, either. Never mind that we want this siege broken as much as they do. They see us and the Regent together, and we're automatically suspect."

Hawmai nibbled the edge of his mustache. "Now *you*. They'll forget how they found you if it suits them. You spent the night in this room, so if they want to believe you're one of us, they will. If we leave you here—which I would certainly prefer—they'll take their anger out on you."

Akhaïdes made an interrogative sound.

"I can't let hostility toward the High King be shown so openly."

"Put back."

"In that cell? Too late. They'll know, and believe you're the High King's spy. Same result."

"Give to . . ."

"The Regent? He'd have to kill you for the murder. But you're Tisamenus's guest now. Orestes couldn't ignore the insult. I'd have to come back here and make war. No one wants that."

Akhaïdes closed his eye and rested his head against the wall.

"Today we're going to the king whose siege this is: Thymoetes of Athens. Tisamenus was his foster son and is married to one of his daughters."

Without moving, Akhaïdes asked, "Stop siege?"

"If I—if he can."

"Only?"

Hawmai's jowls tightened. "What do you mean?"

"You . . . that word you said . . . You despise Tisamenus." Akhaïdes' voice cracked as he struggled with language. He opened his eye. "Maybe you want fail. Tisamenus fail."

Hawmai's temper snapped. "Damn you! Who are you? Where did you come from? Why did you run last night? I didn't need another problem!"

Like a child learning to speak, Akhaïdes answered precisely, "Every problem in the world not yours to . . ." He sought a word.

Behind Hawmai, Sigewas said quietly, "Solve. Control."

Akhaïdes twitched his head to one side, agreeing. "Sometimes kill. Sometimes feed to . . . What is it? Animals. Fire. To get thing you want. You do this." He spoke a long word in a foreign language.

"What?" Hawmai demanded.

"Sacrifice," Sigewas murmured.

Hawmai drew back. "I don't know what you're talking about."

"What with his blood you want? No, not blood." Akhaïdes breathed out, frustrated.

"His honor," Sigewas whispered.

"Orestes' son," Akhaïdes affirmed. "Failing not insult Orestes?

But you Orestes' . . ."

"Tool," Sigewas said for him.

"So," Akhaïdes responded, as if suddenly satisfied.

Hawmai glanced behind himself, where Sigewas was diligently folding a much-folded shirt. He turned back. "You look familiar."

"No." The chain rattled as Akhaïdes' hands closed. "Not born . . . Mycenae."

"An egg in a kennel still hatches a hawk."

"Or snake." Akhaïdes raised his head. "To . . . pick at me not hide what you do. And Orestes."

Hawmai's temper finally slipped. "You sit there like some princeling, stinking like carrion, challenging me, never calling me 'lord.' You're lucky I'll let the boy keep another pet." He shifted his grip on the knife. "Don't defy me, and don't provoke me. Real men have tried that, and what good do you think it did them? Or else try, and save me trouble. It wouldn't offend anyone to drop your carcass by the roadside. I won't even have to light a lamp for you."

The look on Akhaïdes' face made Sigewas catch his breath, but it lasted only an instant.

Hawmai's jaw tightened under his beard. "Interesting, that you mention snakes. I think we *will* take you to Delphi and see what the Serpent makes of you."

Akhaïdes' head sank between his cramped shoulders. The old-straw mass of hair shifted. His hands formed fists, the bonds digging into his scabbed wrists, and he made a coughing, retching sound.

"Finally afraid of something," Hawmai observed, cool again. "And something so ordinary."

Careful not to pollute himself or the knife by touching Akhaïdes' skin, Hawmai sawed through the horsehair bond between the outlaw's wrists and elbows. Still glued in place by dried bloody rags and abraded flesh, it untwisted but did not drop away. Akhaïdes' shoulders loosened in shudders. His hands sank until they lay palms-up on the floor, with the chain between them. The fingers twitched like the legs of a maimed insect.

Hawmai put his hands on his knees and pushed upright. He turned, then had to wait while Sigewas skipped out of his way. He still held the knife as he left the room.

In the quiet that followed, with the other Companions busy packing, Sigewas said to Akhaïdes, "You don't look familiar. I would know. And I know you're not afraid."

Akhaïdes breathed carefully.

"He would have arranged to drop you off some cliff and then apologized to the king for the accident. We all know he was going to do that. By running, you guaranteed that we would take you all the way to Delphi. But what outlaw dares to go there? 'Ordinary,' Hawmai said. Delphi is never ordinary. He talks as if it's nothing, but it's not nothing. I hope you know what you're doing."

"Shut your mouth," Akhaïdes whispered, "my lord."

* * *

The woman was tall and willowy, with narrow shoulders, sleek hair knotted on a long, elegant neck, and the fastidious face of a cat. She squatted before Akhaïdes and showed him a linen fillet such as women used to bind their hair, three fingers wide at the center, with long, narrow tails.

"I am the king's slave," she told him. "And this is for you."

He understood, and let her tie the fillet around his head to hide the fouled eye.

Then, taking a jar from the pouch at her hip, she used a frayed-ended stick to spread balm on his wrists. It smelled of honey and smoke. It bit at first, then numbed. His arms were immediately tired of such a simple task: holding their own weight.

She herself smelled of honey, and something else rich and

clean—wheat, perhaps. He had forgotten wheat until this moment. Her skin was as smooth as a young woman's, but her cool serenity said that she was as old as Hawmai, perhaps older. She tied neat linen bandages around both of his wrists, then rose in a single movement and stepped aside.

He had murdered, or worse, every woman he had ever known. Every one of them.

Oxylus came in, moving deferentially among the Companions. A hemp bag filled with hard angles swung from his hand.

"We have your things here," he said to Akhaïdes. "And now we're going to leave very quietly, the way the baron says he told you."

Akhaïdes turned onto hands and knees, used the wall to climb to his feet, and warily straightened. Oxylus handed the bag to the slave, who set it aside while she fed the chain, the segments of cord, and the balm stick down the floor drain.

Akhaïdes followed Oxylus to the door. The Companions also left, some before Akhaïdes, most after, leaving their baggage for the slaves to carry. All but Oxylus wore the fringed blue cloaks they had wrapped around themselves to sleep in last night.

In an eddy where warm air from the chamber met an icy outdoor breeze, where known met unknown, Akhaïdes had to stop.

Doors, open and closed. Doors to secret places, to the unguarded world. A wicker door at Delphi, opening into the Serpent's grisly chamber. A curtain across a tent's mouth that did nothing to stifle the drone of carrion flies.

He leaned his shoulder on the wooden frame and breathed deeply until his head cleared and his legs steadied. Then he followed Oxylus's broad back across a hall whose stone floor was slick with mire. One final doorway, and they stepped into undiluted light.

Akhaïdes had to stop again, and the man following nearly ran into him and dodged aside with a muttered curse. But Akhaïdes forgot Oxylus, the slave, the Companions, forgot Hawmai's warnings, and raised his face to the sun.

Last winter, he had dug a bear from its den, taking its meat, its fur, and its bed, dozing and gnawing bones through the deepest of the cold. He had only staggered out, stuporous and blinking, when an unseasonable thaw ripened the last scraps of offal beyond even his tolerance. From a more recent shelter—just a gap between rocks—the Boeotians had dug him out in the same way.

That moment came back to him now: glaring light on grass and slick brambles, on cracks and veins in the rock, on the blade of the axe they had kicked from his hand. No one had taken the axe from him before. That the Boeotians could was a sign of his extremity. And it was another sign that he now stood flat-footed and bewildered in the glory of the winter sun.

He remembered this: *Utsir, Utsir, Utsir, nadad tuslaäch.* Please help me. But he wouldn't shame himself further by asking aloud.

"Move on!" Elawon's terse whisper was right under his ear.

Without thinking, he answered, "I will," in yet another language, one he had not heard among these people, but it felt right.

Elawon snapped back in the same tongue, "Do it, then." Then, more guardedly, "What did you say?"

Akhaïdes switched back to Mycenaean. "I will."

"No. You said . . . How do you know Arcadian?"

To either side of them, the Companions strode down into the yard. Empty last night, now it roiled with animals, wagons, men, women, chaos. Each individual bit of this disorder was comprehensible; only the number of bits was confounding: men harnessing oxen to carts and heavy wagons; servants pulling chariots from under the palace eaves; slaves rushing here and there, calling to one another; a few drab-clad onlookers keeping back from the preparations but devouring the spectacle with their eyes. Smoke drifting through all of it like mist through trees. And beyond, the cross-wall, the open gate, and Arne's black ramparts all around.

"Move!" Oxylus snarled. "If you call attention to yourself, Hawmai will burn us all!"

Akhaïdes' two-dimensional sight was deceptive in this fierce light. The stones were slick, with crusts of ice between them. A strip of wet carpet squeaked like a bag of mice but offered more certain footing. He eased down from the porch to the earth.

He felt horses before he saw them: the unmistakable thud and rumble of hooves through the ground. Then came an entire herd of ponies, men leading them in pairs and threes while they pranced and crow-hopped and spattered mud, clearly wild from a night in a strange place. Between jigging hooves dodged Tisamenus's hound. It stopped to sniff Akhaïdes' hands, waved its long tail briefly, then trotted off again.

After the ponies came two horses. The first was white and already wore a riding pad and bridle. Akhaïdes saw that one of its eyes was missing, the lid sunken into its skull. It moved as calmly as Tisamenus's slave, trained to serene obedience.

Between two grooms, a second horse strutted, neck arched, ears forward, gray in color and lean as a hound. The grooms led it to a baggage cart, tied the lead to the cart's railing, and left it there, respectfully circling the animal's rump. The horse jerked at the tether, then settled down to gnaw the rail. When the carter slapped at it, it snatched his sleeve, shook his arm fiercely, then went back to its gnawing. The driver retreated.

Akhaïdes passed Oxylus, passed whatever and whoever, seeing only the horse.

It cast an ear in his direction and cocked a hind leg. He touched its hip with one open palm, and its flank with the other, moving hand over hand along its body. It swung toward him, clapping its lips in warning. He cupped his hands together, and it dropped its muzzle into them. The rims of its nostrils showed above his thumbs. Akhaïdes lifted the muzzle to his face. The horse nodded sharply, pushing his hands away, then rested its lip against his cheek and the side of his mustache. It breathed in deeply, learning him.

"We're going."

He spun, crouching, ready, and both the horse and Oxylus lunged away.

Oxylus recovered and added calmly, "There's a cart for you to ride in."

Akhaïdes straightened warily, feeling the warning stitch in his chest where bones were knitting.

"It's a gift for the High King, from the Regent," Oxylus said, cocking his chin at the gray horse. "Nastiest beast ever sired. There's the cart."

Akhaïdes followed Oxylus again. Behind him came Tisamenus's slave, then three Boeotian warriors in spotted pony-skin armor. He felt the hunger with which the men followed, perhaps to avenge the man he had killed. But when he glanced back, the Boeotians had already stopped, shy of passing the slave who stood facing them without deference or fear.

The gray horse was watching Akhaïdes. So was Elawon, looking uneasy. Akhaïdes pressed a hand to his ribs and cursed himself silently in three languages. Then he added a fourth, just for the practice.

* * *

No, no, no, no. Elawon did not know this thing, this outlaw, this incubus that ensnared Tisamenus, annoyed Hawmai, intrigued Sigewas, troubled even Oxylus, yet spoke in a tone and timbre that squeezed Elawon's viscera tight. Something within him demanded, *You know me; look at me.* And something wanted to run and hide its face in . . . in what? In a voice, a scent, a shirt grasped tight, warm arms.

He had seen Akhaïdes—outlawed, broken, mad, perhaps. Had seen him give his face to the sun so openly, so unself-consciously, that he might be alone on earth. Impossible, yet Elawon knew that posture, that grace, that certainty, that taut profile in the light.

"Master?" A driver, flat-eyed but dutiful, disliking Elawon as all servants did, held a pair of frantically nodding ponies. Elawon stepped up onto the chariot and grabbed the crossbar.

The driver smelled unwashed, but Elawon was resigned to that. He fought the urge to look back at the outlaw but could not stop himself. The scrawny derelict outlaw, all rags and bones, more rank than any driver, with the matted ashen hair and the eye pale as a corpse's, who spoke to him, beyond all ken and reckoning: *You know me.*

| | |

Yours is the shame and sorrow, But the disgrace is mine.[iv]
—*D. H. Lawrence*

The road edged Arne's tall mound, forded runnels of sewage, then looped away to the base of the nearest hill, wasting no fertile soil. Behind Arne stood higher hills, some topped with shattered towers. Far to the west rose Parnassos, broken headed and streaked with snow.

Copais, the vast lake bed that Arne ruled, glowed white in the reflection of sunlight on standing water. From between curving dikes, young flax and blood-brown scrub cotton already forked upward. Wider expanses wore the flush of early wheat. The road's edge was fringed with remnants of Boeotia's original wealth: the tall blue-green centaur grass that grew nowhere else. Paths as punctilious as old ladies' stitching ran along the tops of the dikes. The locks and channels were clean and precise, the water moving obediently along. The Athenians would not harm the gardens they coveted. It was the Boeotians themselves who had charged across their own germinating fields, breaking vines and trellises as they died.

The Mycenaeans stopped where a canal curved between the road and a grove of pomegranates. Here, a portion of the dike wall was deliberately cut away to let animals approach and drink.

The chariot ponies drank their fill, then began nibbling at roadside grass and the grain dropped for them by their drivers. Carters unharnessed oxen and led them forward in pairs while slaves passed among the Companions, distributing bread, dried figs, and catskins of wine.

The slaves crossed a stone slab over the canal to perch like birds in the low limbs of the orchard. Their soft Mycenaean tones played a high counterpoint to the drivers's harsher Argolid accents. They were teasing one another and pinning up their hair, white fingers and napes under toppling black tresses, pretending serene ignorance of the men's attention. But they stopped when Akhaïdes approached the water.

Limping downstream to drink after all of them, even the oxen, he eased himself down to his knees in the mud. He murmured a rhyming children's prayer—all he could remember in this language for moving water. Then he leaned to wash his hands. Black crusts peeled from his skin, and the cold water soaked into the bandages and stung his wrists. Between him and the swirls of silt raised by the animals, minnows as slight as fingernail parings backed and turned and hung. He scrubbed his fingers together, and the minnows darted for the floating morsels. He drank from his nested palms. The cold made his throat knot.

Seeing the slaves, he remembered vanity, although not the word for it. He remembered painted shirts rattling with beadwork; remembered bathhouses, pounded herbs, scented oil; remembered plaited hair, polished teeth; remembered a time when he would not have used the rags he wore now to clean a hound's paws. He did not remember when he had last cleaned any part of himself.

The habit of cleanliness, once remembered, required some action. He raised his hands to untie the fillet that hid his eye, but the knot was too tight. He finally worked it free, feeling his own patience and the weight of his arms.

The cloth came away reluctantly, caked with whorled threads of blood and pus. He spread it on the water and closed his hands over it. Yellow film oozed between his fingers, then spun away.

He squeezed water through the cloth until it ran clean, then used it to scrub his knuckles and fingernails. Leaning closer to the water, he scrubbed his face. The tails of his mustache, once thick and soft to his collarbones, were rigid, broken off at the line of his chin. He soaked and kneaded them pliant, then cupped water over his ruined eye until cold dulled the pain.

"You should get some maggots," Hawmai said behind him. "They heal such things."

"They'll have me . . ." He groped for the words. ". . . soon enough."

"You show no sign of dying, though that would be convenient."

Akhaïdes broke a twig from a bush and used it to scrub at his teeth, spit, scrub, spit.

"The king will want your hands again," Hawmai said.

He raised his head. "What?"

"It's what we do to show service. You kneel and give him your hands. That's how it's done."

"Already did."

"That was a quick acceptance. But the whole process is necessary, to be binding."

Akhaïdes looked down at his fingers, trailing quietly in the water, still holding the twig. He released it and watched it rotate away.

"To his way of thinking, you're obliged to him. He got you out of Arne."

"I was out. He . . . dragged back again."

Hawmai snorted. "I don't want him thinking he can get away with this, picking up every stray he comes across. Don't do it."

"How will I . . . refuse?"

"Who cares how? It's only Tisamenus."

Akhaïdes worked this over: Hawmai wanted him to go to Delphi, but not under even the thin protection Tisamenus could offer. Sigewas was even more right than he knew. *Only Tisamenus.*

"What happened to your eye? Someone did that deliberately.

Why? Who?"

Akhaïdes stayed there, not answering, not moving, until
Hawmai gave up and walked away. Then he rose and turned, weak
legs and back straining, leaning into the sharp catch in his ribs,
forcing the motion to look smooth and strong.

The tall slave was waiting. He felt their affinity, not as man
and woman, but as outlaw and slave. They were not human, either
of them, but the slave was protected by law and custom. He looked
past her to Tisamenus, who was breaking pieces off his bread for
the hound.

The slave retrieved the fillet where it had snagged on grass and
pulsed in the current. She wrung it out, and he held his hair back,
even that small effort making his arms tremble, as she tied the
fillet around his head. She was tall enough that he did not have to
lean. He flinched when her fingers brushed his cheek, and when
she finished he left her without a word or a gesture.

Sigewas Teller still held half a round of his own bread. As
Akhaïdes passed him, Sigewas pressed it into his hand, then bent
and busied himself with a shoe.

Oxylus stood behind Tisamenus's shoulder. The one-eyed
white horse, which Oxylus rode badly, dozed behind him.
Tisamenus occupied a folding stool. Hawmai stood apart, the High
King's man. The three of them waiting, all equally watchful.

Like a dog choosing a master, Akhaïdes eased down to sit on
the ground at Tisamenus's feet. The hound moved over to give him
room.

* * *

"How did you know?"

When Akhaïdes did not sit up immediately, Sigewas drew back
to kick him, thought better of it, and stamped the foot a hand's
breadth from his face instead.

Akhaïdes opened his eye but did not move otherwise.

Sigewas crouched by his head and snarled, "Tell me! Tell us! How did you know?"

Akhaïdes pushed himself up carefully, finally sitting nearly erect in the corner of the Athenians' guest tent, with a scrap of discarded blanket over his shoulders.

He raised his face to Sigewas's. "Assembly bad?"

"Bad? It was a calamity. Thymoetes insulted the king, even though it's his daughter who hasn't produced an heir in two years of marriage. He made the king walk all the way to meet him. He said . . . I forget what he said, but it was insulting. And we didn't get dinner."

Akhaïdes looked past Sigewas at the other Companions, also draped in finery, all red-faced with fury and shame.

"And then?" Akhaïdes asked.

"Isn't that enough? You sat there while we all got dressed and ready, and you didn't say anything except 'Don't go.' And he probably didn't hear you. And then—"

Akhaïdes shrugged the blanket onto his shoulders. "Can't talk before . . ."

"Before permission, I know. But you did say it, just not to any person. And nobody heard."

"You heard."

Sigewas glared, not giving up so easily. "Then Tisamenus—the king—just stood there like a rabbit, not doing anything, and Hawmai didn't do anything, so we got all around the king and took him out of there. And we didn't get dinner. And then—"

"Hawmai not surprised."

"This isn't about Hawmai. I'm asking you, how did you know?"

"Hawmai said."

Sigewas blinked. "He did not. When?"

"This morning. This day. All the time."

Sigewas crouched there, still blinking. The blinking stopped, and he sighed. "Your Mycenaean is improving."

"You keep talking."

Sigewas snorted a laugh. Seeing that there would be no violence, the Companions set about removing and storing their elaborate clothes and jewelry, grumbling all the while.

"Where is king? Hawmai? Oxylus?"

"In mourning, in the fancy tent. At least, they didn't kick him out of that."

"Hawmai doing what?"

Sigewas started to answer, then stopped and considered the question. "I can tell you what he's *not* doing. He's not raging, cursing, threatening, or planning revenge. He's not thinking out all the angles, the way he did when he didn't know what to do with *you.* He looks, um, disappointed."

"Disappointed. Hawmai."

"And smug." Sigewas closed his eyes. "I feel stupid."

"Why call you 'Teller'?"

"Hunh?" He opened his eyes. "Oh. Because I know the old stories and gather the new ones. I know who hides what, where. Who is whose father, who is *really* whose father. Minstrels don't know all I know. When I tell a story, I use the same words all the way through."

He looked beyond Akhaïdes, at the tent wall. "Some stories can't be told yet but should be saved. For later, when they'll be safe to tell."

"Weave word cloth."

"Or scrolls of pictures so even if they can't be told now, we'll have them for the future."

"Save this one."

"You're probably right. It's not finished. I *hope* it's not finished."

Sigewas did nothing more for a while. Finally he said, "Tisamenus was never meant to be a king. The only son of Orestes' last wife, spoiled and ignored like all last sons. There were crowds of grown sons with wives, children, a generous supply of bastards. They all were murdered—all the sons and grandsons, all the pregnant women, all in one night. Now there's only Tisamenus, whose wife still has no child at all."

"How he not murdered?"

"He was fostering with Thymoetes. Six years old or so. His own lawagetas—not Hawmai—got him out in secret. They walked to Pylos, to the king Melanthus, for protection. Just the two of them, hiding from the hunters all the way. In winter snow up to . . . well, very deep snow."

"Thymoetes not protect?"

"The lawagetas was afraid to take a chance."

"Trust Melanthus only."

"No one else."

"How lawagetas know?"

"How did he know in time to save him?" Sigewas raised his brows. "I never wondered." After pondering for a moment, he said, "So even his fostering didn't help him much. He had to get back to Mycenae as soon as possible, after it was safe. He was too young, but what else to do?"

"Maybe Thymoetes still angry."

"Saw that as an insult? Maybe. But then he gave a daughter for Tisamenus."

"To make a High King."

Sigewas considered this.

"A story to save," Akhaïdes said again.

"Yes, it is. And I notice that you don't ask who did the murders. Anyone would ask that." Sigewas unwound a band of fat pearls from his neck, then unclipped his hair.

He started to say more, but a voice spoke outside. Then the tent flap rose, and women entered, carrying bowls of meat with gravy, olives, cubed cheese in vinegar, and stewed greens, which they laid out on the carpet, under the direction of Tisamenus's slave.

"I guess all is forgiven," one Companion said as they knelt around the bowls, jesting and jostling one another, reaching for favorite morsels.

When they had finished, Sigewas gathered a pile of leavings into a bowl for Akhaïdes. Akhaïdes touched his forehead in thanks, but Sigewas lingered until he looked up.

"'Forgiven?'" Sigewas asked.

"Big insult public, small apology private."

"Exactly what I was thinking."

"My . . . fault."

"What? No. Yes, I was angry because, well . . . But it's for something you didn't do—and would have been punished for if you had. But you didn't actually *do* anything wrong."

"Being here. Being."

Sigewas blinked again. "What did you tell Hawmai about every problem in the world not being his responsibility?"

"Different."

Sigewas started to object, then just said, "If you ever want to give me your story, you can. It will be safe with me." He turned and went away to find a sleeping place.

* * *

The High King's road from Boeotia into the hills of Phocis was rutted and gouged, barely passable. Most of the stones had been stolen to build shelters for hunters and goatherds, to fortify the hamlets of warrior-farmers, to pile up the strongholds that shadowed the cliffs and crags. Rather than rising to shed snow, the roadway sometimes lay like a moat, filled with standing water. Then it narrowed to a twisting skein of wheel-worn ruts, with only the largest rocks scraped away.

There was no question of riding, not in the chariots, which wrenched and twisted, or in the lurching, tottering wagons. Oxylus tied the white horse to a wagon and walked with everyone else. The oxen plodded and stopped, plodded and stopped, too calm to fret when a wheel jammed and they must wait while the men struggled to free it. But the constant jostling irritated the ponies until they kicked and bit at their harness mates.

The gray horse neighed all day, every day, its voice mocked by echoes from the crags that closed around them. The ponies had long stopped answering. The men winced and grumbled and glanced over their shoulders at the racket, as if it were the horse's noise alone that gave away their presence in this hostile land. Only Akhaïdes responded, sometimes raising his head to listen. He never approached the animal, though, and if he knew how to quiet it, he never said.

The current king of Phocis had not provided them an escort, and the men wondered if this was only another insulting dismissal, or if it held some grimmer meaning. They treated Tisamenus with cool courtesy: cool in case their vulnerability was his fault, but courteous in case the Phocians might relent and they might find themselves out of favor. Tisamenus himself was subdued and silent. Hawmai made all decisions, not even bothering to glance at the king for token consent.

The oldest land in the world, Sigewas called it, and so it appeared. The gaunt soil seemed mummified, its protruding bones pitted and rotten, its gray trees weary of their own fertility, its springs tepid, its animals already hoary at birth. Spaces that elsewhere would flame with young green pushed out only pale stubs of grass, and the rare stand of robust pines stood out as unsettlingly as the Mycenaean train itself. Sigewas warned of nonhuman raiders, ruthless nymphs, desperate spirits and noontime ghosts, more steadfast than griffins once they chose their prey.

The soil would not hold a tent peg, and the rocks that the men piled to steady the poles slithered down again and the poles fell. So when night crept up out of the fissures around them, Tisamenus, Hawmai, the Companions, slaves, and servants all huddled together under tent cloth draped over bushes and standing stones. And there they winced at the murmurs, taps, and whistles overhead. Oxylus joined that throng, keeping to the outer edge, never touching anyone else. Only Akhaïdes did not seek shelter, but lay with his shred of blanket under the unblinking moon, feeling closer to the animals than to other men.

Normally, they would have been glad for the trees's protection, but no one dared step in among those eerie pines, even to gather firewood. Something so unnatural had to be guarded by terrible powers. The tough bushes they burned gave only grudging warmth, and the fires faded even though wood remained unburned. They used lamps for a short time after dark but mostly hoarded the oil, not knowing how long it might have to last.

The grimness of this ascent suppressed talk and stifled pleasure. Even at the end of the day, the men did not play games. The women did not sing together. And Sigewas did nothing to lighten the mood. The tales he told in the evenings were about murders and monsters and the land of the dead. About Proteus the shape-shifter. About the first king of Phocis, who liked his guests so much that he preserved them in vinegar so they would stay longer. About Tiresias the Wise—first a man, then a woman, then a man again because of encounters with snakes, which, everyone knew, changed their sex each time they changed their skins.

He told of Tydeus, whom Delphi's Serpent—female at the time—had taken for a consort. Tydeus led a cursed army, fought a forbidden duel, and ate the brain of his dying enemy.

He told how, on their flight from Hades and the land of the

dead, Theseus and his friends had come across an outlaw sitting, exactly as he should, by the side of the road. Theseus's group had paused long enough to seize the man, bind him, and leave him as a meal to slow the pursuing Cerberus.

He told about the Good Kinsman of Arcadia, who used the guise of a lost child to dupe a family into taking it in. Then the child murdered all the blood sons and hid their corpses before shedding its human form and flying back to Até, its mother. A new, untainted son was born to the family, but the lost bones still lay somewhere, clothed in flesh, with perytons circling over them, hoping for the dead or the living to come searching so they could steal their places.

One or two of the listeners glanced hopefully at Elawon, who, as the only Arcadian among them, might elaborate on the tale, but he ignored that.

"Monsters can die," Sigewas added. "Even the Serpent won't live forever. But they're the earth's children, so they live a long time. And they can hide anywhere: in caves, trees, clouds, under the sea. And we never know when they might be listening to us.

"That's why we still call Tydeus a king and not a monster. That's why we call a monster 'The Good Kinsman.' 'Good' because, if it's listening, we want to appease it. 'Kinsman' as a way to appeal to any compassion it might recall from its human form.

"It was said that the child called itself Ephialtes." Sigewas gave them time to appreciate that: *Nightmare.* "That's the reason we're careful how we name our children, and the reason we always ask the names of strangers. That's the one thing a monster can't lie about: its name."

No one looked for Akhaïdes, so late in divulging his name—which, Hawmai had noted, was not a name at all. But out beyond the servants, in the unprotected night, Sigewas saw a fleck of cold white luminosity where lamplight for a moment glinted off

Akhaïdes' eye. Akhaïdes usually ignored Sigewas's stories, just as he ignored everything else the Mycenaeans did, but this time he seemed to be listening. Sigewas couldn't help but smile with an artist's contentment.

* * *

With the wood refusing to burn, the slaves could not cook. Thus, the meals were olives, figs, hard cheese, pickle, and dried bread dipped in beakers of the tasteless water. The animals nosed the living Phocian grass and left it ungrazed, so oxen, ponies, and the white horse amicably shared hay the drivers had brought for them. The gray, on the other hand, refused to eat even the hay, just shoving it around contemptuously with its lip.

Akhaïdes slowly shed the stench of his captivity. Sunlight and stony air freshened his clothes, brought color to his face, and even brightened the ashen shock of hair. At first, he moved like a damaged spider, stopping often to press a hand to his side, cough and spit blood, then scuff dust over the stain. As the trek went on, he moved more easily. He stayed scrupulously apart from the others, even the servants and Tisamenus's slave, all of whom grew comfortable with his quiet presence. Although two outlaws might have kept company together, he paid no more attention to Oxylus than to anyone else, never looking directly at them. And—perhaps because his crime had left no marks or stains on his clothes—it was easy to forget that Akhaïdes had killed a guiltless man and escaped punishment. He had passed the three nights and two days that Tisamenus could shelter him, with no objection even from Hawmai.

Only Elawon, when he and Akhaïdes were near each other, would hold the arm on that side closer to his own body, as if an extra finger's breadth would matter, then would tilt his head and breathe in almost contemplatively before twitching his head away.

Sigewas noticed this and smiled at Elawon's familiar fussiness.

Even by day, the Mycenaeans stayed close together, stepping out of sight for only moments when modesty required. Tisamenus's hound, which had joyously hunted rabbits all over Copais, pressed close to Tisamenus's leg and finally took up squatting ostentatiously to pee, proclaiming its harmlessness. And anyway, there was nothing to hunt, not for the hound or for the Mycenaeans, though a group went out daily with bows in hand, only to return with their arrows unused.

"We see wolf tracks all the time," one of the hunters complained. "They must be eating something." He was rewarded with several sets of eyes rolled in alarm, and protective fists clapped against foreheads hard enough to hurt.

Akhaïdes often roamed out of sight while the Mycenaeans repaired wheels and axles. He always left behind, in a corner of a wagon, the sack that purportedly held his possessions—unspoken assurance that he would return. Hawmai glared when he left, but sent no one after him. Outlaws must squat to urinate and must defecate in secret, but Sigewas suspected that Akhaïdes sought solitude for other reasons. He followed several times but quickly found himself alone, Akhaïdes having vanished among the rocks as smoothly and quietly as any serpent.

* * *

Sigewas found Akhaïdes once, in the shadow of a great boulder, his grayed rags a near-perfect camouflage, hands and forehead pressed to the veined surface.

"In the old ways," Akhaïdes said without turning, "one would be naked." He had not spoken in so long that Sigewas had forgotten his accent. "If I take these off, though, they will . . . dissolve."

"Your language has improved. I know; you've now listened to me for half a month."

Akhaïdes turned to face him.

"How did you know it was me here?" Sigewas asked.

"How do I know that you remember your grandfathers speaking to the earth when, for all your respect for their stories, you've never done it yourself? You are as clear as water, my lord." Akhaïdes touched his forehead, passed Sigewas, and went away.

His grandfathers—it had never occurred to Sigewas to do as the old men had done. With great deliberation, he laid his palms against the rock. It was cold and rough; that was all. Still, Akhaïdes was gone and there was no one to mock him. He touched his forehead to the surface between his hands. Nothing. He said aloud, "I hear you."

The answer came in the lowest of vibrations, as if the stone resonated to a distant sepulchral voice. He turned his head to press his ear to it. It made no words, yet it was to him that it spoke. It knew he was here.

He jerked away. The stone stood calm, silent, as patient as forever.

"I'll never do that again!" He declared aloud.

When he returned to the road, he found everyone standing around Akhaïdes, who knelt on a flat spot. Hawmai turned to Sigewas. "You're just in time. You do it."

"Do what?" Then he saw the ox goad in Hawmai's hand.

"He spoke to you first. That's forbidden."

"How do you know he did?"

"How do you think? He came up wanting to say something, so I let him. Use this."

Sigewas put both hands behind his back.

"Or I will. We can't have Eris making trouble." His naming an immortal so casually made the other men flinch, but Hawmai went on firmly. "This is serious business."

Sigewas looked around at faces eager for something, anything, to relieve the tension. Oxylus's expression did not differ in any way from the other men's. Tisamenus actually looked ill.

Sigewas took the goad. It was heavy, flexible, as long as his arm, the handle wrapped in leather. A driver murmured worriedly. The goad must be his. Everyone else was silent.

"I don't want a good tool wasted," Hawmai added, "so leave the shirt on."

Suddenly, Sigewas hated Hawmai. But there was nothing else to do. *Don't yell,* he thought. *Don't give him the satisfaction.*

He swung. The goad whistled and struck. Akhaïdes snatched a breath through his teeth.

"Again."

Whistle, smack, hiss.

"Again."

Again.

"That's enough."

Sigewas threw the goad into the rocks. Its owner darted after it. Sigewas looked around. Oxylus was smiling with apparent relief. Tisamenus was not in sight. Only Elawon, of all people, seemed to struggle to contain his apprehension and uncertainty.

"It's done," Hawmai said with satisfaction.

You are as clear as water, my lord. Then Sigewas understood. "You planned this," he said to Akhaïdes, who knelt in the road, breathing quietly. "You planned it in a second, when you knew it was me behind you. But why?"

Hawmai glanced at the other men. They all turned quickly away, busy with other things.

"Oh," Sigewas answered himself. "You did it so I won't follow you again."

Akhaïdes raised one leg, set his frayed boot on a flat stone, got his balance, rose. He leaned on his knees for a moment, then straightened and walked away.

"It won't work, you know," Sigewas called after him.

"It had better work," Hawmai answered.

Sigewas hardly heard that. He was realizing something so preposterous, he barely understood it. He had always thought himself clever. But he had told Akhaïdes he felt stupid. And he really was.

He had smiled, *smiled,* at the lamplight glint in Akhaïdes' eye.

* * *

The goad had felt more startling than painful. Even now, hours later, the skin of Akhaïdes' back prickled and quivered. The pain was bearable, and it was a useful reminder.

Then, as he stood watching the Mycenaeans labor up the road and out of sight, he felt a powerful urge to turn, to face someone who could not possibly be behind him. He didn't turn, yet a voice spoke anyway.

You don't care if you're caressed or beaten, as long as you're touched at all. But you forgot something.

He raised his head sharply. The voice fell silent, and he knew that those words had not been spoken yet. But they would be spoken, and by someone Akhaïdes could not imagine now, here in the rising darkness among Parnassos's bones.

He had greeted the earth, and it had responded in the first language he ever learned. I am here. *And I am here.* I am coming. *She knows.* Will I be welcome? No answer.

Then that nameless human voice again: *But you forgot something.*

What did I forget?

No answer.

What does the cicada know now of the history you left behind?
What does the cricket know?^v

—Odysseus Elytis

They came into the Pleistos River Valley from its upper end. At one moment, they were creeping over a steeply pitched slope of thorn, vine, and shattered rock that swept up to Parnassos unobstructed. Then the road curled down into a twisting ravine of cliffs and terraces. They slept one last night with the dark air hissing and squealing above them, hiding their heads and numbly waiting for light. Only Tisamenus and Sigewas uncovered their faces to see Akhaïdes, knees drawn up, head raised, gazing unblinking at the moon-tipped peaks of Arcadia.

The next morning, they came to Delphi.

* * *

Parnassos was as multiheaded as a hydra, and in one of those heads was the mouth of the underworld. When the great Serpent came out of the earth, it rose from that fanged throat, crept down a swale of stone, slid between two megaliths and through the spring that rose between them, then slithered on down the valley of the Pleistos River to hunt men at sea. Where the Serpent turned to follow the river lay a puckered vertical vent of stone. This was the bottomless pool where the unforgiven went to swim until they drowned.

The Serpent was black, in mourning for her husband—or, with every other molting, for his wife—and for the eggs that she sought endlessly through caverns and fissures of stone. Sometimes, a frigid stench seeped from the cave and from the spring. It was the souls of men her husband had taken. It was her lost eggs rotting. When the Serpent passed, it could not be seen, but the earth's groaning marked its transit.

Just as fearsome was the nymph Kastalia, the ancient mantis monster who had owned this place before there were serpents at all and was never seen, but the mere scratching of her many legs among the stones could stop a man's heart.

In the midst of all this hung the sanctuary of Delphi: three or four small withy-built structures on a chain of narrow terraces and pathways shaded by black cypress trees. Nothing remarkable about it except its site: cramped into a near-vertical corner of the heart of peril, looking at nothing but itself. In this early light, every surface of water, stone, leaf, or tile, gleamed like shed snakeskin.

* * *

Steps before the small stone bridge that spanned the spring's stream, Tisamenus got down from his chariot. The Mycenaeans stopped and waited while he bent to study a skeleton by the roadside, green with mold and wound in creepers and straw.

At Tisamenus's shoulder, Hawmai murmured, "Outlaw."

"How long has he been here?"

"Ten years. A hundred."

Hawmai turned to look along the Mycenaean train. He called out to all, "We enter sanctity. What lives here is the most ancient and the most revered. It is the fiercest to defend its ground. No man may go armed, on horseback, or in a chariot. There will be no fighting between men. This . . ." He turned his palm up at the roadside remains. ". . . is a warning to us all."

The Companions tied the hilts of their swords and swung the belts around their shoulders so that the scabbards hung down their backs. Tisamenus waved his driver away and took the ponies' reins in each hand, just below the bit. He started over the bridge, the ponies' heads at his shoulders. The Companions hurried to dismount, too. Oxylus slid off the white horse's back and looped the rein over a cart rail. Each man passing the moldy bones touched fist to forehead.

"The trees here," Tisamenus said. "My father planted them, didn't he?"

"Orestes planted cypresses," Hawmai confirmed. "It was part of his reparation."

"They beat him. They beat the High King."

"Reparation."

Farther back, Sigewas told an awed listener, "They only cultivate trees here. The roots hold spirits underground. Vines or vegetables can't do that."

By the time the spring's water reached the bridge, the magic had dissolved and it was ordinary. Anyone could drink it—any animal, any plant. Still, the ponies snorted and tiptoed and balked at crossing. The oxen and the white horse walked nose down, puzzled by the surface under their feet. The gray reared and fought, striking at its tether. The cart dragged it over the bridge anyway, and once across, the horse walked sideways, blowing fiercely, keeping an eye not on the bridge but on the huge stones above.

When Tisamenus had nearly reached the hewn rock steps leading to the sanctuary, he handed the ponies' reins to his driver and went on alone. The hound vaulted out of the chariot to race after him, and the ponies tugged at the reins, wanting to follow, too.

Tisamenus did not look down as he passed more outlaws'

remains beside the road. The hound sniffed each one, then lowered its ears and went on. Furtive as a thief, Oxylus followed, swinging wide to avoid each ancient corpse, keeping both fists at his forehead. Tisamenus climbed the steps into deep shade, out of view.

Coming to the bridge last of all, unnoticed even by Sigewas, Akhaïdes stood a long time studying the remains of the first dead outlaw. He knelt and touched the skull as gently as one might touch a child or a lover. Then he crossed the bridge.

* * *

Hawmai stood beside his chariot, at the outer edge of the road. Just beyond his feet, the ravine dropped steeply away, clogged with boulders, brush, and scrub trees. Its banks were terraced with olives, and in its depths far below, little Pleistos ran, white with foam but too far away to hear. The distant black pool drew his eyes, and he had to make himself look away.

Toward the west, he knew, the vale ran down to a flat basin with a port, groves, and meadows. The steep wall beyond Pleistos hid the Gulf and, behind that, the whole Peloponnesos. But from this spot, Delphi might be all there was to the world.

In his mind, he placed a wall here, a tower there, and was satisfied that a hundred men could hold the place. For what purpose, though? If the time came when monsters could not defend their own, what help could men provide?

He heard a soft step behind him and, feeling benevolent, said, "Well?"

"You plan defenses." The accent was strong but the grammar correct.

"It's a habit."

"Where will you rest here?"

"Where high kings always do: a flat area with a well, down

around that bend."

"The same place? Even if you don't come?"

"Always the same place ready for us."

Hawmai gazed idly at the wall beyond Pleistos.

"Arcadia is there," Akhaïdes murmured.

"Egypt is, too, if you stand high enough to see it. And it's far more interesting."

They shared silence.

"You wanted to come here," Hawmai said. "You came willingly." Both of them let that half-lie pass. "And now you're here. You must be glad."

"Always the same place," Akhaïdes murmured, "even if you don't come."

Hawmai turned to see Oxylus emerge from the shade at the top of the steps, neither gesturing nor speaking, looking at Akhaïdes. Akhaïdes must have felt the silent summons, and turned. Hawmai felt the fleeting urge to wish him luck's help. That urge passed as Akhaïdes crossed the road.

Idly watching, Hawmai considered how most men, when walking, strove to project mass and weight, every stride a declaration of status. Outlaws normally used a mild, rueful slink, like Oxylus's. Hawmai had supposed Akhaïdes' odd gait a combination of humility, pain, and half-blindness. But now he saw it. This low, unassuming stride was partly an old man's limp, but also the prowl of a hunting animal—a seamless fit with the way he seemed to ignore all the men around him, in the same way that a predator never looked directly at its intended prey.

To hunt, Hawmai thought. *But hunt what?*

Then he knew. Knew it so swiftly and with such certainty that he nearly cried out aloud. *Arcadia is there.* He nearly called for Sigewas, for anyone, to collect all the men they could for witness and make sure he was right, or make sure he was wrong.

That first night in Arne, he had planned to go back and cut the thing's throat. Foiled, he planned to drop it off a cliff. No, drag it here because it didn't want to come, and what harm could it do? And so he had escorted it like royalty and delivered it like a gift—to the place he should least have wanted it to be. Watching Akhaïdes ascend into shadow, he drew in a breath and wondered silently, frantically, what would come down again.

* * *

So familiar still was the hiss of boughs and the clatter of water, the texture of the path underfoot, the smell of cypress and stone and mossy ooze, of fear and the offal and brains and blood of the dead.

The sanctuary itself was just a crooked withy shack, the front wall steadied on a line of rough-cut rock. Limed on the outside, but inside, Akhaïdes remembered, all bare dark branches, like a goat shed, a cage, a lair. A bell hung by the entrance. He had once hauled boldly on its cord, certain of a welcome, certain of help. This time, he did not touch it.

You are outlawed, the priest said. *Unclean. You are not wanted. You have no father and no mother, no sons, no daughters. You have no kin, no name, no king. You have no debts, no duty, no protection. Anyone can kill you with no penalty.*

He had knelt with his arms raised, still so sure that they would help him.

A one-armed male servant squatted by the low entrance, brushing ants from Tisamenus's empty shoes. He glanced up at Akhaïdes, then away again. The hound lay panting in a wash of light. It thumped its tail at him.

Beyond the hound, near an old white four-sided column—a stele no taller than themselves—a group of boys watched soberly. Akhaïdes knew they were the sacred children, born with no father to claim them, brought or sent by whatever lord was responsible for the conduct of his people, given no patronymics, the property of the nymph Kastalia. A girl could be a slave, but male slaves were more trouble than value, their masters always fearing resentment and revenge. Only Delphi provided a use for such boys: as servants, acolytes, sacrifices. Most of these lean, vigilant children would not live past their baby names.

He glanced back at the white stele. It was carved down one side with signs that, he knew, represented words or the sounds of words, though he did not know how to read them. Some riddle meant for someone—nothing to do with him.

Now, breathing slowly and quietly, he faced the entrance. *Just move from moment to moment until it's over.* Those sounded like words that Tisamenus might speak, but not yet. He could not say such a thing yet.

He pulled off his boots, breaking the braided grass stems that held them on, and stepped barefoot past the servant, over the threshold stone, out of the world.

The chamber had the same creeping, earthy chill that he remembered. There were no windows, lamps, or furniture—only a floor of rough flags, tilted to follow the land's rise. Light seeped through the Walls's woven willows. He saw shadows moving—people, perhaps—and heard voices murmur. Against the farthest wall, surrounded by tiny clay votive figurines molded in shapes of worship and mourning, a stone waited.

Black and high as a man's waist, it was sculpted, as if by madmen's hands, into a tortured snarl of bones: cow, ram, human, whale, peryton, griffin—all bent and forced together until they could never be untangled. Black spattered the floor around it.

Here were all the creatures of the previous world, eaten by some power when they proved disappointing, their bones regurgitated like owl-vomited mice. When the Serpent went away for the final time, priests would point to a new, white, blameless ornament as its tomb. But that would be a lie.

Light crept brokenly over the stone's surfaces: rib, thigh, hoof, jaw. Neither sun nor lamp, it was the bland, uncaring glance of the stone itself that swung around the room, touching, gliding. When it touched Akhaïdes, in that instant it flared white fire.

He dropped to his knees so hard that someone—Tisamenus?— gasped. He had nothing to cover himself with—had not thought to bring even the shred of blanket. He laid his arms over his head and whispered, "Hear me, Grandfather."

Steps approached, sliding a little on the gritty flags—a sound so like snakeskin on sand that it twitched at his heart. A voice he knew asked, "Who are you?"

Akhaïdes looked up. The red-robed priest stood fiercely erect, eyes like hematite in the massed wrinkles of his face and naked head. Akhaïdes knew that glare, that stance, that thin, judgmental face. Farther back stood Tisamenus and a second priest, a heavy man with kinder eyes. But it was this priest he remembered.

"Who are you?" the priest asked mildly again. Then his eyes sharpened. "You!"

It was an old word, obsolete, meant for weeds, bad weather, insects, or illness. Trees, slaves, and animals, being serviceable, were addressed more courteously. "You," he said again in Akhaïdes' own language, affirming the insult.

Then he switched to Mycenaean, so everyone would understand. "Why has no one put a stop to you? They were never burned or buried. Names not called. Spirits lost."

Akhaïdes forced his mouth to move. "Are you Menetor now? Please hear me."

"Hear lies."

"All lies are left on your threshold, Grandfather. No one would tell lies here."

"You never met Odysseus."

Akhaïdes' heart pounded and thumped like a trapped animal.

"And do *not* call me 'Grandfather.' That is a term of respect you have no right to use. You don't respect me. You respect only your own will. You belong by the roadside, or flying with the perytons you're so fond of. You stink of arrogance and nothing more."

"Grand—" He stopped himself. "Please . . ."

Menetor spoke over him. "No one needs you. No place is empty for you. No one would pluck you from the jaws of fate and carry you home and set you by a fire."

"I would."

Akhaïdes and Menetor froze, not understanding the interruption. Then Tisamenus repeated, "I would do that."

Both Menetor and Akhaïdes barked, "No!"

"You came here with me because you believed I could."

"I came here with you because you would feed me on the way."

"That's not true!"

Menetor overran them. "Why do these things get outlawed, child? To protect the likes of you. Save your treasure for widows and orphans, not this snake food."

The second priest took Tisamenus's arm. The priest's plump face was marked with lines of habitual humor, but none of that showed now.

"My father killed his own mother," Tisamenus said, "but you absolved him here."

"Whom did this thing kill? Not just some woman as Orestes did, but a lineage: men, and all the men coming after until the end of time."

"I don't understand," Tisamenus said. "Who is he? Akhaïdes, who are you?"

"I saved the baby," Akhaïdes whispered.

"What baby?" Tisamenus asked. The priest tightened the grip on his arm.

Menetor said, "A baby isn't a man or even a woman. It has no name. It's nothing." He sucked air through his teeth. "Orestes' friends sent a dragon's hoard of gold for him. The world needed Orestes. The world does not need this."

"Oh," Tisamenus whispered. "I know what baby you mean. I know who you are."

Akhaïdes' hands slid upward until the heels pressed against his temples, and his fingers clawed into his matted hair. "The . . ." He couldn't say it. ". . . It could absolve me."

"The Serpent wouldn't even shit you out after swallowing you. Don't dare think that . . ."

"I don't dare. I plead."

"For mercy. For *pity*," Menetor sneered.

"Only justice."

"Real suppliants make prettier speeches, or at least tears."

"Does that make them more sincere? I kept outlawry. All this time, I kept it."

"And that makes you owed somehow? No. Do something useful, at last. Let a man sharpen his sword on your bones. Go sit by the road, as I told you to do when I was young and you were slightly less stupid than you are now."

Akhaïdes hid his face with his hands.

"Help him," Tisamenus whispered.

"I won't. And the Serpent won't. He'd give any snake colic."

"You won't take compensation from me?"

"That much gold hasn't been minted or mined."

Akhaïdes cleared his throat. "Tell me what else to do, and I'll do it. If you want tears, I'll weep. If you want blood, I'll bleed. But I can't . . . orate. I can only act."

"There is no act you can perform that will matter."

Akhaïdes reached to his hip, where a knife should hang. Seeing that, Tisamenus bent to offer his own gold-worked dagger. Akhaïdes took it, even as the second priest pulled Tisamenus away.

Akhaïdes thrust the blade into his other hand, at the base of the thumb. Blood welled into the bowl of his palm. He lifted it up to Menetor's gaze.

"So. Will you make magic, Outlaw?"

He could not move toward the stone. A hair too close, and his spirit would rip out of his body and flop screeching over the floor like a crippled crow. He palmed the blood across a paving stone, where it curdled, mixed with sand. He raised the dagger to his throat.

"No," said Menetor.

Akhaïdes looked up, moving only his eye. Under his skin, the blood pulsed steadily against the blade.

"You know that's forbidden. No outlaw may kill himself. And you're such a fool, you secretly believe there's some hope even now."

The dagger slid from Akhaïdes' hand and clattered on the floor. He groaned.

But beyond where he knelt, the blood began to move. It crept on its own, over the pavement and down into fissures, even rolling a few grains of sand along as it disappeared.

Watching, Menetor said, "However, you become slightly more interesting. Magic is made. This is enough."

Akhaïdes' head snapped up, but Menetor's face still showed only disdain.

"When a dog loses its way," he said, "it runs until it can't run anymore. Then it walks until it can't walk anymore. Then what does it do?"

Akhaïdes did not answer.

"And what does it not do? You will never again see the land where you were born."

"How will you stop me?"

"You will stop yourself."

"But I know where—"

"You will *not* bargain for the spirits of men!"

Tisamenus said, "If he can release them, why not let him do it?"

Menetor turned on him. "Do you think the Serpent might say, 'Tisamenus Oresteides doesn't care for my laws; I'll change them to something he prefers.'?"

"No." Tisamenus started to say more, then just repeated, "No."

"So one of you, at least, has sense. Explain it to your brother here. Use very small words."

He glanced down. "You may not live where any man lived before your crime. You know this, of course. That's why you left this world for one that you also destroyed."

"How do you know he did that?" Tisamenus asked.

"He's here, not there."

Akhaïdes swallowed. "May I ask something?"

Menetor waited.

"How large is the world?"

"Three thousand rivers and three thousand springs. Each with a name."

"That's not true."

"You didn't ask for truth. You asked for the answer." Menetor turned away, then back. "Remember, both of you, the blood between you." He went out. The other priest followed.

Tisamenus reached to pick up his dagger, but Akhaïdes hissed a warning.

Tisamenus said, "I'm a king. Your blood can't harm me."

Akhaïdes instantly uncoiled to drive a shoulder into Tisamenus's chest, sending him flailing backward. The dagger rebounded off a wall and skidded through the arrayed votives, bowling them in all directions. Akhaïdes caught Tisamenus first by the wrist, yanking him upright, then with an open palm behind his head. And they were face to face, so close. He saw, in Tisamenus's startled eyes, how his own eye glittered like a knot of wire.

He snarled, "That priest once told me that all wrongness followed me out a door that closed forever. But that's not true and it never was. I *can* harm you."

He pulled his hand away, and Tisamenus staggered.

"Now, leave me!"

Tisamenus fled.

Akhaïdes followed as far as the open doorway. Hawmai was striding up the path, but stopped when Tisamenus darted past. Then, seeing Akhaïdes, he set himself.

"If you want that child to live," Akhaïdes said, "keep him safer."

Akhaïdes turned back, alone except for the stone and the votives, arms still upraised or else grasping their hair or wrapped around their bodies—mourning or pleading. Which of those poses should he assume? The stone had accepted his gift and now considered him. Its interest was impersonal and unutterably cold.

The votives twisted around to study him: unformed faces and hungry eyes. Those that the dagger had scattered struggled and rocked, trying to right themselves.

Blood dripped from his fingertips. He sank down, opened his hands, and lowered himself until his forehead touched the floor between them. Cold swelled up in surges, like ghosts rising, wings spreading—a monster's undulating shadow. No one could resist and survive. And no one could surrender and survive.

"We won't give you up," Menetor had once told him. "That's not what we do." And then they had given something so terrible, there could be no returning from it, ever.

Deep below, the earth creaked and shivered. Blood pooled and sucked down between the flagstones. The votives squeaked and swayed and waved their stiff little arms, ravenous but legless and, thus, unable to come and feed.

Ah, you again. What do you want this time? Are you finally ready to look on something truly frightening? Are you ready to look on yourself through my eyes? You believe you are ready. You are not. You believe you have finished. You have not even begun.

Go, follow like a dog at some stranger's heel, or sit by the roadside, or come down to my pool and I will take you now, though you wouldn't like where I would take you.

If you would have what you want, you must give me everything: not this cheap humility, but body, mind, hope, fear, and all the hunger that fed you this long. Come back when this is done. Until then, do not come again.

If I come again, and give all you ask, what will you give me?

Why, nothing, the Serpent said. *Nothing at all.*

* * *

The Herakleid brothers walked together to the sanctuary: Temenus in the center because he would be High King; Aristodemus on his right because he was the oldest and the head of the clan; Kresphontes, the youngest, on the left. Unlike his brothers, Kresphontes wore his black hair long, wrapped around and around a polished wooden rod that was twisted tight and thrust back through the coil.

Aristodemus waved off the Delphi villagers who flocked around them with hands full of clay votives. The villagers gave way without resentment: they knew that the Herakleids had little to trade. "Poor as a Herakleid" was a saying long known here.

Temenus examined a crude winged figure, turning it over and around. His hands were large for him, boxy and practical, with no rings. A villager was sidestepping, keeping pace, keeping track of his goods while rattling off his sales pitch. But when Temenus half closed his canted dark eyes, the man fell silent.

Temenus handed back the figure. The man touched it to his

forehead and retreated.

Temenus asked, "Why is that worth a sheep? We can make them ourselves."

"But we don't," Aristodemus answered mildly.

"We should give a few," Kresphontes said. "The oracle helps us."

"Does it?" Temenus asked. His brothers exchanged glances behind his head. He had behaved snappishly since leaving the thalamus—the augury chamber—the day before, but had not told them what he learned.

"We can't quit just because we don't understand some things," Kresphontes said.

"But they make our goals harder to win," Temenus said. "I am, as usual, a fool to come here hoping. What do we have to give, that the powers will be generous in return?"

Aristodemus said, "If we hadn't lost our mother's dowry . . ."

"It wasn't lost," Kresphontes said. "If someone hadn't stolen it, we could get better auguries." From anyone else, this would sound irreverent. Not from Kresphontes.

"And why did they give us a place to stay so far away?" Temenus asked. "I wanted that spot just below the road there."

"It's reserved for the High King's Mycenaeans," Aristodemus answered.

Temenus grimaced. "They should be *my* Mycenaeans. It should be my place, and that child Tisamenus should be carrying my shoes for me."

"In time."

The curving road straightened here, and immediately ahead stood a long train of chariots and wagons. The villagers took off at a lope toward them. Then a slim figure rushed down the steps from the sanctuary, and the villagers stopped.

"Is that Tisamenus Oresteides?" Temenus asked.

"Who else would come here by land, with a troop so big?" Aristodemus said. "It must have taken a month and a half to get over Phocis with all that gear. And we knew they were coming. Our friends in Mycenae . . ."

The Herakleids kept walking. On the road ahead, Tisamenus confronted an older man, and his voice rose cracklingly high. The villagers backed away.

"Who's that, do you know?" Kresphontes asked.

"That," Aristodemus said, "is Hawmai Aquileides, Baron of Asine. The High King's lawagetas. I met him once, years ago. Rocks are more easily influenced—and have greater imagination."

"Young Tisamenus is looking warlike," Temenus said. "I wonder."

"We don't want to fight here." Aristodemus gazed down the string of Mycenaean chariots, at the warriors who were already drifting forward as villagers backed out of their path. "It's forbidden. And I'm not dressed for it."

Hawmai raised a hand to Tisamenus, gesturing, apparently explaining something. Tisamenus's stance changed from anger to uncertainty.

"I thought he would be older," Kresphontes said.

"He's twenty. Maybe a year or two more. He has no beard, because he has no children yet." Temenus noticed the way Kresphontes stared at him. "What?"

"Don't even think of sleeping with him."

Aristodemus choked and started to cough.

Temenus smiled. "Well, that would be a way to get to know him, though, wouldn't it? Maybe he'd give me Mycenae as a courting gift."

Aristodemus recovered. "Don't."

Leaving Tisamenus, Hawmai came toward them. "Herakleids! Why are you here?"

"My brother's foster father," Temenus answered, "is guardian of Delphi. We have more right to be here than you."

"Thymoetes fostered Tisamenus, too, and more recently. And we are the High King's men."

"Then show respect for the High King Temenus Aristomacheides Herakleides—me."

"That was settled years ago. Echemus Protector dealt with it for all of us. How can you still be festering over it?"

"It won't be settled until I sit where I belong, on the High Seat."

"You won't sit there anytime that I know of."

"This oracle said we will return in the eightieth year. That year is coming next."

Behind Hawmai, Tisamenus spoke up at last. "And maybe that year will leave next, and you'll still be sitting in the swamps, gnawing yourselves."

"And maybe we'll be sitting where we belong, and the swamps will be your tomb."

Tisamenus stepped between his ponies and snatched the reins. The ponies reared, nearly lifting him off the ground. As he strode past Hawmai, the ponies broke into an eager trot. The villagers scattered.

Temenus stepped into the center of the road. Tisamenus stopped. The ponies stamped and snorted as the two kings faced each other.

"Blue eyes," Temenus observed calmly. "You really are Pelopeid, aren't you?"

Tisamenus raised his chin. "Let me pass."

"Let you pass to do what? To tell the world you snubbed the man you robbed?"

Hawmai started forward again. Aristodemus raised a hand, and he slowed.

"Come," Temenus said. "We could talk together and be friends."

Tisamenus flared. "I have friends enough already!"

"Have you?" Temenus raised a hand, but only to touch his own mouth—a gesture both confident and provocative. "Not in this world."

Tisamenus's eyes flickered.

"I would give you a ring as a sign between us, but because of you I can't afford rings."

"And I'll give you nothing."

"Come to me later. We'll see what we can give each other." Temenus stepped aside and swept out a hand, inviting Tisamenus to pass.

Tisamenus jerked at the reins. The chariot rocked backward, then rolled on ahead. As the wheel skimmed past, Temenus nearly stepped on a parched corpse half-buried in the grass. He avoided it, snapped his fist to his forehead, then turned and followed Tisamenus with his eyes.

"An interesting young man," he observed.

"Don't!" Kresphontes told him.

The rest of the train was in motion. Only Hawmai stood still, facing Aristodemus. His driver guided the chariot to the side of the road, clinging grimly to the ponies' heads as they skidded and pawed, throwing clods of mud.

"We could abduct him," Temenus said.

"That's better than seducing him," Kresphontes snapped.

"How so? At least I might learn what his father is planning."

"You know it's true," Aristodemus said. "He can extract every secret a person has by sleeping with him . . . or her."

"Or it," Temenus added just to annoy his youngest brother.

Kresphontes spat into the grass, and a pony snorted at the sudden motion. Kresphontes turned fiercely on Aristodemus, who raised both hands in mock surrender. Turning again, Kresphontes strode toward the sanctuary. Temenus and Aristodemus gazed ruefully at each other.

"Sleep with Tisamenus if you want," Aristodemus said. "It certainly can't hurt."

Temenus smiled.

The baggage wagons were passing. From one seat, a striking woman, a slave by her dress, looked down at Temenus. He looked back at her once, then again. Tethered behind the wagon, the white horse cocked its head to examine Temenus with its good eye. Temenus turned to watch it pass, just as he had watched Tisamenus.

"That," he said, "is one of the things I came here to find."

"The woman or the horse?" Aristodemus asked.

"The horse first."

"They breed them in Boeotia."

"How soon can we conquer Boeotia?"

"You don't want to do that until it's absolutely necessary."

"Why don't I?"

"It's full of Boeotians. Now, come. We really should go up before we drown."

Temenus turned to Hawmai. "You understand my problem, of course. In leading a charge of bulls, much of the art is in keeping enough ahead of them to avoid being trampled."

"That's always true," Hawmai said.

They stood for a moment, regarding each other. Temenus's restless eyes measured Hawmai's stance, the way he held his hands, the calm returned gaze.

"Join me," Temenus said.

Hawmai's jaw dropped.

"We have less likely allies." Temenus winked, then laughed, and followed his brothers up to the sanctuary.

* * *

"Who is that?" Temenus asked.

The Herakleids stood in the sanctuary entrance. The walls wove and rewove dusty threads of sun in the dimness inside. Votives stood in perfect, decorous rows, their shadows a complex geometry of bright and black. The huddled figure on the floor was so still, it might be a discarded bundle of sticks and rags.

"Who is it?" Temenus asked again.

Menetor turned his back squarely to the stone. "It's no one."

Temenus glanced at Kresphontes, who stood with his head and hands raised in reverence. "Is he Mycenaean?"

Menetor did not answer.

"But then who . . ."

"No one," Menetor said firmly. "No one at all."

I would rather feel compassion than know the meaning of it.[vi]
—*Thomas Aquinas*

"Akhaïdes Outlaw."

The sound meant nothing until it repeated, then repeated again. He turned his head. Tisamenus's slave knelt just outside the entrance.

Near evening now, the air was chilling. The stone lay silent, its attention elsewhere. He rose enough to back out of the sanctuary. Only after stepping over the threshold did he turn and straighten. The one-armed servant was gone. The lean young boys sat together on the ground around the mossy white stele, arms around their drawn-up knees, gazing solemnly at him.

"You came a long way for disappointment," the slave said. The hemp bag from Arne lay on the ground beside her.

He sat down on the threshold.

"An injury that will not heal," she said, indicating the binding over his missing eye, "is a sign we recognize. What is so interested in you that it marks you as its own? We know who you were, but who will you be?"

"Don't try to give me hope."

"No. But don't stay longer. This place, this—" she pointed with her chin into the dark chamber "—can break a steadier mind than yours."

Akhaïdes' boots lay beside the door. As he fitted them on and tied them, carefully knotting the braided grass stems, the slave said, "I have been Tisamenus's since he was off the breast. I raised him when no one else would."

"And . . . ?"

"When all the sons of Orestes, all the other Pelopeids, were murdered twelve years ago, it was I, his driver, and his lawagetas who saved him. When Sigewas tells the story, he does not mention the driver and me, because we could easily be harmed. A lawagetas is safer."

"What's that to me?'

"Nothing to you. It is what I am. And my name is Aranare."

"I don't want your name."

"And yet, you have it."

In the distance, the Boeotian horse whinnied, high and plaintive. Akhaïdes glanced toward the sound. The boys mimicked his movement attentively, without irony.

"What does it call out for?" Aranare asked.

"For certainty. For a place and a master."

"Such as the fortunate have. But not you."

Boots on, he sat, arms over his knees.

"The priest waited for you. And there are others, too. More than you know. More than *they* know."

He looked up. "Not for me."

Her tawny eyes were serene. "More than you know."

"You came here to say something that means nothing?"

"And this. You seem to keep changing your mind. But in fact, you never stop bargaining with fate." She thought for a moment, then added, "Everyone believes that you ignore what they do. But you see everything. Judge everything. And there is no mercy in you, only. . ." She looked down at the bag. "You are needed."

He pulled the bag toward him, loosened the frayed knot, and took out an axe. It was made from a single leaf of bronze, as slender as a tool for women. The blade spread from a gather of ribbing at the shaft. On the shaft's other side, the ribbing opened into four spikes, each the length of a finger. The grip was wrapped in leather, and the blade was smudged with finger marks: men had handled it, their curiosity overpowering the law that made it unclean to touch.

He gathered dust and scrubbed the blade until it shone again and all traces of other hands were gone.

Tucking the axe into his armpit, he took from the bag a belt, and a dagger in a leather sheath. The sheath and the dagger's wooden hilt were marked with strings of burnt runes. The belt was strung with pouches of hard leather, the flaps embossed with silver and held shut by loops around small worked stones.

He hung the sheath on the belt and stood. The belt's closure was two stone carvings set in hardened leather, each the size of his palm: a pair of sinuous animals with legs and tails that locked together in an embrace. The sheath rested on his hip. He hung the axe in a stiff leather claw on the other side.

When he raised his head again, Aranare said, "You know my name. Do not forget me." She touched her fingertips to her forehead, rose, and left him.

He descended to the road. The sun, on its way to setting, flooded the sky with gold and emerald. To the west, the road curved down to towns, orchards, cultivated fields, and ports where an ordinary man might find a boat to take him across to Arcadia— or might even swim so far.

Back to the east, in the highlands that enfolded Parnassos, the axe might buy a seat by the fire in some Phocian stone tower until a younger man took even that away. But he could not live where men had lived for so long.

He could return to Boeotia, cross the end of the gulf, and finally see the great ramparts of Arcadia as he had seen them last, climb in among them, breathe the air he knew best. But those roads would remember him. He would be stopped somehow.

Straight down the escarpment lay the simplest road by far: a steep, winding footpath to the pool, already dark with evening—a worthy place to swim one last time.

And right here he might simply sit down and wait for . . . what? Wait for a man with shaded eyes and a mouth Akhaïdes would know well, with a javelin in a leather gauntlet. Wait for a young man with a shockingly familiar face and steady eyes, offering a bloody knife across one wrist. Wait for . . .

Then Oxylus—real, alive, right now—stepped onto the road.

He wore bronze armor and a helmet. One hand gripped a sword with a stepped, tapering tip; the other held a round wooden shield bound in bronze. At the shield's center was a shaman's mark, still wet, smeared across the boss like birth blood on an infant's scalp.

In a movement purely unconscious, the axe embraced Akhaïdes' palm.

"What's that you have there?" Oxylus asked. "Some kitchen tool?"

The tip of the sword rose only a hand's width, but that was enough. Akhaïdes strode straight at Oxylus, who retreated reflexively, then checked himself and thrust the sword forward. The axe leaped to meet it. Bronze clanged and screeched as Akhaïdes joined and narrowed the sword's arc, sliding it past him. Oxylus staggered, and Akhaïdes stepped toward him with an upward stroke. Oxylus whipped the shield down, and the axe sank into wood. Akhaïdes wrenched it free, ripping out a long splinter, as Oxylus backed swiftly away.

Akhaïdes knew, as the axe knew, everything they needed to know. Oxylus prowled, warier now, trying to work himself between Akhaïdes and the still-bright sunset, but Akhaïdes backed as he turned, to prevent it. His other hand slid down until he grasped the axe's hilt with both fists. The cut on his hand was bleeding again, but the leather kept his grip sure.

The sword appeared where he expected. Slipping past its thrust, he hooked it in the curve of the axe, yanked it out of Oxylus's fingers, and hurled it away, all without touching it. Then he went to work on the shield, double-handed — swift, hard strokes that found wood each time. Stepping forward with each stroke.

Oxylus jolted back and back, the shield groaning, wood shattering. He was shouting in a language Akhaïdes did not know. He ducked, crouched, burrowed behind the ragged cover as more shreds and splinters flew.

Akhaïdes swung flatter, and the axe sliced into bronze plate. Oxylus's shriek whistled up beyond hearing. The blade snagged on shards of bone.

Still Akhaïdes did not pause, not caring where or what he cut as long as he kept the rhythm . Fingers scattered under his feet, and the helmet bowled away like a cooking pot. Oxylus rolled, still absurdly fleeing. Akhaïdes stamped a foot onto trailing hair. Perfect spot between ear and shoulder. His muscles stretched, bunched.

Something slammed against his back and hurled him forward.

He staggered, still upright. Men threw themselves on him, bearing him down. He twisted and bit at them, but they pinned him to the earth. Then he could move only his head, gulping in hard, short sucks of air as sweat flooded from his skin.

Above a circle of faces was Tisamenus's, blanched white, the mouth contorted.

"The Good Kinsman," Tisamenus said, and every eye in the circle widened. Tisamenus slung his hair back over his shoulders, the motion itself an accusation.

Akhaïdes swallowed. "Should I thank you for the introduction?"

"I didn't send Oxylus. I didn't know."

"I sent him," Hawmai said from somewhere.

Tisamenus's head whipped up. "Hawmai? *What!*"

"It's my armor. Was my armor."

"But you're responsible," Akhaïdes told Tisamenus.

Tisamenus stared for a moment, then closed his eyes.

Something was coming to Akhaïdes. It coiled up out of the earth — a long arching shadow, not regarding him at all, yet meant for no one else. He could not escape, could not hold what must be held. But he strained to hold it off, to hold his breath. If he breathed, he would scream. If he started screaming, he would never stop.

He heard ". . . die and get it over with." Someone knelt on his hand, prying the axe from his fingers. Faces grew and shrank: Tisamenus dazed, Hawmai impassive, Sigewas wildly alert, the rest stern and fearful. Fits of shaking came, stronger each time. The axe ripped out of his fingers like a limb torn away. His nails buried themselves in his palm.

Then here was the Chou warlord's face, round and hairless, turning toward him, relentless, implacable, as deaf to appeal as the moon. The wide, lipless mouth opened, white as a snake's inside. The warlord said, "I made you a promise once. Do you remember?"

He remembered.

* * *

Menetor was the highest priest of Delphi. Temenus was king of the Herakleids. But there was no question which should show most respect. Temenus bowed deeply and touched both closed fists to his forehead. Then he laid his open hands against the stone floor and lowered his body until he lay prostrate before the priest.

"We have seen you already twice today," Menetor said. "For your augury, then with your brothers. And now here you are again, this time alone."

Temenus did not move. "You know what I need."

"Your augury is as it is. That you dislike it doesn't make it not true."

"I don't dislike it. I don't *understand* it. It was just this jumble of—I don't even know—four kings, wheels, wheat, water, a lion's skin, a woman's skin, both flayed and laid out like rugs . . . a three-eyed man. Grotesque. It made no sense. What was all that? What does it *mean*?"

"No one but you will ever know. That's how auguries are. I shouldn't have to tell you something so elemental. You've been coming here all your life."

"And all my life, Delphi has done nothing to help me."

"How do you know?"

Temenus rose, turned, sat on the floor with one knee raised. He looked up: dark, canted eyes and, like his brothers, a beard with no mustache, accentuating the wide, tactile mouth with deep creases at the ends.

Temenus said, "And there is the other thing I've told you about before: the vision and the dread. Not an augury dream. It can't be. But I can't make a simple sacrifice. Blood of any kind, even a bird's, even a *rat's*. It sickens me."

He ran a hand over his head. "My brother, my cousins, perform the acts I should perform: sacrifices . . . killings sometimes. They dirty their hands for me while I sit like some spider in the midst of it all, touching nothing. I'm unclean. I must be."

"You've never polluted yourself."

"My father and his father had no such fault. And Herakles . . ."

"Be sure."

Temenus's hands closed into fists. "Don't soothe me. Help me!"

Menetor raised an eyebrow, and Temenus subsided. He touched his forehead in apology.

"You always ask the same," Menetor said, "and I answer the

same."

He reached to the table at his elbow, filled two earthen cups with wine, and extended one of them. Temenus took it, offered it to the six parts of the earth—the four cardinal directions, then up to the sky, down to the land of the dead—and drank it all. Then he rapped the cup against the floor. It shattered.

Menetor had not drunk from the second cup. "You are not unclean," he said. "All that you touch remains innocent. The cup was blameless, and so are you."

Temenus ran his hands over his pock-scarred face. "Yet this place marked me."

"For greatness, my lord. When all the children of Delphi died except you, you were not the killer. You were the victor. Fate could not have named you more clearly."

"Then fate can't have meant for me to be so flawed in that other way."

"Fate didn't give your flaw to you. It can't take it away."

Temenus looked up swiftly, but Menetor said nothing more. He pushed himself up and brushed the dust from his hands. Then he sat on the low stool that Menetor had offered when he first entered this room.

"Tell me, Grandfather. Please."

"There is one who might . . . show you."

"And you can't?"

"Not that, no."

"Will it affect so much that you don't want the responsibility? But you've destroyed empires with a word. *One word.* And not cared."

"Go easy, Grandson. It is not just empires this time."

Temenus started to speak, then waited.

"The least likely weapon might kill a man. The least likely physic might save him. The ugliest of changes might make him . . . strong."

Menetor reached out with the second cup. Temenus took it and offered it the six ways.

Then he stopped. "How will I know?"

"You'll never know. Like walking a path that branches and branches until you don't even realize that you'll never find the way back."

"And if I don't want to go back?"

"That would be . . ."

"A very good thing."

Menetor studied the dark eyes, the rough skin, the dauntless intelligence. "I've known you all your life, my lord. Save yourself."

Temenus raised an eyebrow. "Save myself for what? If I never am High King, I might as well have died with the other children here. Or when my father went to his dead. At any time before or after. Today." Temenus closed his hand around the cup.

Old though he was, still Menetor felt as if that big, flawless, ringless hand caressed his own skin. He remembered that Delphi's prostitutes, the sharpest of agents, sometimes served Temenus without a fee.

"Does anyone ever refuse you?"

Temenus blinked. "Occasionally, of course."

"And then what happens?"

"Nothing happens. I'm not a rapist, Grandfather."

"Would you ever want to be a different man than you are?"

Temenus smiled. "Never."

"You met Tisamenus Oresteides today. What are your thoughts?"

"He's not his father's confidant. I saw that the baron Hawmai fills that role, and he won't be seduced or purchased."

"What of Tisamenus himself?"

"Pfft. I eat boys like him for breakfast. There is no counting the number I've taken and discarded. That blue-eyed child is just one more. If I know, you must know, too."

Menetor narrowed his eyes. "Do not speak lightly of the High King's son."

Temenus instantly lowered his face and touched his free hand to his forehead. "Please excuse me, Grandfather. I meant no insolence."

"I know what you meant."

Temenus remained submissive.

Finally, Menetor said, "Leave tomorrow."

Temenus's head came up. "What?"

"Leave here tomorrow. You'll get nothing from staying longer, and you could lose much that you believe is important to you."

Temenus half rose. "Nafpaktos?"

"No. All is well there."

He settled again. "I still need to—"

"That doesn't matter."

"The changing of the moon will catch me outside shelter."

"Do as I tell you."

Menetor could see the questions in those vivid eyes. But Temenus bent his head, and there it was again: that passionate appetite, even in so humble a gesture.

Menetor had to say, "You might lose what you value most."

"I never thought that victory wouldn't have a price." Temenus gazed at the cup in his hand. "My sister Makhawis thought I might look for someone here. A new ally."

"Pass my greeting to the Wanassa. I hope she is well."

"She is. I couldn't succeed without her. And my brothers, of course."

"Your brothers."

"The only people I totally trust. Makhawis, Aristodemus, Kresphontes."

Menetor had to say one more thing. "You'll have no lover afterward. You won't want another."

Temenus's head twitched up and his eyes widened. Then he smiled. "Grandfather, I tell you now, with no disrespect, that you must be mistaken. I've never had a lover at all—not in the way that word is understood. And if you mean a day's or a night's liaison, then what you say can't be true. There is always another of those."

He raised the cup, drained it, licked its edge, and set it back at Menetor's elbow. Then he rose, touched his forehead in deference, and went his way.

* * *

Akhaïdes woke to moonlight, lamplight, and things moving around him. Hands and arms in swinging sleeves. A fire's warmth at one side. Voices. He lay on his back and could not move. Remembering, he began to tremble.

Something brushed his face, and he sucked in a startled breath. Aranare's voice said, "No one's holding you. You're only tied. Be still."

He knew how to do that. Stillness was one of his few remaining skills. The earth was cool against his back. Someone asked a question, and someone else answered it. To be touched, to be cared for, was intolerable. Be still.

His mouth felt astringent. Nepenthe, it must be—the poppy. They had force-fed it to him, making it possible to restrain him without harm to themselves. Now the placidity that always followed the drug drew fear out of his grasp, like a scarf drawn softly through paralyzed fingers.

His wrists burned, but that did not trouble him. He hung between his own arms, carefully suspended, nowhere. A shoulder muscle twitched. He drifted off.

"Akhaïdes? Can you hear me? Can he hear me?"

His lashes ripped apart. The hollow of his eye was wet. Here was a face that he should know. He had to try several times to make a sound.

"King," he finally managed. "King of . . ." He lost the thought, and his lashes meshed. He whispered, "Juchii."

"What's wrong with him?" Tisamenus asked. "Why does he keep weeping?"

Aranare answered, "Why do you ask such questions about a madman?"

Sigewas's deep voice murmured, "Wanax, remember the sources of madness. Any one of them can hurt you, however careful you are."

Push ants back into a hole with a twig, and they will boil out all the faster. Shadow of a monster. The Chou. Akhaïdes shuddered. His wrists hurt suddenly, wire pressing bone, but that pain was relief from the other, which was unfaceable and unbearable. He couldn't flee, couldn't fight. Tears ran silently into his hair.

Aranare trailed fingertips across his forehead. "Be still," she whispered, and the terror drew away.

"If you talk to him," Aranare told someone, "you make it worse. This power is jealous. It can't punish you, so it punishes him. The nepenthe is all gone. And if he bleeds much more, you won't need to wonder what will happen next."

Akhaïdes forced his mouth to shape words. "Hawmai. Sorry."

"What?" Tisamenus asked. Then, "What did he mean?"

"I would have killed him in Arne," Hawmai's voice answered. "Or after. Now we both regret that I didn't."

Tisamenus's silence felt precarious, but he finally just asked, "So who is he?"

"From what mortal father, you mean?" Sigewas answered. "No one knows."

"But you knew that he was the Kinsman."

"I didn't know when I told the story. If I had known . . ."

"If you had known," Hawmai erupted, "then what? Would it have been the only time you didn't instantly blab everything? And how do you know now, when you didn't know then?"

"I'd like to hear the answer to that," Tisamenus murmured.

"It's just a story, Wanax. Was just a story. The right kind for Phocis."

A chilly silence.

Tisamenus finally said, "I listened to it, too. As if it had nothing to do with me."

"It doesn't have anything to do with you," Hawmai said.

"Then why am I here with him? It must."

Akhaïdes whispered, "Don't blame them."

"But . . ."

"Don't punish anyone else because I shouldn't exist. Just kill me."

Tisamenus asked blankly, "Why?"

"I can't stand this. If you want to help, that's how."

"But your spirit will lie like a dead animal underground. Dark forever."

"Better that . . ." He had to catch his breath. "Better that than this. You started it. You finish it."

"You think I shouldn't have gone with the Regent to see you. But I did, and what does that mean?"

"It's meaningless. *I* am meaningless. Ridiculous."

"I'm not laughing."

"Neither am I," said Sigewas.

Akhaïdes tilted his head back. "Please do this."

Tisamenus ran both hands over his own face, then flung his hair behind his shoulders. "I've never done such a thing in my life. I would, just because you ask me to. But I can't and I don't know why."

Hawmai began patiently, "Wanax, I can . . ."

"Take him behind a tent and cut his throat, like a dog with a broken leg? No, not you. You leave him alone."

Every man within hearing sucked in his breath.

"Do you hear me? Hawmai?"

After a long moment's pause, Hawmai answered, "Yes, Wanax."

Tisamenus used his wet hand to stroke tears from Akhaïdes' face, too. He said, very softly, "I'm so sorry."

Akhaïdes shivered, and his eye closed. Hawmai got up and went away.

* * *

He drifted, woke, drifted, woke, each time coming back a little more, until Aranare finally untwisted the bloody wire that bound his wrists to pegs in the earth. Stiff and slow, he got up onto his elbows.

She had mended the lacerations from the wire with a needle threaded with his own hair, closed the gash below his thumb, wrapped both his wrists like a penitent's. These wounds had, at least, hidden the last traces of the horsehair bonds from Arne.

Tisamenus stood a distance away with Hawmai at his shoulder, the hound at his other side. His hair shone pale as ice in the wan light of the hanging lamps.

Hawmai cleared his throat. "The outlaw Oxylus did not act under the king's orders." He stared halfway up the night sky. Tisamenus's eyes were fixed on Akhaïdes. "The king of Lacedaemon knew nothing of it."

Akhaïdes smelled smoke, and something burning that was familiar though he couldn't name it. Something like meat, but not ordinary cooking. The hound's eyes shone red.

Hawmai recited, "Oxylus is outlaw. You are outlaw. There is no offense and no blood debt. Delphi doesn't care."

Hawmai stopped. Tisamenus glanced at him, and he twitched as if pinched. "This is the king's will: go where you choose and do what you'll do."

Oxylus is. So Oxylus still lived. Then Akhaïdes recognized the smell. Some shaman was burning the parts Akhaïdes had cut from the other outlaw, making magic to call his spirit back. Akhaïdes could not imagine what Tisamenus had given for that. It was that one thing, the stink of Oxylus's divination—*he will live, he will not live*—that finally let him move.

The axe lay beside him. He climbed to his feet, leaning on it. Aranare closed the belt around his waist. Her hands rested briefly on his hips. She started to say something, then lowered her eyes and walked away.

Someone had scraped the axe blade clean of blood. Dry grass still clung to the grip after protecting the hand of whoever had done it. He should give the person a gift for that, but a gift from an outlaw had no value.

He hung the axe on its hook. The rims of his sleeves were black and rigid, the front of his shirt spattered. His hands, clean when he had faced the priest, were now cased in brittle gloves of blood, Oxylus's and his own. The bandages on his wrists were the only things clean about him. The contrast was so abrupt, they looked like deliberate ornamentation.

Under the odor of divination, he could smell, from the men nearby, fresh oil, clean fabric, vinegar, a hint of alcohol. While he had crouched in the Serpent's lair, these innocents had contentedly—justly—bathed and changed clothes, had their hair washed. They had eaten cooked food, drunk clean water and wine. Only he, Akhaïdes Outlaw, still wore this absurd primeval filth and infamy. Only he was hungry.

Tisamenus raised his voice for everyone to hear. "The priest said to remember the blood between us, but yours in the sanctuary and Oxylus's now is all the blood I know. For the sake of that blood, and for other reasons I don't understand, I release you."

He spread his hands wide. His rings glittered in the lamplight. "If you ever need anything that I can give you, don't even ask. Just take it."

"Wanax, you can't—"

"Hawmai, shut up! And don't talk to me in that tone, ever again. I'm sick of your contempt."

All Delphi fell silent.

"Go now," Tisamenus said gently. "And may luck and fate rise and walk with you. You are fey. You are untouchable. No man of mine will ever harm you."

Akhaïdes coughed, swallowed, realized that he could speak. "Then next time," he said, "do what I ask."

* * *

So what were the choices, again? At the edge of the road, Akhaïdes stopped. Upward, it led back to Phocis and maybe, for a while, a seat by a bandit's fire; downward it led to towns, ports, orchards, and cultivated fields. All of them, even the bandit's tower, already existing when he had murdered his brothers.

He squatted on one heel before the overturned bowl of a skull. Tangled black hair still clung to it. Under a low trailing mass of weed and rag, the skeleton would be whole to the smallest finger bones, untouched by vermin, contorted only by death and the elements. Any possession, however precious if someone else's, would still be here, since anything given by or taken from an outlaw had no value. The skull would fit perfectly between his spread fingers.

Behind him, Elawon's voice said, "Don't do it."

He had started to turn, to sit here. Now he stopped. "Do they still live?"

"Mother and Father? They saw grandsons. But when I sit at the fire in the evening, I sit with women and children. The brothers who should sit with me—where are they?"

Under his hand, Delphi waited.

"We're Arcadians, you and I," Elawon added. "We know that everything that happens is someone's fault."

Everything that happens, happens for a reason. Everything that happens has happened before. Everything that happens will happen again. Everything that happens is someone's fault. Akhaïdes knew all that.

"But that's why you made up a rubbish name for yourself. That's why you refused to tell who you are. Because you won't admit fault."

"Outlawry releases fault."

"The priests are content with that. Father was satisfied. But what about me? It was you who named me, wasn't it?"

Without looking, Akhaïdes could see Elawon's compact body, black curly hair, clean clothing, soft unscarred hands. "A baby name. I never expected you would keep it, if you survived."

"Mother wanted it kept. I don't know why. And what about you? Did they call you Ephialtes when you were born, and you never got a man's name, either? Did they already know what you would do to them?"

Akhaïdes rose and turned. Elawon stood stiffly erect, a bundle on his shoulder.

"Your hair was lighter," Akhaïdes said.

"Was it? And I always thought you would look like the rest of us, like an Arcadian." Elawon ran his free hand over his head. "In the stories, the Good Kinsman is some foundling monster. Until now, only Arcadians knew whose you were. What family bred you. We don't tell outsiders our business."

They stood a moment, facing but not looking at each other.

"That still made it hard to get a wife," Elawon added. "And now everyone here knows that you and I—I can't sit with them anymore."

Akhaïdes' thoughts were turning like a broken wheel, stopping and jerking. He tacked a few together. "But the priests won't tell. Sigewas doesn't know about our . . . link. The story says that no brother survived. They'll only work it out because you followed me."

"I can use you."

This was easier. "I can't live where any man lived then."

"That's no handicap for what I need."

With the tips of his fingers, Akhaïdes touched his own forehead, mouth, and breast. He reached toward Elawon, did not actually touch him, but repeated the motion—forehead, lips, heart—a finger's breadth away.

"What's that? I've seen it before."

Akhaïdes placed his hands behind him.

"I remember old men used to do it. In Arcadia. What does it mean?"

"It doesn't mean anything now."

Elawon grunted, dismissive. "So, Ephialtes—"

"Never call me that."

"Akhaïdes, then. What does it mean?"

"Do you remember the old language? Arcadian?"

"No one speaks that anymore." Elawon glanced down the road, toward the town. "The Herakleids are here in Delphi."

Akhaïdes blinked at the shift.

"All three brothers," Elawon continued. "The great-something-sons of Hyllus. They live down the coast at a place they made called Nafpaktos, gathering relatives, allies, wanting to take back what they think was Herakles' birthright."

"They want Mycenae?"

"They even want Arcadia. They call their plotting their 'Return.'" Elawon shifted his bundle to the other shoulder. "I hold all our family ground in Ladon. It's good land, for Arcadia. I have a score of dependents. My barns are always full. But I'm on the wrong side of this. The Herakleids have allies all over the north. 'The Tribes,' they call themselves. If I—we—stay with Orestes, they'll take everything. If we join them, they'll let us keep it as a meed, a reward."

"Why do . . . what can you want with me?"

Elawon's brows lowered. "Ladon is still yours. I'm regent while you're outlawed. Although I've held the place as my own since I've worn a loincloth."

Another forgotten word: the garment men wore after they received adult names. Boys wore long shirts. All males wrapped their legs against cold. Only men wrapped their loins, too, but not outlaws. Outlaws were not men.

Elawon said, "Even Oedipus didn't stop being king just because he could never go back to Thebes. Even slaves still have homes, if they can get to them."

"You're sure the Herakleids will win this . . ." Akhaïdes made a vague gesture, uncertain what to call it: war, conflict, reconciliation.

"I saw Temenus Herakleides, their king, today. If anyone can eradicate the Pelopeids, he can. Especially now that Orestes is old and there's only Tisamenus to follow him."

"Does everyone in Arcadia think the way you do?"

"I'm the only Arcadian here. I was Companion to one of the older brothers, but when he went to his dead, Father made me stay with Tisamenus." He twitched his mouth. "I don't know what the tie was, but it was his, not mine."

Akhaïdes could force his mind to practical thoughts. "You can't go to a king with your shoes in your hand. You should send for your own men. Go in strength."

"There's no time for that."

"Take a gift."

"I don't have anything valuable except my rings. You'll have to do for now." Elawon lowered the bundle and leaned it against his knee. "If you're with me, they'll believe that I — we — can deliver Ladon, and the rest of Arcadia."

When Akhaïdes didn't answer, Elawon added, "Nafpaktos is new. When you did . . . what you did, it was an empty swamp. You can live there. It might be the only place you can. And if I leave this way, for you, Orestes can't move against me. He'd have to wait for either Tegea or Pylos, but each of their kings thinks the other is my—our—king. Even if I sent one of them a formal disavowal, a sheep's head, they'd hardly notice."

There had been no sheep in Ladon when Ephialtes lived there—only goats. The kids had slept with their heads on his shoulders. The kids of those kids would not remember him, though he would kill anyone who harmed them.

Akhaïdes asked, "What do the Herakleids want here in Delphi?"

"What kings always want, I presume. Promises of victory. I heard somebody say that Temenus wants a riding horse, but there aren't any here and he can't afford one anyway."

Silence strung between them.

"Well," Elawon said. "I need a place to stay the night."

He hefted his bundle back onto one shoulder and started down the road toward towns, ports, orchards, and cultivated fields.

The baby had slept with his head on Ephialtes' shoulder. He would kill anyone who harmed it. So Akhaïdes followed.

* * *

They stayed in a ruined house at the edge of Delphi Town. Although the wooden door frame still stood, the stone walls had crumbled down to half a man's height, and most of the roof had fallen. Akhaïdes cleared away heaps of dead weed to give Elawon a dry corner, where he slept, wrapped in his blankets as neatly as a gift. Akhaïdes crouched all night in the entrance, uncovered and unsleeping.

He might have risen and gone at any time, but could not imagine doing that. So he crouched and waited, remembering the first night outdoors in Arne. Now he could watch bright lines run across the sky—powers or deities going about their business, as disinterested and harmless as memories of lightning. Now it was the sound of Elawon's breathing that seemed more fearsome than the coughing of tigers.

In the gloom of dawn, as Elawon still slept, Akhaïdes rose and stepped into the thin, chill breeze that crawled down the mountain. From farther west, just out of sight, came the sounds of a camp stirring: men hawking, pissing, and laughing; scents of cooking; the clatter of gear and harness; men not just waking, but preparing to move.

He turned back into the house, plucked a stone from crumbling mortar, and tapped it against another until Elawon woke, yawning and grumbling. He stared around blankly for a moment; then Akhaïdes watched him remember.

"What?" Elawon finally asked.

"Some group is leaving. It might be the Herakleids."

Elawon struggled out of his blanket, pulled his shirt straight, then hurriedly wrapped the blanket around himself again. He said, "I hate sleeping in clothes. We need to catch them before they go." He looked at Akhaïdes doubtfully.

Akhaïdes asked, "How will they travel?"

"By ship, I heard. From Khirra."

"I'll meet you there later. I'll bring a gift for him."

"What gift?" Elawon asked. "You can't . . ." But Akhaïdes was already gone.

* * *

Menetor looked up from his work table and said, "Herakleides. Welcome."

Stopped in the doorway, Kresphontes touched the edge of a closed fist to his forehead.

"No one told me you were coming to see me."

"I'm sorry. Should I . . ."

"No, no. Come in. You want an augury of yourself?"

Kresphontes did not move. His fist stayed closed. "There's no time. And I can't afford one anyway." He paused, then said in a rush, "We came all the way here, and suddenly we're leaving without doing half of what we came for. I don't know why Temenus—"

Menetor still did not rise. "I will not tell you what the king and I spoke of last night."

Kresphontes twitched, then said in a different tone, "I want to give a gift for the ladies."

"Yet you still have a question you can't escape."

He breathed out heavily. "It's just, I doubt that we're following the road we're meant to. My brother can't make a decision without the Dorians, the Carians . . ."

"Without you?"

"Me?" Kresphontes smiled bitterly. "Me, he never listens to." With his free hand, he pulled the peg from his hair, letting it fall in a sleek black tail to his waist. "We drew lots here, my brothers and I, to divide our realm between us. You remember?"

"I remember."

"Temenus won Mycenae, meaning he'd be high king. He and Aristodemus arranged for me to draw Messenia. It was a favor since the land is good and not well defended, and I was so young."

"Yes."

"Who but fate would have put that into their minds? We promised to keep the lots with us, and never cut our hair until we'd finished what we were born for. See? I wear my lot on a string on my wrist all the time. But Temenus? He doesn't know where his is, he set it aside so long ago. And every time some relative dies, he cuts his hair."

"He's obliged to. So are you."

"I do it! I cut the ends, though, just the ends. Our cause is too important for anything to distract us—even reverence for the dead."

"He never listens to you, you say. And yet, he loves you."

"Then he should love me less and heed me more!"

"And your question is . . . ?"

Kresphontes' eyes were as dark and intelligent as his brother's, but transparent, without secrets. He did not answer. Finally he lowered his head.

"Leave your gift," Menetor said. "It will be prized."

"It's not much. It's just . . ." Kresphontes opened the fist to show a tiny clay votive with a crested skull and lifted curved wings. It was common village workmanship, as plain as the disk on his wrist. "I couldn't get a better one. I had nothing to trade."

"A gift is valued for its giver. Place it in the sanctuary if you want."

When Kresphontes hesitated, Menetor added, "The Good Kinsman rested there and survived."

"I saw him." But Kresphontes still did not move.

"I'll place it, then." Menetor reached his open palm across the table, so that Kresphontes would have to come to him, to give it up. When he did that, it was still warm from his hand.

* * *

The Herakleid camp lay on a rocky terrace above the road west of

Delphi Town, near a trickle of water from a cracked clay pipe and a pair of stunted chestnut trees, whose branches bore crows and goats in equal numbers. A low tent with hangings at the sides faced a fire pit, where two men cooked porridge in a shallow kettle while another five or six hunkered around them, cloaked against the cold. A few villagers stood holding donkeys, waiting to load.

As Elawon approached, lean hounds erupted from every corner of the camp. He stopped, set down his bundle, and waited while they sniffed him over. Eventually, one man rose from the group at the fire and came to meet him, kicking at the nearest dogs with every stride. The hounds ducked and slunk out of reach.

The man wore no shirt despite the chill. His paunched torso was thick with white fur, and his bald scalp looked as if it had been cut into pieces, then drunkenly stitched back together. He might have looked fearsome if not for the deep-crinkled, affable eyes.

"Are you an enemy or a friend?" The man spoke Mycenaean, but with a brassy accent that Elawon recognized as Dorian. He had to make a mental shift to understand it.

"Friend, I hope. Maybe you should ask the dogs."

The man backed off a step and examined Elawon. Then his thick forehead wrinkled suddenly. "One of the Pelopeid's men, if I'm not mistaking that cloak. Will he be wanting you back badly enough to give us ransom?"

"No. I'm sorry."

The man waved the idea away. "Never mind, never mind. I'm Xanos Lyceides, Dorian, the Herakleids's lawagetas. The keeper of peace in Nafpaktos. Are you here for trade? We don't have much."

"I am Elawon Hyadeides, of Ladon in Arcadia."

Xanos's eyes widened. "One of the wild men of the mountains? But you look so placid. You're even wearing *clothes*."

Elawon stooped to pick up his bedroll. The protruding hilt of his sword seemed suddenly inappropriate, and he pulled the edge of a blanket over it.

Xanos grinned at the gesture. "Don't worry. We welcome the peaceable, too."

Elawon smiled uncertainly, and Xanos led him to the fire. The men there recited their names one by one. Each had the same black hair and canted eyes that marked them as Herakleid, though one, named Hippotes, stood out in both size and gloom. Xanos sent a boy into the tent to tell Temenus that he had a visitor.

The Herakleids finished their porridge, slurping from handleless cups and passing a knife back and forth between them to shave hard curls from a wedge of bread. Then they rose, glanced again at Elawon, and moved off to finish packing.

"Ah," Xanos said to Elawon. "You're wanted."

A fat man, also of obvious Herakleid stock, stood holding the tent flap open.

Although the walls were rolled up at the back, it was dim inside from the hangings that divided the space. In the largest chamber, Temenus Herakleides sat on a low stool before a short-legged table surrounded by clerks and littered with shreds of pithleaf and scratched clay chips. He raised his head as Elawon entered.

This close, the king looked older than he had yesterday on the road. Perhaps forty, near Elawon's age. Maybe the trim build and the still-black hair had made him seem younger. Elawon touched his forehead in respect.

"Elawon Hyadeides of Arcadian Ladon," Xanos said. "One of Lacedaemon's Companions."

"Welcome, Hyadeides," Temenus said. "Will you take mead?"

"Thank you, my lord." Elawon looked for a place to sit. One of the clerks got up to offer his stool while another rummaged for a pitcher and cups.

Someone poured mead, and the fat clerk herded the others out. Temenus tipped his cup to the six points of the earth and sipped, studying Elawon over the rim.

"So tell me, Hyadeides, what business do we have together? Do you come on the king of Lacedaemon's errand, or the Baron Hawmai's?"

"Neither. I've come to join you if you'll have me—and my land, and my men."

Temenus's eyes half closed. "Who sent you?"

"No one, my lord. I thought—I want to do this."

"Why now?"

"The opportunity is now."

"Opportunity?" Soft, though quick as a whiplash.

"It's a long way from Mycenae or Ladon to Nafpaktos, and how could I know how I'd be received? But here I can meet you like this."

"With little risk to yourself if I refuse. Trying the water before diving in."

Elawon scrambled for a response. "I was sent to the Pelopeids by my family. It wasn't my choice. This is. You are."

Temenus studied the edge of his cup. "When they learn that you've turned to me, your king will take Ladon. Then you and I will have nothing from it."

Elawon had practiced this. "Tegea and Pylos both think I'm subject to the other. Pylos is very far away, and its king, Melanthus, is occupied with more serious business. The king of Tegea has moved so far from the High—from Orestes—that he won't do anything to call attention to Arcadia."

Temenus looked up again. "Surely your leaving Tisamenus might be provocation enough to throw the two of them back together."

"If Tisamenus convinces his father that I left him only to join you, yes. But Orestes never believes what Tisamenus tells him. He believes only Hawmai and a few others. And Hawmai keeps secrets even from Orestes. I think my estate is safe for a while."

"So is there another reason that Orestes might believe instead, for why you left Tisamenus?"

"Yes. My . . . my brother. We met here—well, in Arne. He's the elder, but he can't rule in Ladon. And he doesn't . . ." Elawon silenced himself.

Temenus's gaze skipped to the entrance, then back to Elawon. He said, as if to himself, "Arcadians have their complications, don't they?"

Elawon considered possible answers. Each had disadvantages, especially if presented to a man as quick as this Herakleid. He settled on more silence.

Temenus set his cup down without taking his eyes from Elawon. To be examined so openly was daunting. Elawon didn't know what to do with the cup, with his hands.

Finally, Temenus asked, "What are you to me? What will you do for me?"

"Whatever you need, my lord."

Temenus set his elbows on the table and touched his fingertips together in front of his mouth. "I wonder what you believe I might need."

Elawon said, "My people owe yours a debt. A very old one."

Temenus sat for a long time without expression, like a man counting sheep that he would never own and did not covet, though he still needed to know the number. Finally, he said, "What debt?"

"My mother's grandfather was Echemus Protector." When Temenus made no reply, Elawon added, "Who killed your great-grandfather Hyllus at—"

"Koretoros," Temenus said, still unreadable.

The fat clerk came in so quickly that he must have been listening. "Wanax?"

"Be the witness."

Temenus rose and stepped around the table. Elawon rose

uncertainly.

"Give me your hands, Hyadeides."

Right here? Like this? Elawon set the cup aside, went down on one knee, pressed his palms together and raised them to Temenus.

"Protect me, my lord," he said. "I'm a stranger among your people."

Temenus closed his own hands around Elawon's. "Welcome. And have no fear. My fire is your fire."

"Wanax," Elawon confirmed.

Temenus did not smile. His eyes were clouded, as if his thoughts were elsewhere. Elawon remembered what to do now and kissed Temenus's hands. His new lord drew him to his feet, took his face in both palms, and kissed his forehead.

"You will serve me faithfully, Hyadeides."

"My lord Wanax, yes, I will."

The clerk Koretoros said, "I see this."

As if this had been nothing, Temenus turned to Koretoros. "Are we ready to go?"

"My lord Aristodemus went down to the harbor earlier. Kresphontes is with the priests. Do you want to leave without the tin you bargained for?"

"No, no. Keep a man and a donkey here for the tin. And you stay, too, to make sure it actually gets to the ship. But we can start down before Kresphontes comes back. He'll catch up. Send someone to Aristodemus. Tell him to make certain there's room on the ship for Elawon Hyadeides and his brother, the Good Kinsman."

Elawon's mind jolted. Temenus already knew who Akhaïdes was. Tisamenus, Hawmai, Sigewas, all of Delphi—everyone knew. He could never come back.

"Wanax?" Koretoros asked without surprise. Even clerks knew.

"I presume the outlaw will present some complication. The

Ithacans might refuse to carry him. Aristodemus will need to find a way to convince them."

Temenus turned back to Elawon. "I hate doing business here. They use Phocian measures or Ithacan, Attican, something else, and what you trade for always turns out less than you thought. When I'm High King, everyone will use the same measures."

"Theseus tried that, my lord," Elawon said.

"When I lived in Delphi, nothing was so difficult."

"When you lived in Delphi," Koretoros said, "you were three years old. And you nearly died."

Elawon understood that he was dismissed, but he had no idea how to leave. He finally just backed away. He felt Temenus's attention even after he was safely outside.

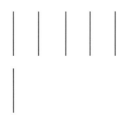

First say to yourself what you would be; and then do what you have to do.[vii]

—*Epictetus*

There was nothing to it. Akhaïdes had never before found a horse so easy to steal.

The Mycenaean ponies stood tied side by side on long tether lines near the chariots, at the edge of the road. But the drivers had left the horses with the oxen on a grassy terrace two levels below the camp.

He came from the far end of the terrace, where it narrowed and then ended in a steep, brush-choked ravine that the Mycenaeans must have thought impassable. Both horses flung up their heads at the sight of him but did not make the noise—the hard, sharp huff of danger—that he had worried they might. They considered him briefly, then dropped their heads to graze again. The oxen, lying in deeper grass farther along the terrace, simply glanced and dismissed him, without a pause in their contemplative chewing.

Both horses wore rope halters with short leads that no one had bothered to secure, but he could reach neither without risk of being seen from above. So he crept along the terrace wall as close as he could get, then, beneath the cover of a tree that blocked the Mycenaean camp, stood erect and stared directly at the horses. One ignored him. The other did not raise its head, but stopped chewing and waited.

He turned sideways—an invitation that either animal could accept or decline. And as he had known it would since their first encounter in Arne, the gray horse accepted.

Then he had only to sidle back to the end of the terrace and start down the steep jumble of boulders, thorns, and cobwebs, choosing as stable a path as possible. The horse lowered its head and wove, clambered, and slid just as he did, choosing prudently how to place each hoof to avoid stepping on the trailing tether.

Finally at the river, where low walls snaked between level stands of olive trees, Akhaïdes glanced back at the complex descent.

Come back when this is true.

He gathered the tether rope, grasped mane, and swung onto the horse's back. Then man and horse moved out together, jumping each small obstacle, to meet the Herakleids.

* * *

Elawon had seen how Temenus wore his hair short, in a simple style, and that his clothes and shoes were faded and plain. While he had always heard that Herakleids were poor, he couldn't fathom why their king, at least, wouldn't dress better for his departure from Delphi. Temenus had stepped out of the tent quietly, with no air of importance. While other Herakleids folded and tied it, he turned to Elawon and said, "Walk with me, Hyadeides."

So Elawon did. Leaving his bundle for a donkey or a villager to carry, he put himself just behind Temenus's shoulder, ahead of Xanos and the other Herakleids, and they all started down the road to the port together.

The villagers who only yesterday had pestered Elawon to trade his rings for their clay trinkets now studied him with interest, even talking behind their hands as he passed. Concerned that the attention might arise from what they knew about Akhaïdes rather than from his own prominence, Elawon spoke to Temenus from time to time, so that these people would see him do so, and see Temenus reply. One time, when Elawon commented on the size of a particular olive tree, Temenus even turned his head to study the tree and agreed that it certainly was enormous, and must indeed be very old. Tisamenus Oresteides had never shown Elawon such favor.

So comfortable with this easy acceptance, Elawon felt an unpleasant jolt when, as the group reached the base of the valley, almost all the way to the port, he saw Akhaïdes standing beside the road, between a withy cattle pen and an olive orchard, under the cool scrutiny of a tree full of ravens.

Akhaïdes' shirt was damp, and the raw ends of his sleeves were cleaner. He had tied his hair back with a shabby string, but that only emphasized the white around his face and the sharpness of the cheekbones crisscrossed with straight, narrow scars. The single colorless eye, the long alien mustache, and the bandages on his wrists made him look all the more derelict. Elawon's gut tightened.

The ravens hopped to the near side of their tree to consider the new arrivals. Like crows and gulls, ravens were untouchable. Few men would risk killing one. Besides, these men carried no bows, and ravens took no other weapons seriously. But rabbits nibbling at weeds under the trees took alarm at the dogs and lollopped away. The dogs raced after, dodging past a horse that raised its head to watch the Herakleids approach.

Temenus stopped so abruptly that Elawon almost walked into him.

"By every power on earth! He's Pelopeid!"

"No, Wanax," Elawon answered. "It was a gift from the Regent of Arne—" Then he caught up. Temenus must mean Akhaïdes, not the horse. "No. It's just a chance likeness passed down from generations before. Who isn't related to everyone else?"

"I'm not." Temenus cleared his throat. "Maybe because the Pelopeids and Arcadians killed so many of my family. And this is your brother. The Kinsman."

The other Herakleid men had continued walking when Temenus stopped. Now three of them gathered around Akhaïdes, nudging and chivvying, daring one another to touch him or to touch the axe that hung at his hip. One of them made a comment that Elawon didn't catch, and the other two laughed.

Temenus watched for a moment, then said, "Get away from him. Hippotes?"

The huge Herakleid whom Elawon had met at the fire moved into the group as if he owned it. Then he turned to face Temenus.

"My lord?"

There was nothing insolent in his words, but the face he showed was hard and lightless. A wide slash of gleaming scar tissue clung like a choker at his throat.

"Your brothers have work elsewhere," Temenus told him.

Hippotes turned back to study Akhaïdes. He tilted his head in some kind of acknowledgment, then glared around at the three younger men. One stepped away; then all of them retreated. With a final appraising glance at Akhaïdes, Hippotes followed them.

Temenus said to Akhaïdes, "That was you in the sanctuary, with the stone. Then you killed Tisamenus Pelopeides' man."

"Didn't kill him." The accent, Elawon noticed, had faded. Akhaïdes sounded nearly normal. Still, the curtness of his answer made Elawon wince.

Hippotes slowed, looking back.

"How did they stop you?" Temenus asked.

"By force, my lord."

"Yes, call me your lord. And what shall I call the Good Kinsman?"

Hippotes stopped completely and turned to watch.

"Call me Akhaïdes Outlaw, my lord."

"'Akhaïdes?' What does that mean?"

"Nothing. Nothing to you."

Temenus lifted an eyebrow at this, then just said, "I won't ask what you want that the Serpent won't give you. That's the worst sort of bad manners. But I will ask, is that for me?"

Akhaïdes turned to the horse, which raised its head and stared at Temenus.

Temenus answered himself, "Apparently so. And is your brother a gift for me, as well?"

It took Elawon a moment to realize that Temenus was addressing him. Then he fumbled, "No, my lord. Of course not. Of course not. That would be . . . The horse, yes."

Temenus turned, looking for someone. Xanos, the Dorian lawagetas with the patchwork scalp, saw this and approached, passing Hippotes, who was following his brothers again. Between them, the dogs came loping back from hunting.

"Temenus!" It was Kresphontes, running. The younger men and the dogs stepped out of his way. "Temenus! What are you doing?"

Xanos changed course and laid an arm across Kresphontes' shoulders. Kresphontes threw it off, and Xanos replaced it more firmly. Kresphontes' voice spiraled up in a furious whine. Flashing a smile at Akhaïdes, Temenus went to his brother.

* * *

Not sleeping after the nepenthe, Akhaïdes had felt almost tranquil. It had been easy to act, to do what he had to. But now he could not hold two thoughts without one or the other slipping away. He could not move, not even to sit on the ground and hold his head with his hands to keep it from falling into pieces. He sat on the ground anyway.

Large dusty boots. He looked up. The Dorian with the patchwork scalp said, "How will you do it?"

"I don't know. Do what?"

"Give that horse to the king. A king can touch an outlaw, but a gift from an outlaw has no value. That's why you can't pay your own reparation, right? Well. And you've handled the tether, so your brother can't hold it to give it to the king. So, how?"

"I don't know."

"If you cut the halter off and then your brother ties another on . . ."

Akhaïdes forced his mind to follow. "Yes."

"Yes, that will work? Or just yes, you hear me talking?"

He closed his eye, too weary to answer.

"Oh. No. We don't own any rope here. When the villagers see that the king really needs it, it will be dearer than gold."

Those villagers, apparently deciding that they would get no more information about Kresphontes or Akhaïdes, had continued down the road toward the port with their laden donkeys. In their wake, the dogs had discovered a tortoise crossing the road and were dashing at it, barking and feinting while it plodded phlegmatically along. The young Herakleids trotted over to watch. Elawon followed, with more dignity.

The Dorian said, "I am Xanos, the king's lawagetas. I keep what order is kept in Nafpaktos."

He stopped as if expecting an answer. Akhaïdes could only wait.

"We Dorians don't do outlawry. We don't go around in sacred horror of miscreants, and we don't expel them so . . . roughly. On the other hand, the Herakleids and most of our allies do. Kresphontes thinks you're a problem, and Nafpaktos doesn't need more problems. Are you cold?"

"What? No."

"You're shaking."

Xanos was right.

"Leave me here."

The time in which that could be reassuringly answered came and went.

Kresphontes was finally listening to Temenus. His head was bowed, and Temenus's hands were on his shoulders. The young Herakleids were cheering the dogs on and tossing pebbles that bonked off the tortoise's shell. One man poked Elawon with an elbow. Another stepped on his foot, perhaps accidentally.

Watching this, Xanos observed, "Your brother seems fearless for a man alone among people who owe him nothing."

"He promises Arcadia."

"Promises," Xanos answered. "Strangers promise things to Temenus all day long, but very few of those things actually appear. And your brother isn't family to anyone in Nafpaktos."

Akhaïdes saw the Herakleids, Elawon with them. No, among them but alone.

"It's easy for Herakleids to teach their dogs to eat strangers," Xanos said. "They do it themselves."

Teach the dogs, or . . .? Oh.

"He is the king's guest," Akhaïdes said. "Protected."

Xanos gave him a patient look.

"They will eat him?"

"Without a doubt."

Akhaïdes did not ask the next question, so that Xanos would not feel obliged to answer. Xanos walked away down the road. Akhaïdes got to his feet, caught the horse's tether and followed.

* * *

Several ships lay on the beach, under the cliffs of Khirra. Men had already run one of them into the water, alongside a wooden wharf. The villagers unloaded their donkeys and led them away. The Herakleids started carrying the baggage out, while the ship's men stowed it aboard. The dogs raced back and forth on the beach, barking and play-fighting. Gulls and terns circled tightly overhead, in and out of the cliff's shadow.

Not far away now, just across the water, rose immense, silent Arcadia out of the sea's low mist. The top of it was equally muted, fading into pale sky. Yet Akhaïdes could feel the absolute weight of that wall and the domains beyond it. Although Arcadia held abundant green glades, woods, and pastures, the places he knew best were hard, dry peaks; tumbled slopes of talus and scree; great mounds of weathered stone; basins of basalt and lime, rich in snakes, lizards, boars, wolves, foxes—the earth in its most remorseless purity.

He had passed years in lands where the sun gave no heat for half the year, where a man could freeze to death in its brilliance. Yet it still was brilliant; it just didn't care. Remorseless purity of a different kind. He gave his blinded face to its regard.

The horse turned its head back, then relaxed its ears. Someone was approaching peaceably.

"I presumed at first," Temenus said, "that you would come with us. Then that you wouldn't. So which will it be?"

"Is it my choice?" Akhaïdes turned. Nearer the ship, an older Herakleid—taller and thinner than Temenus, graying, a little stooped—was quietly arguing with an Ithacan who stood with his arms crossed, steadily shaking his head no.

"Aristodemus will arrange it," Temenus said, as if Akhaïdes had answered yes. "Whatever it costs me, I expect a return of some kind. And you can get my horse aboard."

He waited, then added an interrogative noise.

Akhaïdes twitched. "Yes."

The Ithacan seamaster was already walking away from Aristodemus, his expression signaling disgusted capitulation.

"Well then, please do that."

* * *

"The ship master agrees, but . . ."Aristodemus glanced at Akhaïdes.

"Thank you," Temenus answered, with a glance at Elawon, who had left the younger Herakleids to follow the king again.

The smile that Aristodemus gave Temenus showed misgiving as well as leniency and affection. Elawon felt a pang, realizing that a man could know and yet tolerate another so well.

"Just please make sure he behaves," Aristodemus said. "I don't want Kresphontes complaining. He'll set Hippotes off again, and it's two nights back to Nafpaktos."

"I'm sure he knows how to behave." Temenus glanced at Elawon. "Does he?"

Elawon fumbled for a moment. "Yes, Wanax. Yes. He does."

"No more killing people."

Killing people. Spoken as if what Elawon had seen had been something ordinary instead of spraying blood, splintered bone, Akhaïdes snarling like a vicious dog. A grown man shrieking.

"No, no. I promise."

"And he'll manage my horse." Temenus looked at Aristodemus. "And I won't do *that* with him. Even I have better taste."

"You say so now," Aristodemus sniffed, and Temenus laughed aloud.

* * *

The horse planted its forefeet in the sand at the end of the wharf and refused to move. The Herakleids and Ithacans settled down to watch. Akhaïdes turned it away and led it up the beach, then circled back. The horse went willingly until the moment to step on the wharf. Then it stopped again.

The Herakleids snickered. Temenus shushed them, though he was smiling.

"I wonder," Xanos remarked, "what interest fate has in making a horse walk to Nafpaktos."

Kresphontes said, "On that road, it'll die of old age first. Or Lokrians will eat it."

Hippotes scratched his head, burying huge fingers in the black thatch. "I don't want to get on a boat with one. You never know when it'll go crazy."

"I was on a barge of goats," Xanos reminisced. "Going to Levkas—less than an hour's ride. Porpoises came alongside, jumping to see better. The goats all spun around and ran off the other side of the barge, every one of them. We absolutely couldn't stop them. I wonder if they thought there wouldn't be porpoises on that side."

"Did they swim back to land?"

"Until the first shark noticed them."

Akhaïdes led the horse in a circle. He began to jog, and the horse broke into a trot. Each time they approached the wharf, the horse threw up its head, but Akhaïdes continued past and around. After a few turns, the horse lowered its head, its nose almost trailing along the ground. Then man and animal moved smoothly up the ramp. The horse didn't even flinch at the sudden hollow thud of its hooves on the planking.

Temenus murmured, "Magic."

"Cow manure." Kresphontes rose. The rock he threw missed the horse but rattled into the ship. The horse wheeled and plunged into the water.

Akhaïdes tossed the tether after it. The horse came up, snorting fiercely. Everyone remembered the sharks of Levkas, but the horse was already lunging up the beach.

The dogs had lined up at the water's edge to watch. As the horse bounded between them, they swung around and raced along on both sides.

"I wanted that horse," Temenus complained mildly.

"Oh," Kresphontes answered. "Sorry."

The dogs knew better than to chase any domestic animal. They peeled off after a short distance and stood grinning and panting, watching the horse buck and shy its way through another party's accumulated baggage, scattering crates and donkeys. Finally the lead whipped around an upright post, and the horse slammed to a stop.

Akhaïdes came back along the wharf and past the dogs, who looked away with belated guilt. He maneuvered through the jumbled baggage—the owners arriving to complain, Aristodemus heading off to talk to them—and approached the horse.

It wanted nothing to do with him. As he looped the lead over his arm, it kept its head high and its ears pinned. It did not blink. Akhaïdes turned sideways, busy with the rope. After a moment, the horse lowered its head and breathed out against his sleeve. He led it back to the wharf.

"The Lady of Animals loves him," Temenus said. "What can mortals do?"

"Throw another rock," Kresphontes answered.

Hippotes stood up unexpectedly.

Kresphontes looked at him. "What?"

"I'll help." He drew in his belt.

"You hate horses. Why?"

"I want to go home." He glanced at his three brothers, who had risen automatically to go with him. They settled down again, and he tramped off toward the ship.

Kresphontes called after him, "What do you have to go home to? No wife anymore."

"Stop that!" Temenus snapped. Kresphontes looked only slightly chastened.

Hippotes met Akhaïdes at the foot of the ramp. He asked, "Do I need a whip?"

"Just your hand. Loudly. And duck when you hit it."

"I know. I got kicked once."

Akhaïdes trotted the horse in a circle while Hippotes stood facing away. At the base of the wharf, Hippotes whipped around and smacked its rump resoundingly with a cupped hand. It kicked over his head as he dropped. He was back up instantly, and the second slap echoed off the cliff face. The horse shot up the wharf beside Akhaïdes. Hippotes ran alongside and, when the horse hesitated at the ship, he reached and slapped again. It hopped in clumsily, first the front feet, then the hind.

Akhaïdes led it to the place a seaman indicated, cross-tied it, and rubbed it between the ears. It nodded his hand away, not forgiving him yet.

Hippotes waited for Akhaïdes to come back down. Both were blotched with sand. They walked down to the sea to rinse their hands.

Xanos called, "Is that all?"

"You want more excitement?" Temenus grinned. "We could arrange something just for you."

"Oh, no thanks. Only asking."

* * *

There was no wind, so everyone rowed except for Temenus, the king's guest Elawon, and Akhaïdes. Even Aristodemus took an oar. At the tail of the ship, under the horse's chin and the rudderman's platform, Akhaïdes crouched and watched the land slide by as the men worked, singing quietly together to keep the rhythm.

The boundary between earth and water was uncertain, with the clear water revealing the earth below it as exactly like the earth above. When they passed cliffs, the drop continued unchanged below the waterline. Falls and slides carried their tumbled debris on down. Marshy places barely changed, their grasses turned to seaweed, and slender little long-nosed fishes playing the role that lizards did on land.

"Are there monsters?"

Temenus had turned on his seat below the mast. Over his head, he wore a shawl against the cold. Beside him, Elawon watched the land drift by.

"There are monsters," Akhaïdes answered.

"Do you see them?"

"You never see them."

Temenus smiled. "Until it's too late?"

"You never see them at all."

Temenus held his smile while turning to say something quietly to Elawon. Elawon smiled back at him, like a trained dog.

They passed habitations along the shore: two or three hamlets of fishermen who rose warily from their net mending at the sight of the ship. Temenus called greetings across the water, and after a long delay, cautious hands rose in answer.

"Why do they live right on the water?" Akhaïdes heard Elawon ask.

"They're fishermen." Temenus sounded gently amused.

"Aren't there pirates along here?"

"What do these people have to steal? They don't farm. They trade fish for whatever they need, and trap or pick a few wild things. Their only valuables are their women and children, and they send them inland at the first sign of a boat coming."

"They knew we were coming?"

"There's always a lookout somewhere. But these people know me and my ship."

"Pirates won't go after the women anyway? If they go inland?"

"It's still Phocian territory along here. Land pirates and sea pirates have an understanding about staying out of each other's way—an understanding that doesn't include consideration for the rest of us."

In late afternoon, a smaller boat came out of a cove ahead, moving rapidly on a course to intercept them. The Ithacan ship master rose and stood in the bow, shielding his eyes from the sun.

The ship master turned and called, "Pirates!"

The ship's men scrambled up, pulling in oars, grabbing for weapons. Xanos and Kresphontes set their oars aside and also stood. Then Hippotes lumbered to his feet and strode to the bow, elbowing the Ithacan aside. Raising his shoulders to display his full size, he stared at the pirates, opened his loincloth, and pissed into the sea in their direction.

The pirates's boat slowed; then its rowers dragged their oars and it stopped. The Ithacan ship crossed its bow. Of the ten or more pirates, none rose nor even looked at Hippotes. He stood glaring, holding his member like a weapon, until the ship was well past.

* * *

Before sunset, they went ashore at a pebbled beach with cliffs all around. A deep V permanently marked the sea's edge, where ships had beached since time out of mind. The Ithacans ran out a ramp so that everyone, including the horse and Akhaïdes, who could not touch the rail to climb down, could reach land. At one end of this space, water dribbled from a brushy channel into a pool that then seeped in a plane bright with algae, and into the sea. The water was sweet even after the dogs had drunk their fill and raced through it several times.

Hippotes asked Aristodemus, "May we go up to hunt?"

"Of course. Just don't bring back anything that won't fit in the boat."

Hippotes' mouth quirked at the compliment. Then he glanced at Temenus, busy with the Ithacans, and the incipient smile faded.

"And if you find Phocians," Aristodemus added, "please leave them alive."

The younger men tied javelins to their backs and followed Hippotes, finding the best hand- and footholds in places polished by years of climbers. A few of the dogs scrambled up with them; the rest paced and complained, unwilling to risk the ascent but hating being left behind. Akhaïdes led the horse to a corner where grass grew over fallen rocks and lumps of soil, and sat with it while it sought out the edible blades.

The space was too small to erect the tent, so the clerks set stools around a fire pit. Aristodemus sat talking with them while they built a fire of brushwood they had carried from Delphi.

The hunters returned with two pheasants and a rabbit, and pouches full of last year's grapes, dried by winter, from an abandoned farmstead. Hippotes also carried down a dog that had braved the climb up but was then stymied by the descent.

"Plenty of old deer sign," Hippotes said, "but they've gone higher now that the weather's warmer."

The youngest of the hunters grinned. "If we'd had bows, we'd have brought you six brace of rabbits, Uncle."

Temenus raised his head. "Satnios, don't. Not even as a joke."

The young man looked only slightly abashed.

"We don't use bows," Temenus explained to Elawon. "Herakleids never do and never will. It was a bow in your great-grandfather's hand that killed Hyllus."

Elawon had the presence to say, "I've never used a bow, Wanax. Only a sling or sword," and was rewarded with a smile.

The only clerk who owned a knife skinned and gutted the

animals, then wrapped them in mud and cooked them in the coals. The younger Herakleids devoured the meat eagerly despite its freshness. Temenus and Aristodemus waved away their shares. The rest of the meal was bread, which the men dipped in water to soften, and ate with vegetable pickles and the dried grapes. They tossed bread rinds to the dogs, who growled over them, stole them back and forth, and finally settled down to gnaw them quietly.

Temenus, Aristodemus, Xanos, and Elawon ate together, near the fire. Aristodemus sent food to Akhaïdes by the youngest Herakleid, who said as he delivered it, "I don't suppose *you* use a bow," then laughed so that Akhaïdes did not have to answer.

There was no storyteller among them, so as night rose they wrapped themselves in cloaks and blankets, shielded their faces, and went to sleep early. Akhaïdes lay down next to the horse, which stood dozing with its head down.

He was nearly asleep when he felt a soft approach. Temenus set a stool down near Akhaïdes' head and sat on it. The moon was a bare gleaming splinter, down to its last dry bones on its way to renewal. Only stars limned Temenus's hair and the planes of his nose and forehead, yet hid his eyes.

"I keep remembering you in the sanctuary," Temenus said. "I keep wondering, was it only absolution you were asking for? I don't suppose you will tell me."

Despite the chill, Akhaïdes felt sweat in his armpits and the small of his back.

"What do you think of the way Hippotes stopped the pirates?"

Akhaïdes gathered words. "Clear. Direct. Ingenious. Generous."

"Generous?"

"He is angry with you about something. Yet he did that anyway."

"Not to serve me. To spare everyone else harm."

"Which serves you. How much would your family give, to ransom you?"

Temenus did not answer. They remained that way: Temenus seated, hands clasped between his knees, Akhaïdes at his feet. The sea breathed, both at rest and alert at the same time.

Temenus finally said, "I don't have many tools. I use what comes to hand."

"Elawon came to hand?"

"He did. But so did you. Bringing what I want, but in a form that . . ."

Akhaïdes waited.

"One expects brothers to be similar somehow. But you are nothing like your brother. How can that be?"

This time, it was Akhaïdes who did not answer.

"There is another puzzle, too. You look Pelopeid, but Elawon explained that, and I can't have met you before. Then you spoke. I heard your voice, and I knew you. I *knew* we had met, but not where or when. How can *that* be?"

"It can't be."

Temenus tilted his head, neither agreeing nor disagreeing. "I don't have time for puzzles. I don't like them. And it doesn't help that you're outlaw, so I can solve this one however I please."

From nearby, Kresphontes' voice called irritably, "Temenus! Come and sleep!"

Temenus rose and picked up the stool. He said to Akhaïdes, "Good night."

Akhaïdes remained silent.

"It does no harm to be civil, whatever might happen in the future. Sleep well, Akhaïdes Outlaw."

"And you, my lord."

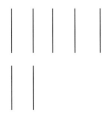

I may not have gone where I intended to go, but I think I have ended up where I intended to be.[viii]

—*Douglas Adams*

Hawmai, Tisamenus, and Menetor: one vexed, one dogged, and one—he would have hated to admit—amused, and all of them outside at nightfall, when spirits rose and monsters stirred. Yet here they were nonetheless, warlord, king, priest, meeting together under a darkening sky with the steeps of Delphi around them, each waiting for another to speak first.

Finally, Hawmai started. "I bring you greetings from the High King, Grandfather."

"Those greetings are well received. Delphi is protected by Athens, but we would never forget our most memorable guest."

Menetor turned to Tisamenus. "And you are welcome also, King of Lacedaemon."

Before Tisamenus could respond, Hawmai said, "The High King needs an answer to a question. To two questions."

"And so do I," Tisamenus said.

"They're the same questions," Hawmai said.

"You don't know that," Tisamenus answered crisply. Hawmai blinked and did not correct him.

Menetor considered smiling at this, then tested it by saying to Tisamenus, "You were not included in the High King's request."

"I am including myself now. Will you refuse me, Grandfather?"

It was difficult to control the smile. "No, young lord. We welcome you. And we are ready."

"We haven't fasted," Hawmai said.

"I ate today," Tisamenus agreed, but made no further apology.

Menetor finally allowed the smile. "You have fasted all your life, young lord. Until today. Come with me. Both of you, come."

* * *

A single lamp lit six steps, each as tall as Tisamenus's knee, the way down as steep as a ladder, the treads so narrow, his feet scarcely found purchase; Hawmai would have an even harder time, he thought, climbing into the well of stone.

Below, a man waited, dressed in a priest's red robe with long sleeves, watching them descend. When Tisamenus reached the lowest level to stand beside him, the priest began talking, not waiting for Hawmai to work his way down.

"The springs of Delphi all arise from one source and branch beneath the earth, as veins branch in the body yet carry the same blood." He turned to face the chamber, and Tisamenus saw that his hair was bound in a tight knot at the base of his skull.

The chamber enclosed a pool of water, beginning at the step where they stood. Tisamenus could have touched the wall at his side, and the priest the wall at his. The far end was not distant at all, perhaps ten strides. In that wall, a vertical black slot reached maybe two cubits above the surface. Otherwise, the walls were an unbroken surface of plain, coarse stone. Even the lamp sat simply on one of the steps instead of in a niche or bracket.

Thin wisps like steam rose and swirled up from the water, but they could not be steam in such cold. Just beyond the edge of hearing, the faintest whispers came to Tisamenus: perhaps the caress of water on stone.

"This," the priest said, "like Kastalia's spring, is the water of life and death, of forgetting and remembering. Birth is forgetting. At death, we remember everything. Drink, and you will never be the same."

Hawmai staggered down to their level with an explosive grunt.

"Bathe; your body will escape you. Drown; your spirit will not leave this place."

From the corner of his eye, Tisamenus saw how Hawmai touched a fist to his forehead. He himself felt no fear at all. He asked, "Grandfather, is this the pool where outlaws swim until they drown?"

"That is outside, at the river under the sky. No outlaw can come here."

"Orestes was never here?"

"Never."

"But he saw himself, he told me. That's what I want, too. Isn't that done here?"

"Here, but elsewhere, too. Outlaws in the pool see themselves as they drown. The purified might see themselves up above, in the Serpent's cave."

"Will I?" Tisamenus heard his own eagerness.

"My lord, you can ask. The lady of this place may be here or may not. She may be willing to see you or may not. The Serpent and its servants go where they wish. They can come to anyone, anywhere. And the Serpent can even devour a suppliant and bear him forth again, changed into that vision of himself forever."

"Like Tydeus?"

"Just like him."

Why am I not afraid? Tisamenus thought.

Hawmai asked quietly, "What now?"

"Now you disrobe. Everything—even any pin in your hair."

They did so, leaning on the steps or the wall, not touching each other. Hawmai set his shoes on an upper step, and his folded clothes on top of them. Tisamenus did the same, adding all his rings.

At once, Tisamenus began to shiver. He glanced sidelong at Hawmai, the bulk of his chest and belly, the thick, furry thighs. His own body must look like a rabbit, skinned and boiled. He did not have to look down to know that his penis and scrotum had retracted into shapeless lumps. Hawmai's penis hung like a hose nearly halfway to his knees. Tisamenus looked away.

The priest said, "You are naked. You are not in your own place. You are alone. You have no knowledge. You must simply wait for what will happen next."

"Will you leave us?" Tisamenus asked.

"I will be here, although you may not see me. Now, drink."

"Where?" Hawmai asked.

"Between your own feet."

"Like oxen?"

"It's the same water everywhere."

Tisamenus crouched, his back grazing the step behind him. He slid his hands into the water, then raised the cup of his hands and drank. He thought, just for a moment, of Akhaïdes and the palm full of blood. Beside him, he heard Hawmai shuffling and breathing heavily, trying to get down without losing his balance.

The water did not taste of stone or dirt, as Tisamenus had expected. It tasted salty and sweet at the same time, full of flavor despite its cold. He reached for more, and as he drank he saw Hawmai reach, too. Hawmai's hands went in to the knuckle, to the thumb, to the wrist, to the elbow . . . With a single grunt, Hawmai pitched forward as if he were diving. Head, back, buttocks, legs—a splash, and he was gone.

Tisamenus started backward, the step hard against his spine. He kept imagining Hawmai bursting up, flailing, arching backward, gulping air. He saw that picture again and then again, like a drawing on a spinning jar. Yet it kept not happening.

Any question died unasked. Hawmai gone, the priest gone, the water unperturbed, and that was all. He crouched alone in this cold space, waiting.

At the far end of the chamber, light on the water stirred as if someone breathed gently on the surface. That disturbance ruffled, glittered, lifted. Then it parted over the rise of a smooth curved surface. It was the back, and then the shoulders, of something sleek and hairless. The hair came a moment later—a clotted mass rising, water seething out of it, and then the body uncoiling upward to show a woman's face.

Still she continued to rise and straighten. She was naked, with long, hanging dugs and thin arms, the eyes open. Her mouth was wide, with dark red lips, her nose and chin pointed, the mound of her hair shifting as if it were a separate living thing. A streak of hair began at her navel, widening downward until the water hid the rest. Her eyes blinked open, and her ribs began to move as if she breathed.

She came wading toward him as any human would, moving her arms for balance. When her hands came out of the water, he saw that they were nearly normal. Only the fingers were strangely long, and perhaps more than ten.

Why did he not think of fleeing? As she came nearer, her hair still moved as if it were below water, bunching and coiling, rising, furling. Although the lamp still burned, the hair did not gleam in the slightest. Not a single strand shone.

Her mouth opened. "Tisamenus Oresteides Pelopeides." Her voice was heavy and sexless, but not a man's. If she had teeth, they were like her hair, absorbing rather than reflecting light. The inside of her mouth was dark as a cave.

Tisamenus had to ask, "Who are you?" He felt surprise that he could make a sound. "Not a nymph. One of the sisters. The Erinyes. The Hunters."

She did not laugh, but her eyes gleamed . The pupils were silver, startlingly like Akhaïdes's. "I am Alecto Ouranou. The Unnamed. Fear me above all. Do you?"

He sucked in breath. "No," he whispered. Then, more forcefully, "No. I don't."

"Then, you are a silly little boy. Tell me how you will die."

So this, at last, was anger. It rose from the root of his body like steam—no, like lava. It hurt. It felt wonderful. "I won't talk about that. I'm not a boy, and I'm not afraid of you. I order you to tell me how to live!"

Alecto's head jerked up, and her hair churned. That black chasm between her lips moved again.

"All Pelopeids come to us sooner or later," she said. "None is blameless."

"I will take all the blame I'm responsible for. None more, none less."

Water ran smoothly off her skin. He saw the hard ends of her breasts, and the V below her navel. But it was the smell of her that moved him: stale and strong like mud, like truffles, like the deep roots of the world. It seeped into his nose, down through his body, into the lowest part of his abdomen, where the anger had begun. There it squirmed and writhed just as her hair did.

She reached out—he could strike her hands away, but what good would that do?—and took his head between her palms, the skin rough as a shark's. As her face came at him, he smelled the breath of that mouth: fish, drowned corpses, the sea bottom.

She did have teeth; they clashed against his. His lip snagged, and something hard darted into his mouth. *Snake,* he thought, but did not pull away.

He had been kissed before, though never in hunger. The coils in his abdomen tightened as her clinging, crawling hair enveloped his head. He groaned, the sound muffled by the suction of her mouth. He couldn't breathe. He was drowning.

Drowning in a cook pot. The smell was like Alecto's, yet at the same time delicious. A man leaned over to stab at him with a huge spoon. Another man dredged chunks into a bowl and ate with his fingers, sucking the bones. The first man said something, then something else. The eating man started, stared, then whirled about and vomited. Tisamenus watched in sorrow his chewed parts spewing. He would never find them all now.

He stood with his back against a wall. Although he wore a thick shirt, the stone chafed his skin. The man between his legs jerked and heaved upward. The man was cursing, but it wasn't Tisamenus's fault; he had only been passing by. The man's face grated on Tisamenus's throat, and his fingers dug into one of Tisamenus's breasts. Oh, he was a woman with his insides packed and burning from the violence of this rape. The man's face was her father's.

Thrust from tight darkness into bright light, he heard women's voices, sharp with dismay. He was another woman, raped repeatedly in another corridor, by another man. He was the man who had held the cooking spoon, stepping into a chamber to see the man who had eaten rise from his wife's sated body, screaming like a panther with the pain. He was a young boy whose father laid a hand on his head and said nothing to claim him. He was a second boy—same father, same act—and this boy would step into old age with his name still unspoken. He was a king fighting to free his arms from knotted sleeves as his wife strode toward him with an axe in her hands. He was the king's slave, strangled with a bowstring for telling the truth. He was the king's daughter, having traveled to a war camp to meet a husband, but instead given as a blood gift to the wind. He was this daughter's mother, shrieking from the walls of her husband's great city, cursing the air that had taken her child. He was a charioteer whose lynchpin broke, the platform sundered under his feet, with only enough time to curse the man who had betrayed him, before the horses dragged him to death. He was another woman so agonized that she could, without noticing, eat part of a roasted child, yet the child lived to do crimes and betrayals that would bear his name forever.

And he was Tisamenus again, standing in that flood of crimes and betrayals, with more still pouring out of the past, like a sinuous rush of weasels. He himself was meat. He wore the bowstring on his wrist, his foot set firmly on a step to nowhere that he could see, his hips steadied by long, scarred, powerful hands that he knew better than his own. He was the lynchpin that did not break. He raised his spear and drove the horses at his enemy.

* * *

"My lord?"

Tisamenus's whole body hurt. He did not want to open his eyes.

"My lord?" He wouldn't wake up for anyone else, but Aranare was special. He cracked one eye. Light stabbed him like a lance.

She smiled. She must have been very worried. He made his mouth say, "I'm all right. Why is it so bright?"

"It's morning. And raining. Do you want water?"

"I'll never drink water again."

"Wine, then?"

Wine? All his bones ached, and his head was pounding. "Water. But be careful where it came from."

She helped him raise his head—cool, strong fingers on the back of his neck—and touched a beaker to his lips. He took a bare sip, then filled his mouth with the clean coldness and let it rinse his throat as he swallowed.

She laid him down again.

"Is anyone else here?"

"Hawmai came earlier, but he left again."

Dragged down with a huge splash and absolutely gone. "Is he all right?"

"He is complaining."

"What about?"

"That you both sat in a well all night and saw nothing. That you fell asleep and he had to carry you back here. That the priest took all your rings for nothing."

"How does he know the priest took my rings?"

"They were gone when he looked for them."

Tisamenus thought about that. Aranare watched him with her usual loving reserve.

"We saw nothing all night, he says?"

"He is sure of it."

Tisamenus closed his eye again. He touched his lip, where a tiny cut, already half healed, felt rough to his finger. Then he placed his open hands on the blanket over his chest, holding his vision to his heart, and fell contentedly asleep.

* * *

It rained all the next day. The horse loaded aboard well enough but then moved restlessly, making the ship rock, never quite settling down. Akhaïdes, stiff with cold, his rags soaked through and clinging, crouched under its chin. Even Xanos wore a shirt, and a cloak over his shoulders. There was no wind, and the men sang only for the rhythm of the rowing. Temenus convinced Aristodemus, who looked tired and sallow, to sit with him and share his shawl for shelter. Elawon might have taken the free oar, but no one seemed to expect him to, so he didn't.

The sea was darkly opaque today. The ship slid past ever-steeper cliffs, some crowned with broken rock, others corniced with rank overhanging forest and pendant creepers. There was even a squat Phocian stockade belching smoke and heaped around with rubbish. It did not open its gates to Temenus's call.

Lokrians lived all around here, Temenus told Elawon, but men rarely saw them—not even the Phocians. Lokrians, he said, built nothing, planted nothing, and despised those who built and planted. They did not have fire. They lived off seeds and small animals, which they trapped and ate raw, and they guarded their forests fiercely. To step off a road in Lokrian territory, even just to piss behind a thorn bush, was to risk never being seen again. Even the Phocians kept to the roads, towers, and open spaces. The few Lokrians in Nafpaktos, Temenus said, either came to trade animal skins and herbs for knives, nepenthe, and ornaments or had been exiled by unfathomable laws.

Lokrian sign was clear to those who knew them: Temenus pointed out paths as narrow and winding as a snake's, and tiny snares at the edges of the water for frogs and crayfish. From his place, Akhaïdes saw other, more interesting code: the skeleton of a mouse reassembled on a tree limb, stones of different colors balanced one atop the other, a human jawbone painted blue. Boundary magic—half plea, half defiance.

Twice when the ship strayed too close to a low shore, stones pattered down, making the horse flinch and the dogs bark fiercely. The young Herakleids chafed to avenge these insults, but Temenus would not let them leave the ship. Lokrians used poison on their darts, Xanos reminded them, and so they sulked.

The moon changed that night—invisibly because of the drizzle, yet they all felt it. They stopped before dusk at another ancient campsite, under cliffs so steep and overhanging that even Lokrians—Xanos hoped—could not figure out how to bother them. They ate quickly, then put overhead every thread they carried. Kresphontes even coerced the Herakleids into giving up their coats to block any leak between the tent panels. Then they all crept together into cover. The dogs tried to sneak in, too, but were evicted. The Ithacans slept on the ship, under the shelter of the unfurled sail.

Aristodemus summoned Akhaïdes, over Kresphontes' protest. An outlaw could not pollute a king's house, Aristodemus reminded them sharply, and that must be true for a king's shelter as well. Then he lay down between the other men and the corner he allotted to Akhaïdes. Temenus stayed, as he should, at the center, the place of greatest safety, and kept Elawon with him there.

Akhaïdes had been outside, unprotected, for more moon shifts than he could count. At the farthest places of the earth, men watched the moon. This was the night that the Bajgani bred horses and cattle, the night that women took any men they wanted. Farmers would spread seeds on roads and rooftops on this night, would marry off their children, but would not bury the dead.

Akhaïdes wondered, did not remember, whether people here did those things. There was no one he could ask: not Elawon, not Xanos, not Temenus. And not Aristodemus. He would not dare to speak directly to so honorable a man as the king's brother.

Sigewas Teller would know and would answer. But Sigewas was as lost to him as was Tisamenus Oresteides—gone as if they had never lived.

The change was always silent, but every man felt in the core of his body how the weight of the sky swung from death to birth in mute explosion. Akhaïdes slept.

While the sea exhaled mist the next morning, an hour's rowing brought them to a place where knife-sharp cliffs gave way to more rounded hills; then those hills rolled back from the water to reveal flat meadows. Behind the largest of these, a narrow road stepped down from the dry heights behind.

The ship stopped here at Xanos's request. With no dry land to run a ramp to, the men swung over the rail and waded up through land more wet than dry, pushing through vines and sinking into peat, the dogs happily splashing along. The horse could not get down without a ramp, nor could Akhaïdes, who could not touch the rails. As they waited on board, Aristodemus dozed, wrapped in a dry shawl, leaning against the mast, his head in his hands.

A mound at the base of the road bore three or four huts, a few trees, and an old collapsed tomb. From a distance the structures appeared intact, but, coming closer, the men saw that the roofs gaped where the stones had slid out of place.

Temenus asked, "Did they leave, or did something happen to them?"

Xanos stepped to the nearest hut and glanced inside. "There's your answer."

Temenus looked. On the hearth, already grown over with creepers, stood a small pyramid of skulls: adults at the bottom, children at the top.

Temenus backed away. "Lokrians? Phocians? Pirates?"

"Any of those."

Elawon stepped up to look, then retreated.

Temenus asked, "When did you hear from them last?"

"At the beginning of winter. We didn't stop here on the way to Delphi. I forgot to wonder about them then."

"They should have stayed in Nafpaktos."

"They were hungry in Nafpaktos."

Temenus turned away. "We can't go anywhere, can we?"

"Outside of Nafpaktos, no. And they were Aetolians, too. We thought they'd be safe. Aetolians have lived along here forever."

Kresphontes came to join them. "Too long ago to find the killers."

"Why kill them?" Xanos mused. "Rob them, sure. Steal the women. But *kill* them?"

He rubbed the patched top of his head. Elawon was scraping at the mud on his shoes with a stick. Temenus glanced at him and then away.

"They had the trees and vines," Xanos said. "Bean fields there, other vegetables. Goats. And they could hunt. Fish. They wouldn't have starved. I don't suppose they thought of this."

"Where are their animals?" Temenus asked.

"Taken, eaten, wandered off. Starved."

"Dogs, too," Kresphontes said.

As if he had called them, their own dogs came to him. He looked down at them as if not really seeing them. They laid their ears on their necks.

"Send some men to Nafpaktos by the road," Temenus told Xanos. "Lokrians don't eat goats. Maybe they'll find them."

The younger men had burrowed into the tomb's debris but found nothing of value. Even the bones were gone. They wandered back to Xanos and Temenus. Elawon straightened from cleaning his shoes and tossed the stick away.

* * *

When the Herakleids returned, less the three that Xanos had sent searching along the road for the lost animals—with orders to be in Nafpaktos by sunset—the ship left immediately. As Elawon picked once again at his mudded shoes, Temenus told Aristodemus what they had found. Everyone else rowed grimly on.

Never looking directly at them, Akhaïdes still watched the king describing ruined houses and mounded skulls. As he talked, everything Temenus said, every movement, was unforeseen. Yet, the moment before Temenus laid a hand on Aristodemus's arm, Akhaïdes knew that he would do that.

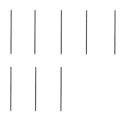

The usefulness of madmen is famous: they demonstrate society's logic flagrantly carried out down to its last scrimshaw scrap.[ix]
—*Cynthia Ozick*

A river descended into a broad delta braided with courses of reeds, vines, and bright sea grass. Birds of all heights and colors stood on spindle legs to watch the ship pass, then turned back to their hunting. At the western end of this marsh, in a tight triangle between cliffs, swamp, and sea, lay Nafpaktos.

The city began at the edge of the sea, on a low bluff of coarse packed sand, then a curve of hutments cramped together. Behind these rose more houses, coil after coil of them, finally topped by a low cupola that must mark the palace—light against the dark ridge behind it. From the water, there appeared to be no space at all between buildings—not enough for a rat or a bird, let alone a person, to pass. Yet here came scores of people to stand and stare at the ship. A gray haze lay flat above the city, and from the ship the men smelled sewage, smoke, and food. The powers, Akhaïdes thought. The other elements.

The horse raised its head to sniff the rank air, then sneezed. Its motion rocked the ship a little. From the rower's bench, Kresphontes tossed a hard look at Akhaïdes, then lowered his eyes to his oar. Temenus gazed steadily at his city, not speaking at all. Elawon sat erect and proud in his shadow.

* * *

The ship passed the city. Just after a tall spine of rock lay a gravel beach with a gentler slope. Here, three or four ships's bodies rose among disorderly heaps of wood. The Herakleids lifted their oars and left the last of the rowing to the Ithacans while they gathered their belongings.

It took a moment for Elawon to realize that the ships on the beach were not ruins; they were being built, not rotting away. He knew nothing about boat building, but these did not look right. He started to ask Temenus, but the set of the king's jaw made him choose silence instead.

The Ithacans drew the ship sideways to the shore and ran out the ramp. Two men trotted up to hold the prow and stern lines while the dogs, the Herakleids, Elawon, Xanos, and finally Akhaïdes and the horse disembarked.

Elawon found himself standing beside Xanos, who had assumed an assertive stance, glaring at the ships. This close, Elawon could see how their sides sagged and bowed. "Is that the Herakleid fleet?"

Xanos snorted. "Temenus thinks something angry with us keeps destroying them—some power we aren't treating well. I think we don't know how to build ships."

He rubbed a hand over the seams in his scalp. "These things will see me to my dead. The wood is the worst quality anybody can find. Most of it is cut from twisted trees so the hulks rip themselves apart as they dry. We can build houses with it, but ships, no. Our armorer can't even use it for his fires. It's too green. The cording is dry-rotted, the pitch is lumpy, the pegs won't swell, and our shipwrights couldn't float a nutshell in a soup bowl. We actually finished one ship last year. See?"

130

He pointed in an unexpected direction: out in the water, a little farther west. Elawon saw a few edges of wood jutting above the surface.

"It knocked itself to pieces against the first wave it met," Xanos said.

"Can't you use other people's ships?" Elawon looked back to the Ithacans, preparing to depart again, none of them so much as glancing at the ruins on the beach.

"The Ithacans won't join the Return. And we can't change their minds with promises or by force, since we can't get at them on their island, since we don't have ships. They promised ships years ago but never delivered. For them to get us to Delphi and back took very dull negotiations. These men won't stay long enough to give us a word of advice. But at least they won't laugh aloud until they're out of hearing."

"This seems a bad place to build a city. Don't you have trouble with pirates?"

"We have had, and will again. The city's too big to raid, but there's a lot of thievery, woman-snatching—that sort of thing."

"Why build here?"

"The Herakleids don't own any land of their own. My kings— Dorians—gave this to them. They didn't have a choice: build here or nowhere."

Temenus came to them, glanced at the ships, and said to Elawon, "Will you walk with me?" as if there might be any question of refusing.

Elawon gathered his belongings. The day was chilly and damp though not truly cold, but he threw his coat over his shoulders so he would not have to carry it.

Temenus glanced at him. "I'm sorry we don't have donkeys. But it's not far to the city."

They walked away from the others. Elawon thought about commenting on the Herakleid ships, perhaps making a mild gibe.

Just in time, he thought better of it. "Your city has no wall." This sounded stupid by itself, so he added, "You must have honest neighbors."

"Nafpaktos is temporary, until I win Mycenae. My neighbors know this and leave me alone."

My neighbors. I win Mycenae. That was how a king spoke. Elawon understood, as if Temenus himself were the city; the people. Orestes must speak that way. Elawon was glad for having left Tisamenus to come to one who owned kingship so surely.

What had Xanos said about pirates and thievery? Elawon didn't remember.

"Don't mistake me," Temenus added. "Nafpaktos has its problems. It is . . ." He looked uncharacteristically baffled for a moment, then said, "I hope you'll be content in my city."

No important person had ever been so attentive to Elawon. He would be happy here.

"And I hope the horse your brother cares for will be contented, too."

Oh, that.

"The damos council will find you a place to live. There's a room in the palace for bachelor men. You can sleep there for now, but it's not suitable for a guest." Temenus walked on in silence for a moment. "Your brother . . . I'm not sure where he can stay."

"He sleeps anywhere," Elawon assured him.

"I've noticed. And when no one else will. How shall we address him? Can't he use the name he was given, before he was outlawed?"

"He could use it without the patronymic, but he doesn't want to."

"So . . ." Temenus's tone had a practiced casualness. "Akhaïdes Outlaw. What name did he have before?"

"Ephialtes, my lord."

Elawon walked along several more steps before he realized that Temenus had stopped. He stopped, too, and turned.

Temenus's eyes were closed, yet his face was utterly peaceful, as if Elawon had spoken the profoundest of truths. He was still for so long that Elawon had to say, "It's not an uncommon name in Arcadia, my lord," even though it was.

Temenus opened his eyes. "When I am High King, there will be laws about giving children such names—in Arcadia and everywhere else."

Elawon smiled, then realized too late that Temenus had not meant it as a joke.

Aristodemus came up and laid a hand on his brother's shoulder. "I'll feel better for warm food and clean clothes. You?"

Temenus's face softened, and the corners of his mouth twitched.

"Warm food," Aristodemus repeated. "Possets with wine and cheese. Onions."

A group of dogs raced toward them, then stopped and stalked, stiff-legged, around the dogs that had gone to Delphi. Ears rose and lowered; then tails began to wag.

"Garlic," Aristodemus added. "Enough to feel as if your head might explode."

Temenus finally smiled. Aristodemus kept his hold on his brother and started him walking toward Nafpaktos again.

"A bed," Aristodemus added.

"With who in it?"

They both laughed.

Elawon moved along beside them, envying their ease with each other, waiting for them to remember that he was there.

* * *

It was as bad as anything Akhaïdes might have imagined—worse even than it had appeared from over the water. Arne was a paragon of spacious order and cleanliness compared to Nafpaktos. Structures leaned together, ignoring the contours of the ground beneath them. The only way to distinguish one from another would be to count the doors—squat, dark openings, like the mouths of caves or kennels. Wherever a cluster of huts conceded even the smallest space, someone had stuffed a pen of animals. The path itself was heaped at the sides with rubble, refuse, weeds, and packed with people, all staring. Right now they were staring at Temenus and his followers. In a moment, they would notice him.

The horse's lead was slick with sweat. He wanted to sidle off the path and out of here, up through the rocks to clean air and light. But ahead, Elawon strolled as if unconcerned, and so Akhaïdes had to follow. He forced himself calm so he wouldn't alarm the horse, and followed his brother into the chaos that was Nafpaktos.

* * *

Nafpaktos opened for Elawon like a pocket of treasure: shelves of houses threaded with pens and passages, all the sounds and smells of energetic living. He had told Akhaïdes that he was rich, and for an Arcadian he was, but with a place like this instead of that crude patch of rock at the top of nowhere—a place no one had ever bothered to try to steal—how rich would he be? And even that barren, ugly space wasn't really his own. He forced himself not to glance back at Akhaïdes in resentment.

The city's population mixed as many types as Elawon had ever seen: heavy brown Dorians, black-haired Phocians, tall, fair Aetolians, Carians in blue shirts and skirts, Illyrians, Dyropians, Ozolians. And even a few who, from Temenus's earlier description, must be Lokrians—slight and dark and furtive in the shadows.

All these people greeted their king with shining eyes and courteous murmurs, touching softly bunched fingertips to their foreheads. Rather than simply accepting these gestures as his due, Temenus returned them as if to say, *I am equally glad to be with you.* After those formal signs, men and women still reached across Elawon to brush Temenus's sleeves, hungry for more of him.

At Temenus's other side, Aristodemus greeted older men who walked beside him, talking quietly and urgently. Behind them, Kresphontes exchanged glances with younger men who stiffened their postures, testing their fledgling manhood.

Xanos, obviously popular, received his own welcome with an immodesty that faded momentarily when one Dorian woman set her fists on her hips to glare at him.

"My wife," he murmured to Elawon. "I must be in trouble for something. I generally am."

"She's beautiful," Elawon said. And indeed she was.

"And as voracious in bed as out of it. What can a man do?"

The path through the houses wound steadily upward. Elawon glanced back, past the rest of the Herakleids. It was interesting to see how the people who leaned toward the king and his brother swayed back from Akhaïdes.

"Don't worry," Xanos said quietly. "No one knows who he is."

Elawon glanced at him. "Not yet. But how do they know he is outlaw?"

"They probably think he's some stockman we snatched to watch the animal. They're keeping away because he looks dangerous."

They climbed a last set of flat, wide steps in uneven tiers. Directly before them lay the palace, its deep porch offering three entrances of varying widths. A young man in a priest's gown, tall even though stooped, limped out to meet them.

Temenus knelt and placed his hands between the priest's. The priest raised his voice to reach everyone. "Our king has come home." His voice sibilated: he seemed to be missing front teeth. "He brought gifts, but the greatest gift is himself, returned to us."

Behind Elawon, people murmured agreement. Temenus kissed the priest's hands. The priest lifted Temenus up and kissed his forehead. Then Temenus turned.

He also spoke loudly enough for everyone to hear. "We traveled to Delphi. The oracle spoke to me. What it said, I will tell in due time."

Temenus gestured to Elawon to join him. Elawon turned and drew in a sudden breath at the sight of so many people, the city falling away behind them, the gulf in the distance, and, beyond that, Arcadia, pale in mist. Directly below, Kresphontes, Hippotes, and the other Herakleids were all looking at him now.

Temenus laid a hand on Elawon's shoulder. "The gifts Delphi gave me, you can see here: this man, my honored guest. And that animal, a sign of our future affluence."

The weight and warmth of the king's hand, the regard of so many . . . Then Temenus drew Elawon into the shadow of the porch, into his new home.

* * *

Xanos watched the Herakleids trail into the palace. Kresphontes, last to enter, looked back a final time, as if slamming a door behind them. Xanos turned to go to his own house and saw Akhaïdes. Oh. He had forgotten. That explained Kresphontes' harsh backward glance. The outlaw stood, his back against the horse's shoulder, at the center of a gathering circle of men.

Xanos hurried over. "Don't any of you have work to do?" The tight knot of men made grudging room for him. "And did you hear the king? The animal is his . . ." Improvising fast, he added, "So is its minder."

The men backed away, then stopped to watch.

Xanos asked Akhaïdes, "Did the king tell you where you're supposed to stay?"

"No."

"You can't go into any house except his."

"I know that. I . . ." Akhaïdes looked around helplessly. Was he really so uneasy in this small town? So unnerved by a few strangers?

"If the king wanted you in his house, he would have said so. I'll show you where you can stay."

* * *

Makhawis lifted her skirt and ran. Startled men dodged out of her way. The group of slaves who had brought the news raced after her. Out of her work room, down a corridor, three steps up, another corridor, two steps down, turn, and finally, she was at her brother's private room. She dropped her skirt and brushed out the wrinkles, touched her hair, and pushed the door.

"Sister!"

Temenus rose from a stool and splashed his feet out of the basin in which his wife was bathing them. He strode barefoot between stooped slaves, his leg wraps undone to the knee and dragging behind. Makhawis's heart leaped with relief: he was unhurt, unharmed, still perfect. She hurried to embrace her brother.

"You're back so soon! I'm glad!"

"So am I."

"I thought you'd be gone for a whole month or more." She leaned away to look into his face. "But what's this? Your mustache grew so quickly? And you smell terrible."

"Time in the Delphi bathhouses is expensive. And they were full of Mycenaeans."

Makhawis glanced toward her slaves who had followed her here. Three of them slipped out.

"You must be starved for a proper meal. Something hot and fresh."

"Oh, yes, yes, yes. Seduce me with food. I love it when you do that."

Makhawis smiled past Temenus's shoulder, at his wife, beautifully dressed, her hair and makeup perfect, her face carefully blank, kneeling beside the foot basin. Then Makhawis and pressed her own face into Temenus's neck, the scent of him, however stale, so dear to her.

"Food, shave, bath. Did Hippotes drive you mad all the way there and back?"

"Mostly he sulked—which is quiet, at least."

She laughed and nosed his hair again. "And Kresphontes?"

"Watching me as the great eagle watches the Serpent, in case of a misstep."

"Aristodemus?"

"He even rowed for a bit."

She stroked his cheek, and he turned his head to kiss her hand.

Then he asked her, "What does 'Ephialtes' mean?"

"'Nightmare,'" she answered easily. "Don't you know? Of course you do."

"Is that all?"

"As far as I know. Why?"

He was silent for so long that she drew away again. His eyes were half closed, full of secrets.

She asked again, "Why?"

He drew her face back to his shoulder. "I'll tell you . . . not yet."

He caressed her hair. She caressed his. He was all right.

Everything was all right.

* * *

Kresphontes touched his eldest brother's sleeve. Aristodemus stopped his slow trudge toward his rooms and turned. In the dimness of the hall, his face was etched with weariness.

Kresphontes asked, "What do you think?"

"About what?"

"The Arcadians."

Aristodemus shifted his balance. "To win one of the High King's followers is a great prize."

"It's not him. I don't care about Elawon."

"The outlaw, then. Why does he worry you?"

"We have so many difficulties already. I don't like the way . . . I don't like it. It will hurt us."

"You're sure of that?"

Kresphontes threw out his open hands. "It's the Good Kinsman!"

"You aren't the only one who knows." Aristodemus grasped Kresphontes' outstretched wrist, and lowered it gently. "Fate also knows, don't you think?"

Kresphontes glowered at him.

Aristodemus's tone was still mild. "Do you know why we hang the heads of our enemies on city walls? Why we post the figures of monsters on them?"

"Nafpaktos doesn't have walls," Kresphontes muttered.

Aristodemus smiled. "We do that to show others how strong we are. 'I tamed this; I can tame you.'"

"If Temenus would hang the outlaw's head somewhere, fine. But to let him walk into the city . . ."

"We don't know the king's plans. Today is only today."

Kresphontes looked away.

"And he's the king. His will is our will. His fate is ours. Everything he does is for us."

"I wish I were as sure of that as you are."

Aristodemus tightened his grip so sharply that Kresphontes started.

"Never question him." Aristodemus's face was as harsh as Kresphontes had ever seen it. "Fate chose him. Fate will do for him what it needs to, and we'll follow as we need to. That's all."

"He's probably asking Makhawis what to do, instead of asking us. He—"

"That's all."

Kresphontes lowered his head and touched his forehead with his free hand.

Aristodemus released him. "The king will consult whomever he chooses to consult: you, me, our sister, or the roaches in the kitchen. Then he will do what he will do, with fate to guide him. As for you, please use that energy to help him, not to fight him. It's always been your way, but you're a man now and a leader of men. We can't afford disloyalty in the king's own house."

"I'm not disloyal! I never would be!"

Aristodemus's face did not soften. "Then go see your wife and daughters, and let me see my wife and sons. Leave kingship to the king." He turned and walked away.

Kresphontes rubbed the wrist that Aristodemus had gripped. He had never imagined that his brother was still so strong.

* * *

The palace was like the city: complex and cramped as a rabbit warren, laced with innumerable chambers and corridors, not one of them straight, no two walls meeting evenly, all dirt floored, with low ceilings and just enough light from the occasional overhead well to keep people from bumping into each other. The range of population outside was reflected inside, with men and women of all types going about whatever their business happened to be, greeting one another, stepping out of one another's path in a complex pattern of social order, Herakleids dominant.

Temenus, with a smooth apology, had left Elawon in the single big room where the unmarried Herakleids slept. One young man showed Elawon a chest where he could place his baggage, and a place on the floor where he could sleep. Nearby, Hippotes and his brothers seemed to be dividing other floor space among them.

The young man said, "This is the best we have. Sorry."

Elawon had imagined a private room, slaves, a bath. He looked at the young man, finally placing him as Satnios, who had joked about bows on the voyage here. Temenus had silenced him quickly and firmly. If the king kept such a grudge against the kind of weapon that had killed his ancestor, what might he really think about a living descendent of that killer, Elawon himself? There was no way to ask anyone. He had not felt a moment's worry since joining the Herakleids. But now . . .

"How old is the palace?" Elawon asked Satnios.

"Which part? It started as a couple of rooms—one of the two or three buildings that were already here when we came. When Temenus came. It still keeps growing."

Satnios's older brother, Meydon, added, "The Dorians gave us this place some years ago, after our fathers and grandfathers went to their dead in the northern wars. Probably to keep us where they could watch us. We came here from wherever we were living after we had to leave Athens. The young ones, like this baby, were born here."

Satnios grinned at his brother.

"But aren't the Dorians all up north?" Elawon asked. "How can they watch you from there?"

"Their kings are twins. One rules in the north, in Trikkala, while the other stays here to help us. They switch every year."

Another king, a Dorian, living under Temenus's rule. Elawon remembered the scorn in the Mycenaeans's voices when they talked about the Herakleids and their friends. Maybe they would feel different if they saw what he saw here in Nafpaktos; so many people, so much energy, and kings under kings, as if to imitate Mycenae itself. As if to replicate it. Replace it.

Satnios said, "There might be food somewhere," and Elawon followed him gladly. As he left the room, he heard the quick scurry of feet behind him and wanted to turn, to see if Hippotes' brothers might be approaching the chest that held his things. But he didn't know how to do that, so did not.

* * *

To the east, Nafpaktos ended with a final chain of linked houses, and a slimy grade down to the great swamp. A causeway led out to a dry hill of modest size, with an orchard on one side and a grassy meadow at its foot.

"This is the king's," Xanos said. "Reserved for the horses he's never had. Goats don't eat grass, and cattle aren't allowed here. One of the few really fertile places, and he . . . Well, anyway, you can stay here."

The hillside against the ridge was tiered in olive trees, their thick, squat trunks twisted and gnarled and pierced with vertical holes like stretched, healed wounds. The branches were so bare, they seemed at first to be dead, until Akhaïdes' eye followed them up to the canopy, so thick with leaves that it blocked nearly all light. He stepped up into the shadows.

For all its apparent abandonment, the orchard was not overgrown with weeds. Only clumps of grass survived, pale in the perpetual shade, like the vines in the derelict fortress he remembered. Broken branches, twigs, and leaf litter formed a mat underfoot that ran to the irregular terraces, held by half-collapsed frames of lichened stones.

There was something else besides: olives, thousands of them, left to dry where they had fallen. He bent to pick one up.

Xanos said, "The orchard belongs to my kings, to Dymas and Pamphylus. They don't need the olives, and the people in Nafpaktos can't have them, since they don't belong to Temenus. So they just fall and rot here."

"No one eats them?"

"Nothing eats raw olives. Not even rats." Xanos paused. "Don't you remember anything about living in these countries?"

"There are no olive trees in Arcadia."

"Why not?"

Akhaïdes looked back up into the orchard. The trees seemed to brood, breathing in the shadows. It was warmer in their shade than in the light. He dropped the dead fruit he held, and wiped his fingers on his leggings. Before he realized he was backing away, he found himself standing beside Xanos in the cool sunlight.

He realized that Xanos had simply been waiting to go away. Without saying anything else, Xanos turned and left.

The horse had already started tearing at the grass. Akhaïdes dropped the lead and walked around the edge of the meadow, avoiding the orchard while looking for anything else out of order.

Then he made another round, higher, in steep scrub. Here were tracks of goats and goatherds, rabbits, hedgehogs, foxes, birds, beetles. Snakes, mice, and lizards would come later, in warmer weather. He returned to the meadow, then thought for a moment and climbed back up.

Some predator—not fox or wolf, but something quite different—had been here. He crouched, turning his head, inhaling slowly and deeply with his mouth half open, tasting the air. Finally, he pressed his palm against a rock, letting the warmth of his skin absorb what it could. He cupped the hand over his nose and mouth.

Cat. The smell was feline, and this spray centered at the height of his shoulder as he crouched here. The animal that had sprayed here was huge.

Tigers had hunted him once, years ago and a world away, but he had seen only their eyes in the dark and their prints in mud, and heard their grunt and purr. He had heard all the stories about lions, but had never seen a live cat any bigger than a woman could carry on one arm. He had traded for the skins of lions, then traded them away again for profit, but had not been able to make out from the crushed, distorted faces what the live animals might have been like. Trying to imagine what had sprayed here, all he could envision was a cat's dim-witted squint. But that would not do for a feline like this.

Lions had lived in these countries, the old stories said, but he had never seen such a beast in Arcadia, however far he roamed with the goats. Only the stories persisted: Herakles and the lion. He pressed fingertips to the rock. It told him nothing, just waited to see what he might do.

Without rising, he turned to see what the creature must have seen as it marked the rock. There below lay the olive orchard, the small meadow with the horse at its center, the path back to Nafpaktos, then the city itself, its chaos strangely tidy from here. What had it thought, looking down?

Herakles had killed a lion and worn its skin. The Herakleids marked their things with a lion-skin symbol; he had seen this already. He thought of Temenus, Herakles' heir, but could not link his face with that of a predatory feline—although perhaps the intelligence and secrecy were somehow akin. He wondered whether Temenus knew of this animal at large within his domain. How could he *not* know?

He rose. It was not his business. If a lion or some such beast had passed by here, it was nothing to him. Three thousand rivers and three thousand springs, Menetor had said. But the world was larger than any priest would know. There was room for lions as well as men, goats, and horses. If it returned, the horse would let him know. He climbed back down to the meadow and found a place bare of the wet, chill grass to lie on. He was hungry, thirsty, his muscles still aching from the fight with Oxylus.

By now, Elawon would be comfortable, bathed and fed and in a room of his own in the palace. Or perhaps this was a trick, a way to get Elawon away from him and then . . . And then, nothing. Just as he could not link Temenus with a lion, neither could he link him to treachery.

Xanos had warned him.

Elawon had walked into the palace with the king's arm over his shoulder.

Kresphontes had thrown a rock, spooking the horse, and Temenus had not reproached him.

Temenus had cared for Aristodemus with his own hands. Of course.

He had cared for Elawon with his own hands. Why?

Xanos had warned him but then put him here, where he could not protect Elawon.

The horse's ripping and champing had slowed as it realized it would be allowed to eat its fill. Now it grazed contentedly, raising its head from time to time, comfortably watchful, chewing with placid enjoyment.

The scent of cropped grass was so old in Akhaïdes' memory as to be almost unfamiliar. The grass where he had lived more recently looked and smelled different, tasted different.

Grass on a steppe would blow like waves on water. Silver on one side, it would then turn and blow gray. It had no bounds but went on forever, to the ends of the earth. And after its end, there was no end. And after that end, there was also none.

He was already asleep.

* * *

Xanos's wife said, "You're back so soon."

He had sat down just inside the door to pull off his shoes and socks. Wherever he might put them would be wrong, so he just dropped them beside his bare feet.

"Don't leave them there," his wife said.

She stood over him, her fists planted on her hips as if that were their natural resting place. She smelled of camphor and something else—some potion from Temenus's shaman, perhaps. Meant for what purpose? He dare not ask. But she also smelled of rich, ripe woman. He wondered how difficult getting around to having sex was going to be. The usual path full of traps and brambles stretched before him. He pulled his mouth into a toadying smile and got on with it.

* * *

Makhawis's bath was widely known and envied. A small room buried deep in the palace, it had a clay stove in one corner that burned only smokeless charcoal, frescoed erotic scenes on every wall, and a tub in which a full-grown man could submerge his entire body. The tub had a fitted drain that could be opened to release the used water and oil down a clay pipe and under the wall, into an open channel in the nearest corridor.

Well-fed and briefly sated by hasty sex with his wife, Temenus relished the hot scented water that soaked away dust and sweat. He opened one lazy eye to see his sister sitting on a stool at the side of the room, watching him with shrewd delight.

He felt almost too lazy to speak. "You know so well what I miss when I travel."

"Pleasures, comforts, duties," she answered.

This warned him that the woman he would have after the bath would be, again, his own wife. Makhawis was right, of course: he should keep to his wife today. After such deprivation, the likelihood of creating a child was strong. He should create that child for his family, for the Herakleids. He suppressed disappointment.

"So, who did you bring us?" Makhawis asked.

"One of the High King's own. Elawon Hyadeides, a Companion to Tisamenus. An Arcadian chieftain who turned away from the Pelopeids, making all the usual promises. But something else; his mother's grandfather was Echemus."

"The man who killed Hyllus, and he's here with us? That has some value."

"I hope so. What value, I don't know. I was expecting more. Someone more unique, special. He's . . . ordinary. Maybe he's only meant as a sign from fate. If so, I'll take that."

He raised his eyes to the beautiful frescoes: men with women only, since this was a woman's room. Nearly life-size, with impassive faces, they struck poses even more evocative for being so stylized, their nakedness all the more erotic for being broken by belts, rings, necklaces, earrings, sinuous ribbons in flowing hair. Hands and mouths outlined, organs immense and in florid detail.

Makhawis was still watching him.

"There was someone else, too," she prodded gently.

"Elawon's brother, an outlaw. Delphi rejected him and I suppose he has nowhere else to go. But he brought a horse I want."

"A riding horse? Where did an outlaw get such a thing?"

"Don't tell anyone yet. About Elawon and Echemus."

"Because?"

Keeping secrets from Makhawis was satisfying. It reminded him of their childhood, when he would hold a beautiful stone or an iridescent beetle between two cupped hands, and she would wait, eyes blazing, for him to show it to her.

He would share everything, of course. But there was no hurry.

* * *

One of the three young boys asked, "Are you alive?"

Akhaïdes had identified them without bothering to look, as they were still approaching. He opened his eye. Yes, three, wearing oversize loincloths and tattered shawls, their feet in ragged shoes but their long legs bare to the cold. He had not worried about them, because they had approached so openly. Had they meant trouble, they would have tried to come without noise.

Now they stood together in a formal row, watching him warily.

"I am alive," he answered without moving.

"Are you hungry?" They showed him some rounds of bread, a grubby shard of cheese.

He sat up.

The tallest of the boys studied him gravely. "Is there something wrong with you, that you're out here instead of in the city?"

"Yes, there's something wrong with me."

"Are you sick? What happened to your eye?"

"Someone took it."

"Why?"

"I caused him more trouble than he liked."

They blinked, solemn as owls. "Are you a fighter, like Hippotes Herakleides? He's Nafpaktos's great warrior. He's our hero."

"He should be."

"Is that a horse?"

They all looked at the gray horse. It looked back at them.

The second boy said, "Rousa was right. They're bigger than donkeys."

"Rousa is your friend?" Akhaïdes asked.

"He's one of the armorer's helpers."

"Why don't any of the Herakleids wear knives?"

"Because you have to give metal to the armorer to get a metal thing back. And Herakleids don't have any metal. Rousa told us. Even the king doesn't have a knife, even though he made that rule and he's the king."

Another reason not to mistrust Temenus: he obeyed his own rules.

The first boy asked, "Can we give you food? Is that allowed?"

"Yes, it is. You can't take food from me, though. Only children and animals can."

"We aren't children. We have loincloths."

"I see that. So you have to be careful."

"You can't touch us?"

"Never."

"We could touch you."

"But don't."

"Are you . . . poisonous?"

"Venomous. Yes."

They tried that word, whispering it among themselves. Then the second boy nudged the third, who surrendered a piece of the bread charily, snatching back his hand. Then they all hunkered down at a safe distance to watch Akhaïdes eat.

* * *

Temenus leaned back as Makhawis kneaded scented oil into his bare shoulders. He said, "The priest told me Elawon Hyadeides would be important. Born from the line of Hyllus, of course he is. But his estate in Arcadia is so small that Orestes might not even care if he loses it. When I think about what he offers, I don't see his value."

"And when you do anything else with him?"

"I haven't done that. I don't even want to."

She stopped moving.

He laughed. "Really. I look at him and nothing happens."

"You've been known to close your eyes." She resumed the massage.

He closed them now.

"Keep him, of course," she said. "You need all the allies you can find. It's a good link, back to Echemus. And the priest was sure he'd be valuable otherwise?"

"He said that I'd meet someone important to me, if I left Delphi early. And if I keep Elawon, I can figure out how to keep the horse."

"You've always wanted a horse." He heard the smile in her voice. "You didn't tell me how the outlaw got it."

"Stole it, they say, from Tisamenus. It was meant for Orestes, which gives it value."

She clicked her tongue. "Is it right, for you to ride a stolen horse?"

"If I had taken it myself, of course. But now that it's passed through an outlaw's hands, who can say? Even if he just gave it to me, is it tainted? I don't know. And how can I take it now, even from an outlaw? What would my people think of me? Take from an outlaw, maybe later I'd take from a man. They have to trust me."

"Something you want so much, but out of reach."

"So it seems."

"And the outlaw? What about him?"

"The land in Arcadia is his by law. He's the oldest."

"I wonder if anyone remembers. Does he care enough to make trouble about it?"

"Maybe not. But if he wanted to, someone might listen, just to be able to act against me."

"Ah."

"He came with Elawon, but they ignore each other. He came like—I don't know—like an old dog following its master around just because it has nothing better to do."

"So he's like most outlaws: no spirit."

He had to say this now. "He nearly killed a man in full armor and carrying a sword. With some little hand axe."

Makhawis's fingers stopped moving. "Yet you brought him here."

"He killed a man in Arne. To get away from the Regent's cells."

Even after this, his next words felt like letting a snake loose in this warm, scented room. "He is the Good Kinsman."

"There is no such real person." Her tone was flat, unconditional. "Even if the story is true, it was so long ago, he couldn't possibly still be . . ."

"It's true. It's him." It was time for the final secret. "And his name is Ephialtes."

He could almost hear the machinery of her mind bump into motion, grinding turbulent thoughts into order and calm. Coarse grist in, smooth flour out.

She finally said, "Well, don't think of keeping him here. No outlaw will live in this house. I'm sure Kresphontes won't allow it. And neither will I."

"No, no, no. Of course not."

Compliance was quick, automatic, but he remembered a mind perhaps even quicker than Makhawis's, quicker than his own, and a voice so familiar, softened by an alien accent: *How much would your family give, to ransom you?*

The smell of flowered oil suddenly sickened him. He twisted out of his sister's hands and stood up. All the slaves in the room raised their heads.

As if his revulsion were only a boy's whim, Makhawis said calmly, "If you want the horse, take it. The Shaman will purify it. The Arcadian—Elawon?—keep him on a short leash. You know how to do that. Flattery, promises, comfort."

So much unruffled sense. He felt himself relaxing.

"And as for your outlaw . . ." She waved a hand. "He can't be a very competent murderer, if he killed all his brothers but one. Why leave one? And now, why leave *him* to trouble your life?"

Comic theater. Murder. But, of course, to kill an outlaw was not murder. It was nothing.

She reached up, drew him back down, and began the massage again. "Really, my love. You sometimes make the simplest things so complicated."

* * *

"Lawagetas?"

Xanos glided up from sleep, from warmth, from luxury, his wife in his arms, his face in her hair, his sex against her thigh.

"Lawagetas."

She smelled of flowers, bread, semen, babies, wood smoke, hair oil . . .

"Xanos Lawagetas!"

He rumbled, "If you aren't a Herakleid, your dead are already on their way to collect you."

A soft chuckle. "Sorry, then. It's Satnios Herakleides."

"Aw, fuck me."

"I'd as soon not."

"All right, all right. I'm waking up. I'm coming."

He crawled up out of the blankets, into a shawl and shoes, out into the dank chill, and he needed to piss but instead had to trail after Satnios, who walked far faster surely, than necessary, whatever the problem.

And this was not such a complicated problem, anyway. Just a horse on the king's porch in the early dawn, and an outlaw holding the lead.

Not complicated at all, until Xanos stepped through the crowd of gawkers at the foot of the steps and the outlaw turned toward him. Then the complications began. For between the outlaw and horse and the palace entrance stood the Arcadian Elawon, with his hair mussed and his clothes disheveled—and, Xanos could see from here, a blackened eye.

It was only reasonable to ask, "What?"

But no outlaw had the right to answer, "You are responsible for this," in a voice no louder than a serpent's hiss, though it carried well enough.

Nearly under the outlaw's elbow, in the first rank of onlookers, three or four young boys shared grins and glances.

Xanos turned to Satnios. "What happened?"

"An accident. Mistake. Nothing." But the young man's eyes slid away.

"You idiots." Xanos turned back. "What do you want, Outlaw?"

The answer came like a snake's strike. "I want to trust you."

The last thing Xanos expected or wished to hear, aimed like a well-thrown javelin. He wanted to lighten this, but the outlaw's fixed glare made that feel like not so good an idea.

Instead, he asked Satnios, "Is Aristodemus awake?"

Satnios's face went suddenly solemn at the family head's name. He shot up the steps, around Akhaïdes and Elawon, and into the palace.

As they waited, Xanos said, "So that first day, when I warned you about this place, you actually were listening."

Akhaïdes did not answer.

* * *

Xanos watched Satnios come out of the palace quietly, his head down and his hands clasped in front of him, looking like a penitent child.

Satnios said to Elawon, "My lord Aristodemus says that the palace will give you a house of your own." He glanced at Akhaïdes, whose face had not changed. "Both of you. And we are very, very sorry."

"For?" Xanos asked.

"For treating the king's guest like . . ."

"Like?"

Satnios ducked his head.

Like some ordinary visitor of no special rank, kin to none of them, from a place they had never been, bringing nothing of value except an animal none of them could use except perhaps to eat, and what might he have in his baggage? Anything worth stealing?

The outlaw was right. Xanos was responsible for keeping order, even though the Arcadians' being here was just another whim of Temenus's and he would forget them soon enough, maybe already had, yet he had dragged this outlaw into Nafpaktos, as if Xanos needed any more—yes—complications, and if mistreated enough maybe they would leave, and leave him to more normal complications.

But instead, they would get a house.

Oh, fine then, Xanos thought. Just fine.

154

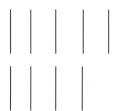

Reason is a whore, surviving by simulation, versatility, and shamelessness.[x]

— *E. M. Cioran*

Elawon paced three strides to the end of the hovel, then four strides back, ducking to miss the single rafter. Three of the walls were those of adjoining huts—slabs of unfired mud laid on foundations of stacked stones. The front wall was mud brick as well, slumped and crumbling at the top and dribbling gravel.

He said, "Temenus might be angry about this—about me leaving the palace."

"With me, certainly. But he *should* be angry with his younger brother, not with you."

It was raining. A fat cockroach dodged Elawon's heel and continued on its way, clambering through mushy straw like a rabbit through brambles. Water already ran through gaps in the roof tiles and down the broken ends of reeds.

Akhaïdes sat on the cobbled threshold, facing outside. The horse stood under the roof's overhang, almost leaning against the flimsy wall to get out of the rain, its head blocking the light.

Elawon said, "You don't care if the king is angry with you?"

Akhaïdes didn't bother to reply.

"I ate with them last night," Elawon said. "There were boiled beans, bread, dried fruit, wine. I had a place to sleep."

"A warm pallet. A private room. Slaves."

A narrow space between other men, on a cold dirt floor. An attack in the dark. "Better than this, anyway."

Akhaïdes said nothing.

"Don't sit out there like that. Come in."

"I can't."

"It's like where we stayed in Delphi."

Akhaïdes said, "That place had no memory of ownership, no roof. This place is closed. It could remember."

"But it was built after you . . . well . . . Anyway, if it belongs to anyone, it belongs to the king, and you can be in kings's rooms. They wouldn't give it to us if you couldn't live in it."

The horse bumped Akhaïdes with its nose. He stroked its face and picked dried crust from the corner of its eye.

After a moment, Elawon slogged to a corner where the piled straw was still dry on top. Something in it stirred at his approach, and he backed away, stepped past Akhaïdes, and went outside.

This was the lower limit of the town. The hovel entrance looked away from the city's sound and warmth, facing the weather and the one direction Elawon didn't care to face: across the water to Arcadia.

Only steps away, strings of refuse rode up and down on the lip of the sea. The dwellings on either side rattled with life: men laughing, women complaining, children crying and calling. They might well be talking about Elawon and Akhaïdes, the king's guest and the outlaw, suddenly dropped into their midst. He turned and saw his own doorway, the only one with no sign of life except a horse's bulk under the overhang, and Akhaïdes crouching there with it, too still to be asleep. Shame and anxiety gripped him for a moment. He suppressed it and went back in.

* * *

Akhaïdes cleared the sodden straw from the hut, using his hands for lack of a fork. Elawon offered halfheartedly to help, but he said no. He carried load after drooling load, seething with roaches, centipedes, and lice, out into the sea and flung it over the water—even garbage that he had touched posed a hazard for the unpolluted. Then he took a heavy, curved roof tile and used its serrate broken edge to scrape the mire down to firm soil. He even convinced the huge rat that lived in the corner to leave, escorting it courteously through the door while Elawon pressed himself against the far wall, begging him to kill it.

Finally, looking at the floor, Elawon asked, "Why is there still that awful smell?"

Akhaïdes glanced down at his shirtfront and leggings, saturated with muck. He turned and walked along the beach, lowering his head every time he passed someone, whether man or woman.

Elawon watched until he realized where Akhaïdes was going: to the last stony, muddy flat where the river met the gulf, where the water carriers worked. These were families given by custom to the work of carrying waste from the finer households and delivering water to them.

A few carriers were there already. Though wearing rags of the most advanced decrepitude, they moved with dignity, waiting in file to empty their buckets of lees into the sea at a single spot. Then they trudged away up the river to fill the buckets again with clean water—a long, slow circling from house to sea, to river, to house, bearing pollution away, bringing back purity. It was the same place where the corpse tenders washed themselves, and then, last of all, Akhaïdes. For the five orders of purification never changed: smoke, river, shaman, king, and—last, highest and most final—the great Serpent of Delphi. And the serpent had refused him.

Elawon picked up his bundle and went inside.

The rat's corner was the driest place, so Elawon opened his blanket on the floor there, folded an extra shirt for a pillow, ate some bread that he happened to have, and lay down for a nap.

He woke later to see Akhaïdes shifting the roof tiles this way and that overhead, cutting off one leak after another. The residual stink was gradually fading, and it appeared that he had cleaned his clothes somehow.

Elawon said reluctantly, "I can help with that."

Akhaïdes did not stop. "You won't know what I've already touched."

Elawon went back to sleep.

* * *

Akhaïdes sat in the doorway all night, every night, plaiting a flat cord of hair plucked from the horse's tail. Whether he slept or not, Elawon could not have said. Before dawn, never waiting to see Elawon safely awake, he led the horse out to graze, then led it back, to stand tied through the modest warmth of the afternoon, while he sat under its dozing head and the cord slowly lengthened in his hands.

Boys often gathered to stare at him, eventually to speak with him. Smaller children used the space near him for refuge, for even the most obstinate bullies would not come near enough to tease a child in his shadow. After a few preliminary frights, mothers accepted the babies' confidence and let them stay.

And it was without irony that those same mothers sang their babies to sleep:

"Sleep, my child, my arms will mind you.
Neither dreams nor the Kinsman find you.
Life is dear and love is dearer;
Night is coming nearer, nearer.

While he walks the dark behind us,
Loving is the light that finds us.
Safe and cozy with each other,
Sleep, my child, and trust your mother."

* * *

As in Mycenae and the other cities Elawon had known, all the grain, olives, beans, meat, wine, and oil were grown on the king's land or traded under his control. Carefully measured shares were then distributed, from storehouses around the palace, to every chief or clan leader. These men then shared the goods downward among their own dependents. Even for those entitled to full rations, the king's food was barely enough to live on. Some also received rations from their own chiefs, brought or sent from their home countries or provided from rights to land near Nafpaktos.

The lists of approved residents were kept by clerks and maintained by the damos council, but the king controlled rations. Elawon's name was on both the resident list and an allotment list, but with no amounts shown. Day after day, he trudged to the palace and waited in a long queue of men, women, slaves, and messengers. And day after day, he watched impatiently as one clerk or another ran a finger down the lists of names, found his, pointed to the blank space next to it. And Elawon had to walk away empty handed.

Nor could Akhaïdes help. No outlaw would be approved as a resident of Nafpaktos or be entitled to the king's food. He offered to show Elawon how to forage outside, in the woods and wilderness. Wild mustard and comfrey grew in the meadows, and one could always snare a rabbit or lime a few larks. But Elawon was ashamed to eat such fare. Old women gathered green weeds, and dogs caught frogs and lizards. Men ate bread, beans, and real meat.

Elawon complained to the nearest damos council member, a

toothless Ozolian who promised to investigate the problem, then went back to his sour wine and ogling his neighbors's young daughters. Elawon complained to another council member, who consulted the first. Whatever they decided resulted in neither of them doing anything. So Elawon went to the palace itself. A clerk agreed to deliver his message to Aristodemus, the council head, but the lists didn't change.

Elawon foraged in his own way, killing sparrows and doves with his sling. He could not cook the birds, though. Only women cooked. So he traded them to the neighbors's wives for shares of the cooked food they prepared. Again he declined Akhaïdes' offer to show him more edibles from the wild pantry.

Akhaïdes volunteered his belongings, saying that perhaps Elawon might take them to a shaman for purification, then use them for bribes or trade. But all that Akhaïdes owned were the rags he wore, an axe so alien that no one could want it, a frayed belt clasped with stone in place of a buckle, and pockets whose contents Elawon could not imagine and didn't want to see.

From time to time, Elawon found a food gift beside the entrance. That angered him because Akhaïdes was not a madman, to be fed by law. Still, the offerings were a welcome addition to their stores. Those that were immediately edible, Elawon ate. Those that required preparation, he traded, again to the neighbor women, eyeing closely the shares that came back to him.

Back at the warehouses, a clerk explained that Elawon had erred in his earlier complaint: the council controlled only residency and land rights. Elawon should have spoken to certain of the clerks responsible for maintaining the king's ration records.

Could Elawon speak with that clerk now? The clerk was with the king at this time of day. When would he return? Don't know. Could Elawon wait? No, he was blocking the queue. Would this clerk speak to that clerk? Of course, of course.

Nothing changed.

Days turned to a quarter month before Elawon finally thought to offer the clerks gifts of his own. One bronze fitting from his clothing got him a twelve-weight—twelve times its weight—in beans or barley, an eight-weight in coarse flour, or a four-weight in meat. This was too little to feed on comfortably, and every time he replaced a beautiful hook or button with a wooden peg, he felt a pang of resentment.

Elawon had gathered and spread clean sand, to a hand's depth, on the floor of the hut. The hut still had no door, since neither he nor Akhaïdes could find anything to serve as one. In Nafpaktos, even the shabbiest of rags were used over and over until they dissolved.

The hut also lacked a hearth. The king forbade private fires except in pots: so much fuel, even brushwood, could not be spared. But there were still some crude, secret hearths down here, where public ovens were few and the time to use them expensive. There were even some clandestine open fires set in small beds of stones, most of their heat wasted. Elawon never saw one burning, but he could sometimes smell them.

Akhaïdes laced three sticks together with grass, then asked Elawon to set within this frame the broken base of a clay bowl. Akhaïdes explained that he had purposely not touched it but had carried it between two sticks. In this awkward contrivance, Akhaïdes kindled a small fire every evening and morning. The neighbors all had lamps as well as illicit firepots and hearths, and this light, leaking though the three shared walls, was enough to live by between sunset and sleep. Shrews and roaches had nibbled Elawon's shoes, leaving the edges jagged enough to scrape his feet raw.

Elawon piled dead grass to spread his bed on, to keep him off the cold ground, but such a flimsy pallet flattened overnight. Then Akhaïdes showed him where to find dried seaweed. Springy and stiff, it provided comfort, although the sea stink disturbed his rest. Akhaïdes had already used his dagger—an ugly, primitive thing with its rune-burned wooden hilt and stone blade—to dig a shallow trench around inside of the walls, to catch the rain leaking from the neighbors's huts or running down the insides of their own walls and channel it outside. But none of that solved the most basic problem.

Finally, one morning, Elawon said to Akhaïdes, "There's nothing to eat. I don't know what to do."

"Go to the king," Akhaïdes told him immediately.

"The clerks . . ."

"No, the *king.* Himself. He took your hands. He's responsible for you."

Memories of Temenus's quick, sardonic glance, the arm across Elawon's shoulders, made him hesitate.

"He's just forgotten me. Maybe he'll remember on his own."

"That king never forgets anything. If he knows you're here, he knows you're hungry." Akhaïdes thought for a moment. "*Should* know you're hungry."

"So why doesn't he do anything about it?"

"Only he knows."

* * *

Elawon combed his hair and went to the palace. That night, when he returned to the house, Akhaïdes looked at him keenly.

"The clerks said no. I waited and waited."

Akhaïdes' gaze slid away. "Something is wrong. Someone . . ." He looked directly at Elawon and said, very softly, "Ah."

* * *

Hunger woke Elawon the next morning. Light came in bright needles between the roof tiles, and the air felt dry. Another day without rain, perhaps. He turned over, dislodging a fly, which spiraled noisily upward.

Akhaïdes was not in the entrance, but the little slow-burning fire he made every morning was glowing away in its makeshift pot. Elawon untangled himself from the blanket and unrolled the shirt that was his pillow. His back and hips ached despite the seaweed pallet. He leaned over the fire, warming his face and chest, then straightened and stepped out into the raw air. Three sparrows stared down at him from the roof's edge, their quick heads turned at three different angles. A thin mist glowed low on the water, but the sky was already blue.

He tossed the shirt up over the edge of the roof, dislodging the birds, to let it freshen before he put it on. He leaned outside to spit, stretched, and looked around.

In the distance, he could see water carriers emptying their buckets at their usual spot. Crows strutted about the sand, insolently near the carriers, upending trash with their beaks and poking through it with swift, confident jabs. Smaller gulls shifted from foot to foot, waiting, then rushed in behind the crows to squabble over their leavings. Elawon would never eat a crow or gull, of course—both untouchable—but still they recognized him as a killer of birds and kept a wary eye on him.

Other men, too, staggered out of huts to spit and stretch and scratch themselves awake. Elawon smiled at their bantering complaints, even though none spoke to him. He walked, as if one of them, down to the sea.

The chill of the water made him sneeze. He blew his nose between his fingers, spent a moment examining the floating snot, then waded out to mid-thigh depth. Untying his loincloth, he squatted, cringing at the water's touch. When he finished, he scrubbed himself with his hand and retied his loincloth.

As he climbed out of the water, he saw the gray horse coming toward him on the hard sand just at the water's edge. Akhaïdes was not leading it, but rode on its back. The horse's neck was arched, its tail raised, hooves working in a high, slow, gaudy trot, flinging up glittering water with every strike. The water carriers parted, and Akhaïdes bowed his head as he passed between them. Crows grudgingly took flight and curved away.

Elawon had never seen any man ride horseback except clutching, sliding Oxylus. Horses and ponies were for riding behind, not sitting astride, and he had never imagined that riding could look effortless. Neither, it seemed, had the neighbors. One after another, men turned their heads toward the hooves' thudding rhythm. Then one after another they rose and gaped, whatever bit of work they held drooping in their hands.

Then Akhaïdes did the strangest thing. He leaned sideways until he surely had to fall, until he could touch the ground but reaching farther yet. A crow took wing too late. Its head leaped from its body, and Akhaïdes rose up again, axe in hand. The headless bird fluttered and slumped. The horse never broke stride.

Men's voices exclaimed, all together. Akhaïdes made no movement that Elawon could see, but the horse rose suddenly upright, forelegs tucked against its chest, and marched forward in powerful strides of its hind legs.

When it came to Elawon, the horse lowered to all four feet and stopped still, then stretched its head down and forward, dragging the rein through Akhaïdes' loosened fingers. Elawon saw that the rein and the bridle were made of the horsehair cord Akhaïdes had plaited. The bit was a smooth rod of wood.

Akhaïdes was wearing his belt, the silver now polished, the stone weights swinging. The axe again lay along his thigh, in a gaudy sweep of gold streaked with the crow's blood. He laid the rein on the horse's neck and flexed his hands.

Elawon looked up at him, shielding his eyes from the rising sun. "What are you doing?"

"Talking with the king."

"What?"

Akhaïdes drew in the rein. He made no other motion that Elawon could see, but the horse moved off instantly at a walk, then rose into that thrilling high trot again, tail raised and flowing, drops of water sparkling like flung jewels.

"Ride that horse!" someone shouted, and a score of voices laughed.

As Akhaïdes rode around a bend and out of sight, one man, then another, turned toward Elawon with dawning interest while small boys gingerly approached the oddly truncated crow, still not understanding what had happened to it.

* * *

"So," Temenus said a short time later. "Welcome to my room, Akhaïdes Outlaw."

The space was small, with a simple plastered bench built against the wall and spread with cushions. A firepot and an overhead well gave some warmth and light. There were two or three beautifully made stools, but Temenus had not invited Akhaïdes to sit.

"You must be busy," Temenus added, "so it was good of you to come here. And how is your brother?"

"My brother does not believe that you've deliberately refused him rations."

Temenus blinked, then recovered. "But you believe that."

The young page who had fetched Akhaïdes edged toward the door.

"My brother is the chief of a very good province. You treated him like a respected guest. Now you treat him like a camp follower.

I wonder why."

"He left my house."

"Your house was unwelcoming."

"He had food from my own hand, a place to sleep among my kinsmen, my friendship, but he preferred to live with the poor. With you. And with his own resources from his own people."

Akhaïdes waited.

Temenus asked, more quietly, "What is it I don't know?"

"Ask Satnios."

Temenus blinked again. "My sister's son?"

"Ask your brother Kresphontes."

"Why ask them when you're right here?"

"Because I don't know everything. I might be wrong."

Temenus glanced at the page. The boy looked away.

Temenus asked softly, "What is it that you believe?"

"That your family doesn't want me here."

"Of course. Why would we?"

"And they hope that if Elawon leaves, I'll go, too."

"If someone does hope that, is he correct?"

"Yes."

"And if Elawon stays?"

"I will stay."

"And so we will have to deal with you. That seems simple enough." Temenus tilted his head and half closed his eyes. "What are you not saying now?"

"That such a thing would seem simple only to a Herakleid, my lord."

Temenus's smile was instant and unguarded. Then he straightened his face, tightened his lips, and touched them with the tip of his tongue. "You and your brother are truly nothing alike."

"And you and yours?"

"That's not your business."

"I agree. So make it stop being my business."

Temenus's head jerked up.

"My lord, leash your family. One of them could get hurt."

"By what? By you?"

"By something. Who can tell what?"

"Did you just make the most reckless threat ever spoken?"

"Not a threat. A warning, spoken in all humility."

"You're insolent!"

"And you're the king." Akhaïdes bowed, touched his forehead with both hands, and left the room. He heard a soft, explosive curse behind him.

* * *

That afternoon, Elawon squatted on his heel among other men, watching women simmer barley gruel over a shared illicit fire. These men were his neighbors, casually including him in their group at last as if they had always been this deferential and attentive. They would share the meal. Elawon already held his bowl in anticipation.

When the king's page approached, it was all Elawon could do to keep from shouting in triumph.

The boy said, "I come from the king. That horse belongs to one of you?"

Ordinarily, a man would not stand to speak to a child. But this was the king's own page. The men nudged each other, murmuring at the boy's clean hands and colored clothing.

Elawon rose casually from among them as if to stretch his legs. "I am chief of Arcadian Ladon. And yes, the horse is . . . it lives here."

The boy's head bobbed. "My king, Temenus Herakleides, asks your company tonight. For a great allcall."

The other men glanced around at one another, eyebrows hitched high.

Elawon half-closed his eyes, trying to look casual. "I'll be there."

"The other one. Your brother."

Elawon opened his eyes again. "He's outlaw."

"The king said."

"Yes," Elawon snapped. "Fine."

"At the right time, someone will come for you both."

"Thank you."

The boy peered into the pot, then touched his forehead and left them. Elawon squatted again, among men awed to silence, but with his own spirits quashed.

* * *

"Hawi?"

Makhawis closed her eyes briefly. She had avoided Hippotes since his return from Delphi, by keeping to her own quarters. But she could not avoid him here, in the unmarried-men's room where he now lived again. She had come here, with her usual escort of slaves, to visit her second-eldest son.

Satnios was suffering from nothing worse than a nasty hangover. Groaning that he was dying, he had asked for the Shaman, and his older brother Meydon had raced to find their mother. But Makhawis just gave Satnios a stinking potion to drink, to make him stop vomiting. He had sucked that down, gasped something unintelligible, wiped his mouth on Meydon's shirttail, and immediately fallen asleep. Meydon had left the room hesitantly—some job needing his attention—and now Makhawis slid a healing talisman under the pillow, then rose and faced her ex-husband.

"Wife," Hippotes said to her. "When do I come home again?"

She answered, "This is your home now."

"You know that's not so. You know where I belong." He glanced at her women, all alert but wise enough not to intervene without a sign from Makhawis. Hippotes stepped between them and their mistress, his back to them, blocking their view. "I'll come tonight, after the allcall," he murmured.

Makhawis retreated in the only direction she could: away from the exit and her women. "I won't let you in. Not tonight or any other night."

"Do you know what happens to runaway women?'

Her heart jerked. "I divorced you fairly, before the king."

"Before your brother, who gives you everything you ask for!"

"Before my brother *the king.*"

"And you sent me back here to live with boys. But I'm not a boy. I'm a man. *Your* man. And you're my woman."

She retreated still, with Hippotes following closely. She had been a moon and longer without him, without any man. Now she smelled the male heat of his body, felt the size and weight of him, and her own body began to soften.

He smiled, showing his clean, square teeth. He knew it. Damn him, he always knew. He murmured, "I'll come tonight."

"I won't marry you again," she whispered.

"I don't want marriage. I want . . ." And he used a word so vulgar that her womb twitched even as she gasped with shock.

Then he repeated, "I'll come tonight."

"Yes," she whispered. "All right."

* * *

Akhaïdes returned to the hut at sunset, leading the horse by the bridle he had made for it, looking so shabby and deferential again that the neighbors hardly noticed. Elawon rose from their company and went to meet him.

"What happened?" Elawon said. "You saw the king?"

Akhaïdes stopped. "There are numbers for you on the lists?"

"I got oil, grain . . ." He glanced toward the nearest fire pot.

Akhaïdes looked past him to the men, who were passing around a beaker of mead while carefully gazing in other directions. "Will there be an allcall?"

"How did you know?"

170

It seems to me that men do not rightly understand either their store or their strength, but overrate the one and underrate the other.[xi]

—*Francis Bacon*

It was Xanos who came to fetch Elawon and Akhaïdes for the allcall. He sat outside the hut on a stool borrowed from a neighbor—who had offered him a cup of wine, as well, which he accepted—while Elawon fussed about what shirt to wear, and other neighbors glanced and whispered. Akhaïdes sat on the hut's low threshold while the horse stood dozing nearby.

Across the gulf, Arcadia rose, flat and featureless against the darkening sky. The ground was littered with stones. Xanos pushed at a few with his feet. It wasn't right to sit silent in company, even this company. He finally said, "They don't look like much, those mountains."

Akhaïdes answered immediately, "There are taller, and more beautiful." His Mycenaean was no longer hesitant, but the accent remained, mild yet distinct, and unlike anyone else's.

"Still," Xanos said, "they're important to us. Our landfall on the Peloponnesos is there. Our first battle with the . . . with the Mycenaean pretender. Orestes. Right there."

He felt Akhaïdes' surprise.

"It's agreed between us. Between Temenus and Orestes through years's worth of messengers. We meet there on the first day of next year, just a year from now."

"Will you be ready?"

Elawon strode out of the hut, wrapping a shawl around his

shoulders. He did not look down at Akhaïdes as he passed. "Do we go now?"

"Right now." Xanos rose, set the empty cup down, and brushed his broad backside with both hands. He turned to Akhaïdes, who had not moved. "Well?"

Akhaïdes looked up at him. "I can't drink, can't speak, can't touch furniture. Can't sit with men. Can't enter a clean man's house."

"It's the king's house. It's safe for everybody. And whether you can drink, talk, sit, or not, the king wants you there."

"For what—an exhibit of Mycenaean ignominy to amuse his friends and family?"

Xanos heard an unsteady note in Akhaïdes' voice. The derision must be meant to hide it. "We all do things we don't want to do. Why should you be exempt?"

Akhaïdes closed his eye. Without that distraction, Xanos saw how strained he looked. "You're strangely finicky for someone in your position. You can always quit it, though. You can always just leave."

"That's impossible."

"Are you angry with me specifically, or just with everything?"

"This is not anger, Lawagetas."

"He doesn't have to go to the allcall," Elawon said hopefully.

Back on solid ground, Xanos said, "Yes, he does."

Akhaïdes rose with no further objection. He wore the belt, dagger, and axe.

"Weapons aren't allowed in an allcall," Xanos said.

The horse had raised its head when Akhaïdes rose. He spoke to it in some foreign tongue. It shook itself and lowered its head again to doze.

Xanos said, "Nobody could touch your things, anyway, even if they wanted to."

Elawon added, "You could wash yourself. And wear another shirt. You're filthy."

Not fair, and Xanos nearly said so. The shirt had obviously been cleaned, but the leather fabric was worn thinner than muslin, shredded at the tails and torn at the armpits, all gray. The tattered ends of the sleeves bore dark stains—from what, Xanos didn't want to know. The bandages on his wrists were stained, too, but otherwise clean. The leggings, of heavier hide, were split at the seams and worn through at the knees. The high boots were patched over and over, the soles, he had noticed, stuffed with layers of rawhide and leaves. But the man himself seemed remarkably clean. Still, with his shrouded eye, the mat of colorless hair down his back, and those sorry clothes, he could never look anything better than disreputable.

In answer to Elawon, Akhaïdes said mildly, "I don't own another shirt."

Xanos said, "It's cold. A coat?"

"I don't own one."

They started off, Xanos and Elawon together, Akhaïdes behind them, striding through the gathering dark. As they climbed among better houses, women were setting lamps out on porches. Men called greetings to Xanos. He replied good-naturedly, but whenever he turned his head, he saw from the tail of his eye the silent figure following, and felt an edginess he could not ignore—a tension between his shoulder blades and at the back of his neck—at being stalked by Elawon's eerie brother.

Xanos was relieved when they reached the king's house and he could move among men he knew, in lamplight. He scaled the porch and led Elawon from group to group, greeting men who were hardly distinguishable under their hats and other wraps against the cold. He finally led Elawon inside, down a corridor, through open double doors.

The floor of the megaron, the king's formal hall, was laid with flat, roughly fitted stones. The space, with a round, flat hearth in the center, four pillars supporting a plastered ceiling and a tall open cupola, wells cut in the roof for light, was large enough to dignify any king. Three wooden chairs with arms, cheaply inlaid with wire and colored stones, stood against the wall to the right of the entrance. Of the three, the center one had the highest back and the most elaborate decorations. Above it, set in the otherwise plain, roughly plastered wall, were four large tiles painted with a lion's skin, each tile bearing a quarter of the image. Hanging lamps provided illumination, now that the light wells and cupola were full of night.

The hearth held a modest pile of smoldering coals. Between that and the lamps, the hall was warm despite the cold outside and the open cupola, and men removed coats and shawls as they entered. Stools were scattered around the room, and a few small children played quietly or dozed, heaped like puppies, in the corners.

"Whose children are those?" Elawon asked Xanos. "Why are they here?"

"Orphans, most of them. The Herakleids's own children tend to come here, too, for the company." Xanos unwrapped his coat, leaving it hanging from his shoulders.

"Orphans? Shouldn't they go to Delphi?"

"Temenus thinks so, but his sister won't hear of it. We call them Makhawis's pets. Come. You can sit with me and my own king."

As Xanos led Elawon through the clutter of stools to a group nearest the chairs, the talk throughout the megaron dropped off abruptly. He turned to look back.

Akhaïdes stood in the entrance. He had clearly paused only for a moment to accustom himself to the light, but all heads were turning toward him. Sidelong whispers passed from man to man.

In this bright room, among the unornamented but neatly dressed Herakleids, and other chieftains in their jewelry and embroidery, Akhaïdes looked as out of place as a crow in a pen of bright cockerels. But then, Xanos thought with resignation, he would look out of place anywhere on earth.

Every face in the room looked, some with curiosity, others with wariness or outright suspicion. Xanos thought of pack dogs, emboldening themselves to attack the outsider. But Akhaïdes stood quietly, his eye moving from man to man, alert but seemingly unimpressed. Then he simply stepped to one side of the doorway and dropped down on his heels, his back against the wooden frame. He rested his arms on his knees and let his hands hang loosely. Xanos realized that Akhaïdes, having consented to serve as an exhibition, would exhibit himself in his own way: without defiance but also without deference.

A Dorian of about Xanos's age, squat and thick in the middle, with shoulder-length graying hair, and bulging, faded eyes peering out through tangled brows, turned to Xanos and said, "Well, that's unusual."

"Hadn't you heard about him? The outlaw? I thought I told you."

"You did." The man arranged the tails of his shirt over his wide thighs, sat down, and laid his coat on his lap. "But hearing is nothing to seeing." He set a big, scarred hand and a knobby, handless wrist on his knees. "I presume you told him to leave his weapons at home."

"I did."

Elawon stood, looking uncertain. Xanos told him, "My king, Dymas." The one-handed man and Elawon exchanged greetings. "You sit with us." Xanos lowered himself to a stool and indicated another nearby.

Before Elawon could sit, the young page darted in and announced in a bold treble, "Temenus Herakleides!"

Temenus came in from a smaller doorway beside the chairs, followed by his brothers, and went straight to the highest seat. Aristodemus, leaning on a stick, took the chair to his right; Kresphontes took the most modest, to his left. The men in the megaron, disrupted by Akhaïdes' presence, which made seats near the entrance less desirable, were still sorting and resorting themselves and furtively stealing one other's places. Elawon quickly claimed the stool Xanos had indicated, before someone else could. As the men shuffled about, Xanos watched Temenus's eyes find Akhaïdes. The king's mouth flexed, his back straightened, and his hands went flat on the arms of his chair.

The tall young priest who had met them on arrival in Nafpaktos limped to the hearth and tossed a spray of powder over the coals. They sharpened and snapped. "This is the king's allcall," he declared, his voice hissing through the gap in his front teeth. "Everyone will hear and be heard, and the king above all others."

The priest surveyed the room. "Truth is here, and Accord. Eris and Ate, conflict and chaos, may not sit among us. Every man here has the right to be present. As he feels in his heart, so shall he speak without fear. This smoke purifies men's hearts and men's words. May there be peace among and between us all. The king commands it."

All the men in the hall touched their foreheads, and the priest retreated to a low stool beside Aristodemus.

Then, as the rest of his dependents finished settling, Temenus himself said, "Peace is with us all, indeed, and may we all be heard. May the powers that hear us respect our desires." Temenus modulated his voice to be heard clearly, without stridency. "We are the Tribes, the Dispossessed—so many men, so many lands, so many families, all lost but then joined together. Even the least among us is here under my hand, under the hand of all the powers and the hand of fate."

Faces turned again to Akhaïdes, who watched only the king.

Temenus said, "Hear me, cousins and friends. Here are two who have joined us. Elawon Hyadeides is chief of Ladon in Arcadia, and a recent follower of the Pelopeids. But now he has come to me. He has given me his hands and called me 'Wanax.' He is the first of what will be many defections from the Pelopeids to the true high king." Temenus tightened his lips and touched them with the tip of his tongue. "As for his heritage, you should know that he is a distaff great-grandson of Echemus Aeropeides, whose name you must recognize."

A murmur ran through the room.

"Yes," Temenus said. "We remember Echemus. He sent the great Hyllus, son of Herakles, and my own great-grandfather, to his dead. It is Echemus who was responsible for our exile, all these years and generations, up to this very night. But Echemus was more than that. He was great-nephew of the first wife of Herakles. Another distant aunt of Echemus was Herakles' final wife and the mother of Hyllus. We are cousins, then, this Arcadian and the Herakleids.

"And there is more. With Elawon Hyadeides—whom we greet tonight with respect and affection, an equal to us all—has come another soul. He is an outlaw in the first degree, the lowest of all stations, the most unforgivable and unforgiven."

Kresphontes started to speak, but Temenus raised a hand and he did not.

"Akhaïdes Outlaw is birth brother to Elawon. Although outlaws can make no claim to kin, these two have chosen to retain the link that bound them. Akhaïdes is not a name. It is only an appellation that he has chosen for himself. His own birth name, he does not use. His patronymic, he cannot use. Nevertheless—"

"The Good Kinsman," Kresphontes interrupted.

Temenus's mouth tightened for a moment, but then he said, "Yes, he is known to the world as the Good Kinsman."

The megaron was silent. Someone finally asked, "From the tales?"

"The same."

The megaron stirred, men murmuring to one another, asking questions, answering. Xanos could scarcely believe that most of those here did not already know that the Kinsman had come to Nafpaktos. No one had tried to keep it a secret, for all the good that would have done. Perhaps rumor was one thing, but a meeting in the king's own palace was another.

Satnios crawled out of his drink-induced infirmity to ask, with a shadow of his usual puckish tone, "Can you tell us, Uncle, is this really good luck, or really bad luck?"

His older brother Meydon, who sat with one hand on Satnios's shoulder, shifted that hand—joking but with a purpose—to Satnios's throat. Satnios briefly pretended to strangle, then grinned, silenced.

"Luck," Temenus said, "is often spoken of as if it were an immortal itself. Yet I believe that luck is not outside ourselves. I believe that luck is simply the art of being ready to receive and use what fate hands you—even unexpectedly."

"Clever man," Dymas murmured, scratching his thigh with the stump of his wrist.

"That which we call this . . . apparition, 'the Good Kinsman,' is a euphemism for a name far too terrible to speak aloud, just as we call the Sisters 'Erinyes,' the peaceful ones, to flatter them and soothe their violence. But what violence do we have to fear from one who sits so humbly at my door, asking only a place in the world to warm himself and to lay his head in peace?"

Temenus waited while whispers passed again. Kresphontes, meanwhile, stared straight ahead, looking like a man forced to eat raw lemons.

Hippotes rose from his seat among his brothers. Huge in the

lamplight, with his wide, sloping shoulders and his long hair cut straight at the jawline, he said, "This outlaw came with us from Delphi and did no harm. He minded the rules perfectly."

He paused, and his face closed a little, as if he was reluctant to continue. "But to live with him in a city is another thing. We were warriors, all traveling together. But there are women and children here."

Xanos leaned and whispered to Elawon, "If you look closely at Hippotes, you'll see Kresphontes' hand up his neck, making his mouth move."

Kresphontes himself took up the argument. "It asks for a place to rest, you say. But what of those who will come hunting it? It might sit here by your door; it might defer to every soul in Nafpaktos. But like a frog to a snake, like a rat to a dog, an outlaw is the Erinyes' rightful prey."

Hippotes took his turn again, with more conviction. "What if the Sisters come for him—it? Who else will they take once they've tasted souls in Nafpaktos?"

Xanos felt sweat start over his own bare scalp. He hadn't thought of that, Temenus having mentioned the Sisters so calmly. He glanced up at the open cupola, as did every other man in the megaron except Akhaïdes and the king.

Then Temenus spoke. "You're right when you point out that the outlaw—not your women, not your children, not yourselves—is the Erinyes' prey. You, Hippotes, and you, Kresphontes, traveled with him on open water, through the clouds of spirits rising therefrom, without protection. You slept with nothing but tent cloth between your heads and the monsters of the night. You sat with the outlaw under the thinnest of shelters as the moon changed over. And yet, you survived.

"And he? He slept at least two nights that we know of, not under tents, not in shelter, but under the raw, open sky, where anything that wanted him could have stooped down and seized him. Yet he also survived. Now, here, in a place of roofs and walls and weapons by the hundreds, you suddenly fear for your safety in his company? I think that Nafpaktos is stronger than you apprehend."

"Very clever man," Dymas murmured.

In the whole megaron, only the sound of breathing and the whispers of the children could be heard.

Temenus went on. "How many times in his life was Herakles outlawed? Yet the number of those who sheltered him is beyond counting. I say that in memory of our own ancestor, in memory of our own histories, this outlaw has a place here, by the king's door, in the light of the king's fire and in the warmth of his care."

Temenus paused again, letting the silence draw out, showing his mastery of this room. Kresphontes' face was a picture of exasperation, but he did not interrupt. Then Temenus said, more quietly, "Why did the Good Kinsman come to Nafpaktos? Because he, like all of us—like Herakles himself—seeks something. What is it that an outlaw might seek? What might there be left for the Good Kinsman to want? I can't tell."

He paused again, holding all these men quiet as they waited for him. "But I can tell that the Good Kinsman, Akhaïdes Outlaw, still lives after so many years. His life did not end when the great Serpent itself drove him away. It continued all this time."

His gaze moved unhurriedly around the room. "And why would it continue, except that his business in this world was not yet finished? Just as Herakles' was not finished. Just as mine is not finished.

"Killed, this outlaw would not make clean bones any more than I would." At this, Kresphontes shot him a startled glance. "He would not go to his dead, but would roam the world unsatisfied, just as I would. That is the law, they say, for outlaws. But it is true also for those like me, like all Herakleids alive, who are unfulfilled, who still have business with fate. No man's life is finished until it is finished, until a king sits on the throne he was born to occupy. Until a hunter lays his hand on the head of his prey and can finally rest from his hunting."

"Extremely clever man," Dymas murmured. "I've always said so."

"So you have," Xanos confirmed.

"I fostered him, you know."

"I know."

Temenus spoke again. "Nafpaktos has roofs, and walls, and weapons by the hundreds. Yet the hands of its king are empty." He raised those hands from the arms of the chair, palms up. "Why is that? What am I lacking? What do I need?"

As always when dealing with Temenus, Xanos remembered his own relative dullness, then settled down to watch the master do what he did best: have his own way.

Temenus asked, "What is an outlaw to a king? What can he be?"

Kresphontes said quickly, "A wolf in your sheepfold. A rat in your granary. A weevil on your plate."

Aristodemus whipped around, openly astonished that Kresphontes would interrupt his king. But Temenus overran whatever else his younger brother had to say.

"You say the calls you hear in the night sky are the Erinyes, hunting. But I say they are the voice of Hyllus, calling me to retribution and justice."

Temenus flung an arm toward Akhaïdes. "The murderer's own children sit here now. One of them even crept out of legend to join us. I met him first in the home of the great Serpent, where he humbled himself to the power that had cast him out, and that power did not destroy him. Instead, Delphi and the Serpent gave him to me."

The megaron was silent, all the men listening, even

Kresphontes.

"Look at him. See how he resembles the Pelopeids. Then tell me it is not Pelops's blood as well, somehow removed—Pelops himself, come to make everything right. Maybe it's this, this coming to me, this act of atonement in Pelopeid guise, that will heal Echemus, heal the Pelopeids—even heal this outlaw—of their evil and shame."

He paused. There was only silence.

"A leaf, in an immortal's hand, is a sword. The mightiest blow can be struck with the frailest of rods, should that blow be struck justly. Even aside from the ties that already bind this outlaw with all of us Herakleids, in bringing about our own righteous homecoming at last will anyone tell me not to use a tool that has been placed in my hands, just because it is misshapen and not beautiful?

"Should I risk everything that is owed to me for the sake of such fastidiousness? After so many generations of broken-hearted exile, can I *afford* that?"

He turned his whole body toward Kresphontes and demanded, "Can I? Must I throw away a weapon given to me, just because you disapprove of its provenance? Is that what you ask of me, brother?"

Kresphontes was studying his own fingers. The waiting drew out until, finally, he raised a blotched, furious face and snarled, "No!"

Temenus turned back in his chair so fast that everyone winced, but it was only to catch his page's eye. The boy stepped forward, pulled something from the pouch at his belt, and tossed it on the floor among them: a crow's head, the feathers awry and the beak daubed with dry blood.

"Perhaps," Temenus said directly to Akhaïdes, "these tools will serve me well. And they are beautiful in their own way, are they not?"

Akhaïdes blinked as if waking. At the last moment before rudeness, he bent his head to the king and touched the fingertips of both hands to his forehead. A shared exhalation pulled the strain out of the room.

No one cared to speak until Aristodemus finally said, "Our guests are welcome. The council concurs."

Kresphontes mumbled something, though not loudly enough to be reprimanded.

Temenus finished. "There is welcome here. As Herakles was welcomed wherever he wandered, so are all wandering souls welcome here."

With that, a throng of slaves bustled in. They wore identical costumes—loose, cream-colored muslin dresses with scarlet hems, belts, and sleeves—and carried trays of earthen cups. They scattered through the room, distributing cups to the ordinary Herakleids and chieftains. Only Akhaïdes received none. One of the women nearly stepped on the crow's head. Her grimace of revulsion needed no words.

Then another woman came through the curtain. Broad hipped and erect, she was dressed in intricate, flowing black that emphasized her white skin, black hair, and black eyes and the wide Herakleid bones of her face. At her entrance, all the men stirred and straightened. The children who had not fallen asleep crowed and toddled toward her, to be waved off by the other women.

She carried her own tray first to Temenus, then Aristodemus, then Kresphontes, so that each of them might claim his own personal cup.

Elawon leaned toward Xanos. "Who is that?"

"That is Makhawis, the king's half sister. His father's only daughter."

"Not how I would picture a woman with a man's name."

"Indeed. She's the family treasure, born outside marriage but acknowledged the same hour. Rich in her own right—lucky for her. Wed early, wed often. A bribe, a reward, and bait in any number of traps. Those two are her oldest sons."

Elawon looked at Meydon and Satnios, busy teasing each other though they were nearly grown men. He said, "I can see how she collects husbands so easily."

"Invitations to the king's bathhouse are popular."

"Bathhouse?"

"We call it 'the Mycenaean welcome.' Temenus adopted it for his favorite guests."

"No one uses the bath in Mycenae anymore. There's something wrong with the drains."

"It's Makhawis who presides in Temenus's."

"I'm the king's guest, but I haven't gotten a bath invitation."

"You haven't been invited to walk on bare knife blades, either. Makhawis was recently divorced from Hippotes. He didn't take it well."

Hippotes' eyes were following Makhawis. He held his cup with thumb and two fingers, as if holding a dainty bauble, but when he drank, it rolled into his palm and disappeared.

"She was married to him?" Elawon asked.

"Yes."

"Why?"

Xanos laughed. "Many, many reasons. As with all Herakleid reckoning."

Elawon glanced that way again. "Is that why he was so foul tempered on the way from Delphi? The divorce?"

"Oh, yes. I suspect he'll make life, um, uncertain for any new husband. For bathers, maybe not, since the only sex they're having is with her slaves. But still . . ."

Makhawis came to them, lowering her head to Dymas, the Dorian king, as he took his cup from her tray, then moving to

Xanos. Xanos tried to see her as Elawon might for the first time: black hair veined with silver, soft pillows of flesh around the jaw and chin. Her fine, crow's-footed eyes with their painted lids, even though cast demurely downward, never stopped moving. Like Temenus's eyes, but without his ominous vigilance.

Xanos took his cup from her tray and said to her sweetly, "The sun rises in the nighttime, my lady, if you appear."

She bestowed on him a suddenly impudent smile, kinked by a white scar across the upper lip. Two gaps in her teeth, upper and lower on one side, emphasized the whiteness of those remaining. "Ah, Lawagetas, you lie so beautifully." Before Xanos could protest, she added, "May I meet your new friend?"

"Elawon Hyadeides, chief of Arcadian Ladon, my lady."

She gave Elawon an amiable smile while he blushed and mumbled and finally remembered to take a cup from her tray. Then she turned, regarding Akhaïdes across the open hearth.

"And why does that one sit by the door? Has he been wicked?"

She was prepared for this, Xanos realized. She already knew about the outlaw, though he knew nothing of her. Nevertheless, as if she had called to him across the busy, noisy room, he suddenly raised his face into the lamplight.

Makhawis twitched her head away, the braids on her neck slithering over one another like live things. One of her women took the tray from her hands and replaced it with a long-spouted pitcher. She turned and went to fill the king's cup.

Xanos saw their eyes meet. Though they said nothing to each other, the glance they shared was full of some urgency that only they might understand, and that the likes of Xanos might only worry about.

Then Temenus rose. Every head in the room came up, alert again. He said, "This is my own cup. With it, I welcome my most honored guests."

He came down toward Dymas, at whom he glanced

respectfully, toward Xanos, but stopped before Elawon. This close, Xanos could feel Temenus's energy like fever's heat.

Reaching out with the cup, the king enunciated very clearly, "Welcome, Elawon Hyadeides."

Elawon quickly set his own cup on the floor, took the king's, offered it, and spilled a libation, then sipped from it and handed it back. And as Temenus sipped from the opposite side, Xanos realized what he would do next.

Temenus said, "An outlaw may not touch a man, may not touch a man's property, may not eat or drink in a man's company, may not enter a man's house. But I am no man. I am the king."

And crossing the megaron, he squatted down on his heel before the outlaw. Eyes on Akhaïdes' face, he lifted the cup between them. Akhaïdes watched without expression.

Temenus said, "You came armed to my allcall, but I am not offended. I understand your uncertainty, but I ask you to set uncertainty aside for me.

"No man here will drink with you. You and I will drink alone, then. The others will drink after we do, and we will still all be together. And you will be with us. With me." He held out the cup to Akhaïdes. Akhaïdes hesitated, the muscles in his jaw working. Then he took the cup in both hands and touched his forehead to its brim.

Temenus said quietly, though everyone heard him, "Welcome, Akhaïdes Outlaw."

Xanos glanced at the priest, who sat watchful but not disapproving. Aristodemus had reached with his walking stick across Temenus's chair, laying it against Kresphontes' chest, keeping him seated.

Xanos looked back at Akhaïdes in time to see him whisper something that only Temenus heard. Then Akhaïdes raised the king's cup and drank. Temenus took the cup back, turned it, and drank from the same place Akhaïdes had.

"I wish he wouldn't do such things," Dymas murmured. "But I'm sure he has a reason."

Xanos answered, "Likely ten or twenty, as usual."

Temenus rose and went to Makhawis to refill the cup. Watching, Xanos realized that the cup was empty and had been since Temenus took it back from Akhaïdes. Akhaïdes had drunk all the wine in it so that . . . Temenus had pretended to drink after him so that . . . He had then gone, himself, to his sister for more wine, with everyone watching, so that . . .

Xanos felt like closing his eyes and thinking about simple things.

Temenus sat again between his brothers and said, "If anyone still would challenge the king's welcome to his guests, let him."

No one spoke. "Then let us drink together and be one people. Including the least of us. We are the Tribes."

Xanos sighed and did as the king suggested, as did everyone else in the room. Even Kresphontes touched his cup to his lips.

As talk began to rise again, Dymas asked Xanos, "What did he say?"

"The outlaw? To Temenus? I didn't hear." He glanced at Elawon, who didn't respond. "But Temenus seems pleased." He could mention the empty cup. Too complicated.

Dymas said, "Temenus always seems pleased when he's getting his way."

"As we all do."

"When will he get better wine? This is some dreadful swill." Dymas drained his cup and summoned a refill. A slave came promptly.

Xanos answered, "He'll get better wine when someone gives him better wine. They're not going to produce any better than this in Nafpaktos."

The children had given up on following Makhawis and were

sitting on the floor in a group, staring after her. While Xanos watched, a tot in a rag-tailed shirt got shakily to its feet and wobbled across the open floor. Moving under the talk like a newt under water, it climbed guilelessly into Akhaïdes' lap. Xanos expected Akhaïdes to snatch it violently away, but he did not. As the grubby face snuggled into the front of his shirt, Akhaïdes calmly looped his arms around the small body. Xanos saw that Makhawis also saw, her face a study in bafflement.

Temenus and his brothers rose together, and the talk dropped off. The priest came from his chair to stand before the king, facing the hearth and the roomful of men.

"The king has come from Delphi," the priest intoned, "the center of the world. He went there seeking information, and what he found he will share with everyone now." He fished for a moment in the pouch at his waist, then scattered powder over the hearth's coals. They snapped and spat, and tiny colored flames shot up. "Listen, all men who love the king and his cause."

The men all touched their foreheads. The priest returned to his chair. Temenus and his brothers sat down. Makhawis gave her pitcher to a slave and went to stand behind Meydon and Satnios. Then she glanced down, lifted the cup from Satnios's hand, and passed it to a woman who had followed her. Satnios grinned up at his mother, then turned back.

"My priest has spoken well," Temenus said. "I have returned from Delphi, from the place of all knowledge. And I'll tell you who I met, what I saw, and what I learned."

He paused, giving everyone a chance to settle. "Who did I meet? I met these two new allies. And I met a young man, Tisamenus Oresteides Pelopeides, king of Lacedaemon." Temenus paused again while the men murmured to one another. "We spoke of matters that you and I all know of. We spoke of war, and the boy ran from me."

Xanos felt a jolt like lightning. Looking for the source, he saw Akhaïdes' back suddenly straight, his eye wide open, his face stripped of caution, recklessly alert. Then Akhaïdes stopped himself, crimped his eye shut, and dropped back into passivity. The child on his lap rooted lazily in its sleep, barely disturbed. No one else had noticed except Makhawis, whose eyes narrowed in Herakleid calculation while she laid her hands on both her sons's shoulders The brothers moved nearer to each other, into their mother's protective touch.

Xanos scanned the room again, Was it only he and Makhawis who had noticed Akhaïdes' response? No, Temenus also had seen. Temenus was still speaking, but his eyes were fixed on Akhaïdes, and he looked pleased, as if he had insulted Tisamenus only to provoke this reaction. "The boy fled not only from Herakleid power but also from what we already know are the terms of battle. We still will meet on Rhion Plain, next New Year's Day."

Every man in the megaron made an audible sound: a sigh, a laugh, a triumphant snarl.

Temenus gave them their moment of exhilaration, then continued. "The priests would not speak to support us. But I got an augury."

Every man snatched a protective fist to his forehead. Makhawis, standing behind her seated sons, shaded her eyes with one hand. The slaves all set their trays and pitchers on the floor and covered their ears. Akhaïdes alone did nothing, merely kept his eye closed.

"The augury of Delphi showed me four kings, with wheels in place of their legs, racing through standing wheat and, at the same time, through water. Their leader wore a lion's skin on one shoulder, and a woman's skin on the other, but he had no face. And a three-eyed man rode before them all." He cleared his throat, then tightened his lips and touched them with the tip of his tongue.

There was a bewildered silence.

The priest said, "I have studied this since the king returned. I can't unravel it."

Dymas said, "The lion's skin is obvious: your totem. And water means your ships."

"His ships," Xanos muttered, and Dymas elbowed him discreetly.

Someone asked, "Wheat? We're supposed to plant wheat instead of other grain?"

Aristodemus said, "We already know that wheat won't grow here. Perhaps it means the season—that the New Year is too early."

Kresphontes said, "Boeotia. It means to take wheat land we don't already hold."

Temenus looked startled, then thoughtful.

Xanos muttered, "This is where they tell me to collect five or six spearmen and a donkey cart and go conquer Arne." Elawon smiled at him.

A Carian said, "No man has three eyes," glancing at Akhaïdes.

"Four kings," mused Dymas. "But the three of you, Pamphylus, and I make five, not four."

"I'm not a king yet, nor is Aristodemus," Kresphontes said. "We won't be kings until we take the lands we should rule. And you and Pamphylus take turns, so that's only two, or three including both of you. Or five, yes, if it means the future."

The Carian said, "Don't forget my king and the Dyropian. That makes five now. But the Aetolians make six. And the Ozolians, seven."

"Are there four southern kings?" someone asked.

Temenus said, "Athens, Argos, Nemea, Tegea, Corinth, Elis, Lacedaemon, and Pylos, with Mycenae over them all."

"Tiryns?"

"A barony."

"Megara?"

Aristodemus said, "They only keep the wall. They never leave the isthmus, and they never join wars."

"Will we have to fight for Elis?"

"The king is old," Temenus told them. "His Companions promise not to interfere."

Hippotes spoke up suddenly. "Elis is mine. You all know I'm its real heir."

Temenus did not look at him, but went on. "Lacedaemon will fight us, but Tisamenus has both Lacedaemon and Mycenae."

Kresphontes said, "He doesn't have both. Not until Orestes dies."

For a moment, the room was clumsily silent in the echo of the high king's name.

Kresphontes added, "Don't count Tegea. Arcadians won't fight for Mycenae." He didn't bother to glance at Elawon for confirmation. "And Thymoetes fostered me, so Athens won't oppose us."

Meydon said, "So that makes . . . how many? We need a clerk."

"Five," Elawon said.

Aristodemus glanced at him, then smiled. He said, "Wheels might mean chariots."

Xanos said, "I've heard of men fighting from chariots, but only where the land is much flatter than here. Assyria. Still, some could be useful for managing battle."

"Better simply from horseback," Temenus said.

"Horses are harder to control, and they eat more than ponies do," Aristodemus said.

Xanos added, "I can't picture a warrior with weapons also managing a riding horse. In and out of a chariot, yes. Especially with a separate driver. That's what the Mycenaeans do."

"Can we get chariots?" Temenus asked.

"Melanthus of Pylos controls all that trade. He has the best wrights this side of Assyria. Even Mycenae gets its chariots from Pylos. But Melanthus won't deal with us. And we have no ponies at all."

"Donkeys?" Aristodemus asked.

"Too slow," Xanos answered.

"My brother has a herd of ponies," Dymas said. "We ate some this winter, but there are a lot left."

Satnios arched his neck back to look at his mother upside down. "A woman's skin,'" he said. "Ready for your next round of husbands?"

Makhawis laughed, but a wordless rumble cut it off. Everyone looked as Hippotes climbed to his feet, his huge knotted hands swinging against his thighs. The men near him stepped hurriedly away. Hippotes' bearded chin thrust forward, and his lower teeth glittered as he snarled, "No more husbands!"

The Carian raised a hand. "Surely it's the king's right to say—"

Hippotes crossed the space between them in a single step. One rising arm lifted the Carian off his feet and slammed him backward against the wall. The Carian, eyes wide, slid slowly out of sight behind other men.

Xanos murmured, "That's two gold bits's penalty. Three if his nose is bleeding."

"Temenus will pay it," Dymas said. "He always does."

Hippotes turned a circle on one heel. The men nearest him showed him their open hands, palms up and spread apart—the sign of submission.

Aristodemus rapped his stick on the floor and snapped, "Hippotes Herakleides! This is the king's allcall. Sit down and never do such a thing again!"

He looked at the priest, who hastily joined in: "There will be a penalty for this. Hippotes, come and see me tomorrow. And you, my lord"—this for the Carian, who, with the help of several friends, was scrambling back to his feet—"you have been wronged and insulted. Come to me tomorrow for your compensation."

The Carian glared from the safety net of arms holding him back. "Fine! I'll be there. And he . . ."

"He will be there, too," Aristodemus assured him. "And so will I, to make certain that you are satisfied."

The Carian brushed his clothes, wiped his nose on the back of his hand, and sat down at last. His friends returned warily to their seats.

Finally, Dymas said to the assembly, "It's clear we won't make any sense of this augury tonight. And if it's going to cause conflict, that's just as well. Let's all study it privately, and talk again some other time."

The priest said, "The king of the Dorians speaks sensibly."

"As always," Temenus agreed. "So I present this augury not as wisdom received, but as a riddle that wants an answer that we must devise together. We will meet again and discuss it further."

"Which leaves us with damos business now," Aristodemus said. At that, Makhawis signaled her women, who uncovered their ears and picked up their trays again. She drifted to one side, to stand behind Satnios.

"The damos has an issue for my allcall?" Temenus asked. "What can't you settle it for them?"

"They are troubled about the lion."

Temenus looked undisturbed. *Of course,* Xanos realized. He was expecting this. Aristodemus and he must have discussed it already.

Aristodemus added, "It's come back, as it comes every winter. It took two sheep while we were gone to Delphi. The council says it must be killed. But lions are sacred to Herakles."

Hippotes commented, "Ordinary men can't kill a lion. They don't have the skills." The Carian he had struck glared at him, as if trying to work an insult out of this.

Dymas said, "The sheep the lion killed were kept by Dorians."

"All the sheep here are Dorian," Aristodemus said. "There isn't enough pasture for a flock of our own."

"And so we should depend on you to protect them."

Kresphontes said, "Why don't you go criticize the Phocians? It only comes down here in winter. They could kill it anytime they want, in summer."

"Because," Dymas answered pointedly, "I'm not the foster father of a Phocian."

Temenus glanced around the room. All the Herakleids were watching him alertly. "And what if it's a sign, sent by powers to bring me Herakles' own strength? If it is killed, what will happen to that strength?"

"Your augury showed a lion's skin," Dymas said, "not a living lion. And you already have Herakles' own lion skin in your treasury. It hasn't harmed you."

Temenus thought this over. "You could hunt it, my lord."

Dymas snorted. "We cleared out all the lions up north years ago. There aren't any left in the world, except this one. Now Dorians are farmers and herders. We don't go chasing over the hills like wild dogs anymore."

There was a dismayed silence. Dymas rubbed his nose, looking slightly abashed.

Xanos noticed a movement from the doorway. It was Akhaïdes, trying to attract Elawon's attention. Xanos elbowed Elawon and pointed in that direction.

Elawon mouthed at Akhaïdes, "What?"

"Tell them," Akhaïdes said aloud.

Temenus was saying, "The Aetolian king—"

"Tell them what?" Elawon asked Akhaïdes.

"Tell them I'll kill their lion, if it's allowed."

He spoke so quietly that at first, no one seemed to hear. Then heads began to turn. Temenus sat straighter, eyes searching. Makhawis, standing with both hands on Satnios's shoulders, looked straight at Akhaïdes.

"Who said that?" Dymas asked finally.

Elawon cleared his throat. "We did. My brother . . ."

Someone piped up, "One man can't kill a lion."

Xanos found himself saying, "We don't lose anything by letting him try."

Dymas reached for his cup, got his fingers in the wine, then raised it and drank. "Kill it," he said. "Kill it, by whatever bizarre Herakleid laws will allow it."

Aristodemus asked, "Can he be counted as a Herakleid, making it forbidden?"

"Not if he's outlawed," the priest answered. "And even if he weren't, his blood ties originate in Herakles' life before he took his own lion, so the lion wouldn't be sacred to him as it is to you. And as an outlaw, whatever his family's status is, means nothing. He must give compensation, of course, but only what any man gives for killing a beast."

"Compensation for killing animals!" Dymas said. "That's the most antiquated . . . You Herakleids!" All the Herakleids glared back at him, adamant. "Fine. If the king's outlaw kills the lion, *I'll* give the compensation."

The priest said, "With compensation, the killing can be done."

Kresphontes finally spoke up. "Don't do this. Don't!"

Temenus laid his hand on his brother's, but Kresphontes shook it off. "Don't give this thing such important work!"

Xanos heard the child in Akhaïdes' lap whine faintly, but it did not wake.

Aristodemus asked, "Why not?"

"Because then it can claim a reward, and then you're stuck with obligations that no king should bear to an outlaw."

Everyone seemed to ponder this.

Temenus said, "An outlaw may speak in assembly, with permission. Talk to us."

"I am no man," Akhaïdes said. "I make no claim of kinship, as you imagine. I would not accept a reward even if offered. But if you can take my brother into your assembly of tribes, you can take this service from his hands."

Kresphontes started to object again.

"And if you would reward someone, reward him for bringing me to serve in this way."

Xanos watched, intrigued.

"He's looking to shame us," Kresphontes said. "To make us look incompetent."

Dymas snorted, "When a family the size of yours can't rid itself of one single sheep snatcher, you don't need an outlaw's help to look incompetent."

Satnios yelped a laugh, then ducked the flat of his mother's hand.

Dymas added, "I say he does this."

Aristodemus exchanged glances with several men, then said, "The damos agrees."

Meydon said, "You'll want dogs."

An Aetolian said, "And beaters. I'll go. How many do you need?"

"No dogs, no men," Akhaïdes said. The words were mild, given like answers to questions, rather than refusals, and no one looked offended.

Aristodemus said, "See my armorer for weapons. Whatever you need."

"Thank you, my lord." Then Akhaïdes looked at Temenus. "In your honor, Wanax, from my brother's hands."

"He belongs to me," Temenus agreed, "and I will give him up only for you."

"Clever man," Dymas murmured again.

Xanos knew that it was not Temenus he meant this time. "Why do you say that?"

"He just got Temenus to promise lifelong safety for your friend here, even if the lion eats him."

"Yes, yes, but what was that last part, about giving him up?"

"I have no idea. No one but Temenus ever will."

"What?" Elawon asked.

* * *

"The king likes us," Elawon said. He and Akhaïdes were descending through the dark, guided by lamps on the porches they passed. The Wolf Moon was waning ice-white above Arcadia, and a night bird whooshed past them and away. Three dogs on some business of their own trotted in file beside them for a moment, then turned off between hutments.

After the talk about the lion, Elawon had drifted into a daze, lulled by heat, wine, and the dimming light as the lamps went dry. Even the present moment's night air did little to rouse him, although it felt harsh as sand in the depths of his lungs.

Akhaïdes either did not hear what Elawon said, or did not intend to answer. Elawon repeated, "The king likes us."

Akhaïdes glanced at him briefly, his eye dingy white in the light of the last guttering lamp. "The king likes you well enough. He doesn't like me."

Elawon pressed his mouth tight. "He made a wonderful speech defending you."

"That isn't what it was."

"What did you say to him? When he gave you his own cup?"

"I told him he should be more careful."

"You can't talk that way to a king!"

"It doesn't matter. He won't listen."

Elawon tried another subject. "That woman is beautiful. I'd love an invitation to her bathhouse."

They walked some distance before Akhaïdes asked, "What does that mean?"

Elawon noted that he had not asked, "What woman?"

"A bath," he explained, "includes all bodily services."

A moment's quiet. Akhaïdes asked, "You want sex with the king's sister?"

Elawon hadn't expected that leap. He started to explain that any sex would be with slaves, not with Makhawis herself, but then simply replied, "What man wouldn't?"

"Why not just put your head in a sack and hand it to him?"

Whatever that meant, it did not sound like approval or agreement. They went down to the hut, with Elawon maintaining a stiff silence. The horse greeted Akhaïdes, then drooped its head again to sleep.

On the doorstep lay a woolen coat, neatly folded. Elawon lifted it and let it fall open. It was a fine garment, a bit worn but thickly woven, and light in his hands. Better than his own.

A neighbor's head came out of the next doorway. "That's for him." The man jerked his chin toward Akhaïdes. "The boy said."

"One of the king's pages?"

"Not the same one that came before."

"Who is it from?"

The man withdrew.

Elawon turned. Akhaïdes was backing away, hands behind him. Then he stopped, seemed to think this over, and reached out. Elawon felt a pang as the polluted hands took the coat out of his possession forever.

For the first time, Akhaïdes lay down inside—on bare earth and sand, but wrapped in the coat's embrace, with one arm under his head.

———— |

What am I to myself
That must be remembered,
Insisted upon
So often? [xii]

—*Robert Creeley*

Makhawis glared at her needle in the lamplight, as if it and not the seamstress were to blame. Then she pulled it off the end of the thread and started picking out her last few stitches.

A slave bent over her, the scarlet sleeves of her dress swinging down over her hands. "Lady, I could do that for you."

"I'd rather you finished that fur vest for my brother. You know I'm even less skilled with a bronze needle than with bone."

"But your weaving is lovely."

Makhawis smiled at her. "It is, isn't it? Anyway, it's time to sleep."

"And meet dreams," the woman said.

"You all know me too well," Makhawis complained contentedly.

The slave raised an eyebrow in mocking amusement.

It was late to be awake still, but they had returned from the allcall too restless to sleep. The potency of so many men together, the great subjects discussed, and the king's energy had affected them. A few minutes's needlework settled them, and now they moved around the room, their shadows slipping over the rugs as they arranged bedding, snuffed lamps, latched shutters, brushed tapestries.

Makhawis threaded her needle again and studied the

recalcitrant embroidery. Not so intricate, and this skirt was her favorite: long and full, double patterned all over with cranes and doves. She had only to fix this one fault.

What a pity that only women sewed. Surely that outlaw could create great beauty if he chose to, with those hands. She had lingered in the megaron to see how he would handle a cup of his own, but her women, correctly, had not given him one. Besides Makhawis, only Kresphontes and Xanos had seen the outlaw's reaction to Temenus's slur on Tisamenus Oresteides. She had lingered to watch how he could be so wary of men, yet with what immaculate sweetness he sheltered a sleeping child nestled in his lap. A woman could crave a man for much less. But an outlaw, never.

Her slaves stopped what they were doing, and turned toward the outer door. She raised her head. She heard it then: a stroking, humble knock. The women looked at her, and she lowered her eyes in consent.

Hippotes hulked in. As if walking on razors, he placed his enormous shoes delicately on her pale rugs and stood with eyes cast down, hands held together in front of him. As out of place as a boar in a nursery. But here in her domain, like a giant child. A slave closed the door behind him.

He murmured, "My lady."

Her women circled him, never looking away. He came across the room and sat, huffing and groaning all the way down, at her feet the way her own children did.

"You're angry with me," he said, staring at his hands. Lamplight shone on his thick black hair.

She made a deprecating click. "It's naughty to hit someone in an allcall."

He didn't raise his head. His voice was muffled. "I know. But what he said . . ."

"What he said is true. My brother decides whom I marry. It has nothing to do with you. Besides, you need a nice young wife. Someone to live with you so you can raise your own children."

He tipped his head back. Light fell along his broad nose and forehead. "I don't want more children. I want you."

"And once you're married again, you can look to the rest of your duties. You're renowned enough to foster a reputable boy."

"I don't want children."

"It's your duty to help other men raise their sons. Others will help you by fostering yours when they're old enough."

"I don't even know where mine are. You manage that—you and Temenus."

"It's Temenus's right." She breathed calmly. "And you'll be grateful when . . ."

His eyes narrowed. "I won't hang on the hopes of babies, like some old lady. No man will give me his son to foster, or take mine. And no woman with a dowry will marry me. Where will I live with a wife? Under a tree? How will I live? On her dowry, like a drone bee? I had to hand over my sisters to anyone who would take them, since I couldn't give them dowries. I can't get wives for my brothers, thanks to you and Temenus, because you put me out into the street, like a dog."

"You live in the palace."

"I live in a room with boys. But I'm not a boy, and I won't be treated like one."

He looked straight into her face. "I don't care who you bathe for your brother. But if you marry another man, I'll kill him. You know I will." The scar on his throat gleamed like metal.

Makhawis whispered, "That won't get you anything—just penalties you can't pay."

"Your brother pays my penalties, because I'm worth it to him."

He cupped one hand over her knee, covering half her leg, it seemed. He had killed with that hand—thrust swords and spears through other men's bodies, cut a throat so deeply the spine separated, throttled a man with a linen cord, done other things whose details she didn't know—only that they had happened. Temenus had paid and paid again the penalties for Hippotes' temper, and had used that temper just as often for his own ends.

And for what ends had the outlaw killed? The Good Kinsman had killed his own brothers, yet here was a surviving brother, alive, well, and unafraid. How . . ?

Hippotes' voice went low and wheedling. "Hawi, Hawi. Pretty lady . . ."

The hand moved up her calf. Her thigh shivered reflexively. Her sex was already moist. She had to try twice to say, "I can't make a baby with you."

His voice rumbled, abnormally muted. "Then I'll just touch you. I know how to touch you. Don't I?"

Oh, he knew. She closed her eyes. She didn't have to see. The pleasure was purer without seeing. What she saw in her mind was more perfect: the big scarred hand creeping under her skirt like a thief's, huge enough to hurt if it moved too fast, but never moving too fast. Always crawling so slowly, one fingertip, another . . .

But not Hippotes' hand this time. Another's. Danger. Hippotes growled his satisfaction at feeling her wet heat. Makhawis tilted her head back on the mound of pillows and stopped thinking at all.

* * *

Elawon woke with a fever. He twitched and shivered in his blankets while Akhaïdes fed the firepot. Outside, the horse rummaged through the heap of grass Akhaïdes had cut and carried here. From time to time, Elawon would sneeze but not apologize. To do so would have freed Akhaïdes to speak, and Elawon did not want to hear what he might say. He waited until the thirst was almost unbearable before asking for water.

Akhaïdes rose and left, then came back almost immediately, followed by a neighbor woman.

The woman squatted beside Elawon, wrinkling her nose at the smell of the seaweed pallet and, perhaps, of Elawon himself. She lifted his head for him to drink from a clay cup. Her fingers felt cool under his neck. In the cup was not just water, but warm broth from some illicit cooking pot, with the flavor of meat in it, and a few lentils clinging to the rim.

After Elawon drank it all, the woman laid him back down. Then she did a strange thing. She turned toward Akhaïdes and touched the fingertips of her free hand to her forehead, as if in respect or righteous fear. Then she rose and hurried out.

Elawon cleared his throat. "When do you hunt the lion?"

"When a priest or a shaman says. But not while you're ill."

"You don't need to stay. Neighbors can watch me."

"They may be flattered by your company, but they're too poor not to be practical. They won't feed you for nothing, and we have nothing to give them if you can't go to the warehouses."

"If you kill the lion, we'll have plenty of gifts."

"And if the lion kills me, you'll have nothing."

"The king promised me a place."

Akhaïdes spread his hands to indicate the empty, doorless hut.

The woman looked back in and said, "There's something outside."

"What is it?" Elawon asked. "A madman's gift?"

She winced. "I don't think so. I don't know."

"Can you bring it in?"

"If the . . . if you wish."

She stepped in and set a small gray jar beside Elawon, then touched her forehead toward Akhaïdes again and went out.

It *was* a madman's gift, Elawon thought, but then realized

that it couldn't be. It was clean, new, its mouth closed with wax, cloth, and a seal. A pattern was fired into the side of the jar: an upright oval with three dots at each side. The short sign for salt.

Salt? He lifted the jar—heavy for its size, clearly full—and examined the seal. It was an oval, badly carved but clearly a man standing with a sword in the air, stepping forward to meet a rearing lion. It must be Herakleid.

Akhaïdes asked, "What is that?"

"Salt, of course. Can't you read this?"

"No. What does salt mean?"

"We share bread and salt to make peace. Salt for loyalty, bread for trust. You don't know that?"

"Without bread, salt is still valuable?"

"As valuable as gold. The king must have sent it." Elawon showed him the seal.

"Why would he?"

"It's a promise to take care of me. So I don't need anything else from you." He set the jar on the highest part of the floor, where it would stay dry. "Except one thing."

Akhaïdes sat back against the wall, elbows on his knees, arms extended, hands dangling.

"Tell me," Elawon said.

Akhaïdes' head twitched up. "Don't ask."

"Why not talk about it?"

Akhaïdes' jaw muscles clenched, and he turned his face away.

"I haven't asked before." Elawon hitched his blanket up around his shoulders. "But now it's time."

Akhaïdes drew a hard breath. "Look," he said, "I'm sorry I left you. But even now I can't see another road."

That was completely unexpected, yet it resonated deep inside Elawon like the true and perfect note of a bell. The scent he knew so well, the lean, strong arms, the stubborn heart beside his ear so unquestionably his that his own small heart had matched its rhythm. And then sudden, cold loneliness.

As much against this as against Akhaïdes' words, he had to protest. "But you would have killed me! Only Mother saved me from you!"

Akhaïdes' eye closed. "Yes. Never doubt that."

"Is there something else to know? Something different?"

"Nothing. And you're sick today because I slept in here last night . . . Ah!" This came out in a distorted whisper, through clenched teeth.

He reached down suddenly, but only to pick up a small stone. His hand closed on it for a moment, as if on a weapon's hilt. Then it opened and began to manipulate the stone, passing it between the fingers and back again, as if in a shaman's game.

Elawon waited and waited. Finally, Akhaïdes turned his hand up, opened it, and looked down at the stone as if he could not account for it. He said, "I will give you anything that's in my power to give. But I will not give you that."

"I just want to know."

"Pray you never do." Akhaïdes tossed the stone outside, then rose and walked after it.

* * *

In a dream, he sat on dry, warm earth, in grass as high as his shoulders. Under his arm, a young woman leaned against him, as she had done from time to time all her life. No longer a terrifying infant in his hands, not yet the laughing mother of infants who would be murdered with her for his sake, she rested peacefully, trustingly. The scent of her thick black hair bothered him, yet he already knew that one day he would be willing to trade all the kingdoms he had ever seen for one more breath of it.

* * *

In a dream, he drove one bare foot against the throat of his Bajgani kinsman by marriage, raised a digging stick to the full height of his reach, and plunged it down through the man's chest. The bonus's resistance, and then yielding, was wildly satisfying. He hauled the stick free and stabbed again just as hard, and again, until the stick sank deeper this time and rose with its sharp end covered in mud. Only then did it occur to him that it was probably safe to stop.

* * *

Before dawn, Akhaïdes led the horse to graze in the king's meadow. He brought it back by noon, to rest through the early afternoon, then went out again until sunset. He didn't ride again. Anyone who wanted to see either the horse or the outlaw who would hunt the lion must go down to the sea.

The paired attractions, horse and outlaw, created such traffic that all the thin salt grass wore off the area between the hut and the water. Akhaïdes completely ignored the attention unless someone spoke directly to him. Then he would listen carefully, respond in as few words as possible, and immediately look away. This courteous inhospitality discouraged no one.

The babies who gravitated to Akhaïdes still came, crawling and staggering. He would hold their gnawed crusts until they wanted them again, wipe their bottoms, take away the bugs and sticks they tried to eat, shelter them in his shadow while they slept. These things he did with neither sentiment nor solicitude, as if he himself barely noticed. Young mothers, relieved of that portion of their endless labor, would even steer their little ones his way, knowing they would be protected with a fierce diligence that the mothers themselves could not spare.

Small boys still came to stare at the hunter and the horse and discuss their every movement in shrill, unguarded voices. Talking inevitably led to wrestling, squabbling, or play, and only rarely were fewer than half a score of small boys dodging and shrieking between the hutments, their vestigial rags cast off in their excitement despite the cold, and their bare little nubs bobbing bold and innocent as minnows.

Slightly older boys, dignified in their kilts and sandals, came to lounge in the sun's new warmth, to talk and share food snatched from unwary cooks. The boldest among them stood daringly near the hunter, alertly nonchalant. All on their own, the boys took to sharing their looted bread with him, proud that their adolescent thieving might be a skill appreciated by an adult as interesting and undemanding as the hunter. Elawon, still fevered and coughing but collecting rations every day, recognized these as free gifts rather than placation—unlike the offerings of adults—and let Akhaïdes keep them.

Bigger boys, already wearing loincloths and shaving their first downy whiskers, often managed to find some business or other near the shacks by the sea. At their age they were pollutable. Any accidental contact, even Akhaïdes' shadow, could harm them, and they bore themselves with a care the younger boys did not require. But still they came. Even fathers, grown men, happened by on obscure errands and lingered to attempt conversation from a safe distance. Most accepted Elawon's offers of bread and wine even though they must sit on the ground to enjoy it.

* * *

Aristodemus's armorer, a Herakleid with a braided beard and ropy, fire-scarred arms, searched through baskets of spearheads to find the right one. It was not the sleek, modern almond shape, but a massive, elemental thing, green with age, broad as a man's hand

and twice as long—meant to go in and stay in, to drag the life out of the body by its sheer weight. To kill by force, not subtlety.

The armorer looked pleased when Akhaïdes agreed to it. Then he watched while his apprentices—the boy Rousa and two younger than he and, thus, unpollutable—calculated Akhaïdes' height, reach, grip, and center of balance. They did not comment on his partiality for the left hand over the right, but simply accommodated it.

At one point, the armorer said quietly, "You've never handled a spear. You've never before done such a thing as you promise to do."

The apprentices stopped and stared at their master, and he waved them back to work.

"Neither have I," he continued. "I don't know anyone who has. But I think that you must not to throw the spear but hold it, brace it into the earth, and let the lion impale itself when it springs. That means forcing, and then facing, the charge."

Akhaïdes tilted his chin to the left: consent, acknowledgement. The apprentices shaped the ashwood shaft while Akhaïdes tried it again and again, until the armorer was satisfied.

* * *

That evening, Elawon asked, "Shouldn't you have two? Hunters carry two spears."

"If I lose even one, I'll never be able to replace all that bronze."

"But a lion . . ."

"I'll be alone. If I don't kill it with one spear, it will be too late to kill it at all."

"It might kill you." This tentative concern sounded flat.

"If you'd take a bow and arrows . . ."

Akhaïdes stared at him, momentarily alarmed. How could Elawon know of all the years when a bow had been so natural to him? How he had sat on the snow-crusted brim of a river to mourn Echemus's bow, carried for so many years and then lost, in a careless moment, under the ice? How he had killed an elephant with only three arrows? How he craved to hold a bow, the most honorable of weapons, once again? He could hit five herons in flight with six arrows from the back of a galloping horse. Even Ulaän Usu could not do that.

But not here. Not for this king. And Elawon was only talking, anyway.

Akhaïdes said, "You know how angry the Herakleids are that Hyllus was killed with arrows. They wouldn't accept this killing if it were done with a bow."

"You keep not giving them what they want, but this one thing you're going to do their way? The Dorians say that killing something is just killing something. It doesn't matter how."

"The Dorians are new to these places. The Herakleids are not. And we are Arcadians, older than any of them. We know to follow the land's own laws."

"Old men's superstition."

"You won't eat crows or gulls."

"Of course not. They're—" Elawon stopped.

Akhaïdes did not add, *you won't touch an outlaw.* Even so, it was the longest conversation they had had since Delphi, and no more satisfactory than any other.

* * *

The fifth morning after the allcall, Xanos found Akhaïdes sitting cross-legged in the sun, braiding leather strings under the critical eye of a half-score boys of various sizes. An infant or two gummed bread rinds in his shadow.

Xanos's approach was silent, and he was pleased that Akhaïdes started when the shadow fell across his hands. He was not pleased that Akhaïdes gave him only the briefest glance before looking down again, decorously dismissive.

"Good morning," Xanos said.

Akhaïdes acknowledged that with a sideways twitch of his head.

"What's that you're making?"

"Khazaär," Akhaïdes said, then corrected himself. "A bridle."

Xanos had noticed the knife before, but hadn't realized that it's blade was stone. Akhaïdes worked the tip of it between the braided leather strings, fitted a new thread into the pattern, and wove it around and through. His hands moved with unexpected elegance. It was more than just the depth blindness linked with the hands's structure. It was as if they were sentient, sovereign beings in their own right. To watch them work was a pleasure.

Xanos moved his head out of the light. "That's an odd knife. Where's it from?"

"China."

Xanos glanced around. The children watched him with crows' eyes, alert and calculating. Finally Xanos said, "Where is China?"

"At the edge of the farthest sea."

"Atlas."

"The other way. East."

"The Pontus?"

"Farther."

"There isn't any farther sea." Xanos waited, but Akhaïdes did not contradict him. He tried, "The end of the world?"

Akhaïdes repeated, "The edge of the sea."

"Same thing."

"Yes, Lawagetas."

Xanos glanced at the boys. Small eyes narrowed, calculating. They had provided the leather strings, he realized, and he chose not to ask them from where.

"The priest says to go tomorrow, to hunt the lion. Something about the moon."

Akhaïdes forced the knife blade into the leather and slid the end of a new string into place. "It's waning. A risky time for risky work, is it? Or something else?"

"What else?"

"I don't know priests's business, nor kings'. But I know my brother is not well."

"Isn't he? Maybe he needs divining. Did you ask the Shaman?"

"I can't talk to a shaman, and Elawon is ashamed to ask. He has a fever. But he goes to the storehouses every day."

"About the lion: the king says—"

"I won't leave Elawon alone. The king will have to wait."

"He won't wait."

"How not?"

The boys nudged one another.

"What do . . . what can be done?"

Akhaïdes finally looked up. "Send a shaman to divine my brother. Get the king to give him proper rations—not one day at a time like a beggar'. Find my brother some useful work to do. He mustn't go on living like this."

"Like what? You have shelter and food and—"

"Not good enough."

"I can't do all that!"

Akhaïdes dropped his eye to his work. "Then do nothing," he said. The stone blade creased the pad of his thumb. One of the boys sighed.

Xanos rearranged his weight. "I need to tell the Shaman your thyreos—your family sign.

"For divining Elawon?"

"For your hunt."

"I can't use it. And your shaman can't sacrifice for an outlaw."

"She says she needs it anyway."

"I don't want the moon to know me. It's very . . . precarious."

"The king says."

"Tell the king no. Never mind." He measured a thread, then let the braid drop onto his thigh. "Crane. The red crane."

"And the maternal sign?"

"A crested boar."

"Crested? You said a *crested* boar?"

"With that thing on its back."

"I know. I thought that family line was gone. From what I know of you Southerners and your clans, that's Diomedes and Oineus, isn't it? Mad Tydeus? I thought you were related to Echemus on that side."

"Echemus was my mother's grandfather, and he was related to everyone. I don't know how she kept that sign, but I remember it."

Xanos might ask if Akhaïdes needed anything for the hunt, but he feared getting another impossible list. He had meant to warn him that the king's page would come later. But he didn't. Let the ingrate deal with it unprepared. It would serve him right.

"Good-bye, then," he said, and left without waiting for a response. He had to walk some distance before the tightness between his shoulder blades loosened.

* * *

In the late afternoon, Elawon returned from the storehouses, jubilant. He carried a large bag of lentils, a jar of oil and one of olives, and a cheese the size of his head. Shortly after, while he was still fussing over how best to store these treasures, the Herakleid page delivered a folded leaf of beaten pith. Elawon put on his blandest face to accept the leaf, as if kings routinely sent him written messages.

"Will you wait for an answer?" he asked the boy.

"Those aren't my instructions."

"Go, then," Elawon told him. "You've done well."

The page glanced down at Akhaïdes, who sat on the ground nearby. Then he went away through the crowd of neighbor men who had gathered to learn his business here.

Elawon came to the doorway, where everyone could see what he held. He opened it showily, raised it high before his face, and read it to himself.

"It's an invitation," he said loudly. "From the king."

The neighbors murmured with awe.

"It's for his own bathhouse tonight." Elawon's voice quivered with triumph.

All the men looked at one another. The boys, not understanding, yet catching the men's energy, crowed with excitement.

Then Elawon stopped. He tilted the leaf and studied it. It was wrong. Were Temenus's clerks as incompetent as this? While the men all waited, he tipped his head in the opposite direction, to examine the writing more carefully.

Finally, he lowered the pithleaf and let it hang by his side. He looked through men's legs at Akhaïdes. "It's for you."

* * *

"No," Akhaïdes said. They had stepped inside the hut for the slight privacy it provided, but even if they whispered, every neighbor would hear.

Elawon thrust the pith at him. "You can't refuse. Temenus wrote this himself."

"A clerk wrote it. I can't read it. You go. You want to."

"I can't. I'm not the hunter. The king is honoring you."

"No. He's doing . . . something else."

"Well, what, then?"

"I don't know!" This came in a sharp eruption. "But I know he would feed me to his lion, cool as snow, if that would poison it. So this doesn't make sense."

"The point is—"

"You can't begin to know what the point is."

"Keep your voice down! The neighbors . . ."

"This king should do this for important men he can't get any other way. Why me, since I already promised to kill his lion? Why even you, since you're already in his pocket? I don't know why. You don't know why. Maybe even *he* doesn't know why."

Elawon snapped, "A woman might be exactly what you need!"

Total silence.

"I won't insult a king in his own city," Elawon added. "You've done enough of that for now."

* * *

Temenus had not written the invitation himself, but he had worked with the clerk to ensure that its meaning was clear. He had watched the page carry it away and had spoken with him on his return. He knew that it had been delivered—and that it would not be refused.

He dined with his brothers, and they talked about the day's trades, problems, ideas. Then Aristodemus and Kresphontes went to their private rooms to end the day with their wives and children.

At the end of his day, Temenus liked to rest for a while in his courtyard or his private chamber, alone except for a slave's discreet attendance, sitting quietly behind a screen in the corner in case he should want anything.

Often, he used this time to meet someone, man or woman, who had caught his fancy. Both the courtyard and the chamber had cushions and privacy enough to pass a relaxing quarter hour.

Tonight, there was no new slave to sample, no visitor with motives to explore, no spouse or ally with fidelity to test. But the courtyard was cold, so Temenus wandered to his private chamber to sit, sip wine, think, and wait.

He had told Makhawis directly, as was their custom, "Sister, I need you to do something for me."

She had known at once and was agreeing almost before he finished speaking.

He added, "He is wary of me. But you heard how he spoke in the allcall."

"Direct," she said. "Humble, in a way. But unyielding, for all that humility—even with so many men who owe him nothing."

"And he's been far more direct in private, I assure you." Temenus smiled ruefully. "If I thought he might be dangerous now, so long after . . ."

"I don't feel that," she said. "And this brother survives, and lives with him."

"You are the key. You and your bathhouse. I need to know . . ." He breathed out.

"To know if the priest of Delphi was mistaken. Or if you misunderstood."

"I need to be certain."

"Yes, of course."

"This is the perfect opportunity. I can't send him on this errand looking so shabby. And there's nothing wrong with rewarding a deed when it's promised, as well as after it's done."

They stood alone together amid the inevitable traffic of slaves and servants around them. "Do it tonight," Temenus added. "And later, come tell me everything you've learned."

"I will," Makhawis murmured.

"Be careful." Then he smiled again.

"What are you thinking?"

"That's exactly what he told me privately, in the allcall: to be careful. Can you imagine anything less likely than to be warned by an outlaw? By the Good Kinsman himself?"

Makhawis returned his smile. "The Shaman will know what to do for me, in case I accidentally touch him."

After supper, on his way here to his private room, Temenus had stopped to watch his sister's women preparing the bath: lighting charcoal; heating water; gathering towels, lanolin, oil, pillows; shooing the water carriers around. The rush of resentment had surprised him so, he had to stride swiftly away to keep from showing it.

Now he sat in this chamber, alone except for the attendant behind the screen.

Soon, Akhaïdes would step into the bathhouse. As he had done upon entering the megaron, he would stand perfectly still, openly examining every detail of the room: the things in it, the pictures on the walls. He would make no effort to hide that scrutiny; he would show no expression. Silence was his habit, as were the simplicity and clarity of his movements. Could the outlaw ever dissemble? Temenus thought not. He could lie, no doubt. He could hide any thought, any emotion, and show the most maddening indifference. But he could not pretend. What else he could and could not do, Makhawis would learn.

The women would peel away the scraps and tatters of his clothing. They would help him into the great bathing vat. When he stepped forth again, he would shine like a deity. But not a deity. Not even a man. Only Akhaïdes, with the skin and hair, the muscle and bone, the face, the hands, the structure of body and mind, uniquely his. Then, under Makhawis's direction, in her sight and hearing, within her reach, a woman would take all that into her hands.

And later tonight, Makhawis would come and tell Temenus everything. But now . . .

He asked aloud, "Who is here?"

"Deione, my lord." A face tilted around the screen. "Would you like more wine?"

Bless Makhawis and her good sense. This was a slave he had acquired a year or more ago. She had seemed clever enough, so he had lent her to Makhawis so that his wife's lazy, sullen women would not spoil her. He had never had sex with her.

"Ah, Deione," he said. "Come and . . . come and talk with me."

* * *

The bathing basin, with a rim like a monstrous seashell, was set in plaster against one wall of a tiny, windowless room. The heat, the steam, the smothering closeness, the weight of perfumed water pressing on him like one of those great snakes he had heard about that had only to envelop you and wait for you to suffocate.

He closed his eye against the light and the women's quiet talk and baffling activity, but it was all still there: the lamps, firepots, jars, boxes, stools, pillows, and rugs, the ornamentation on the door posts and walls, and Makhawis, directing everything as calmly as if she did this every day. And she might, of course, for all he knew. She was as strange to him as any Chou—stranger yet. And this dungeon of warmth, light, luxury, and excess surely hid a thousand hazards.

The women had peeled the clothing from his body, cut the bandages from his head and wrists. Their detachment made it bearable: they had handled him as if he were a piece of furniture. Then they had stood back to let him step of his own accord into this basin—like hunters watching prey place one foot, then the next, into the snare. Like cooks watching dinner climb into the oven.

His tattered shirt and leggings had been beautiful once, presented with well-deserved pride by one whom they would long outlast. The dyes and beadwork, the stitching, the suppleness of the leather, the perfect fit—how well she had known the proportions of his body. Only in losing them did he remember when he had worn them the first time. He could not have dreamed that so strange a time as this would be the last.

Makhawis had spoken only a formal greeting. Her voice—he had not heard it before—was low and clear, like the bell he had once found in a hastily abandoned temple and hung for a time from his horse's bridle. In other settings, her voice could have been soothing, calming, warming. Here, though, it scraped his nerves. Eventually, she would speak to him again and expect him to answer. But words were so alien, so deceitful, so unlike their meanings, they could never be relied on. "Love" was a barren noise, "mercy" a brutal one, and "fear" had no link to that emotion's vast hunger.

The dead yellow light was hot, without shadows. They rode swiftly up the valley, too frightened to be careful. The stench was heavier than the trailing smoke. Children sprawled underfoot like wads of rag. H'olgaichi's tent was the only one standing.

He shuddered and came back. The light was too bright for a moment; then his eye adjusted and the room was again itself. Lamps hissed like owls from the steam that gathered in the high corners of the room.

He could not look at the walls. In the frescoes, the people's faces were impassive, their organs precisely rendered. They did their work like machines, like wheels turning and levers lifting. The depicted sex left Akhaïdes unmoved, but the repeating images of hands touching bodies, arms, faces—those chilled him to the heart. Touching . . .

Tisamenus Oresteides had touched him, had stroked his face with scalding tenderness. Temenus Herakleides had taken his hands formally, yet so honestly that it startled him alert. Soon, a

218

woman might touch him.

To fight a man was easy: he had only to face him, read his thoughts, then push back with such violence that the man would never try again. To resist any woman would be wildly complex, reckless, and would get him nothing. Still, that nothing would be far more than he could hope for in not resisting. To submit—that would hold horrors indeed.

He could not do what she expected. The decorations in this room only confirmed what he already knew: his sexual power was as threadbare as the clothing he had worn. He could no more perform one of the deeds so lavishly celebrated on these walls than he could fly. Flying, in fact, seemed the more likely—certainly the more desirable.

A shadow touched him, and he jerked awake. White-frosted hair, wide bones, fine skin, soft mouth, and flat-lidded, intelligent eyes. Makhawis stood over him.

"You look like a sacrifice waiting for the knife," she said.

She was correct. His fingertips were numb, his knuckles white from his grip on the fluted edges of this basin.

"My women will bathe you, but I'll be right here. They are slaves, and I have been prepared, so don't fear polluting any of us."

He raised his chin in bare acknowledgment.

"And if there is some service you'd prefer before they bathe you, just tell me. We are accustomed to men."

He managed to whisper, "No. Thank you."

He heard the terrible smile in her voice. She said, "You're a strange one, even for an outlaw. Be at ease. There's nothing here to harm anyone."

There had been nothing to harm that other woman, yet he remembered a fan of hair caked with blood; a foot tangled in clothes; two ragged black eyes on a narrow chest, no other face; black-crusted fingers like the hooked feet of dead birds, like upturned cages of human ribs; squirming larvae disturbed by light. He remembered . . .

He woke with a gasp. These women were gathered around him like birds around carrion. Sleeves rolled up, hands filled with weaponry: sponge, cloth, jar, comb. Jaw clenched, he shrank against the wall of the basin.

But they were implacable. They pulled the stopper, letting the hot water drain off, carrying with it the dirt, blood, and grease it had soaked away. Then they drew him in among them and washed his body, not roughly, but as impersonally as if they were scrubbing clothes or the floor. They wiped away stains and scabs, chafed off calluses, trimmed his nails, unraveled his hair, cut the stitches away from his half-healed wrists, bathed his slashed eye and soaked it with ointment, massaged his skin with oil. They poured jars of scented water over him, rinsing everything into the drains.

Despite their restraint, something was happening. A shadow coalesced above him. It was his own monster's, hanging high on the wall of this pretty room.

The boy snatched his bow and ran for his horse. He threw his head up and screamed his war cry. A cataract of arrows hit him.

Here lay Chinowa Wolf, grass growing up around him, clutching a feather doll. Reaching but never touching him, the hand of H'olgaichi's daughter was nearly severed at the wrist, her arm wrapped in the cord of the baby hacked from her womb.

The boy's face was suddenly, finally open to him: shock, horror, dread, anger. H'olgaichi marked them one by one, like an inventory of trade goods.

He felt only relief.

H'olgaichi was on his knees, arms outstretched and a Chou hand in his hair. The warlord sat on his huge yellow horse, holding the reins in a fist like a rock. The round, naked head turned toward him. "What might it take, to turn the likes of you . . ." The warlord sought a word in this language. ". . . to make you grovel and whine? It will be interesting, very interesting indeed, to learn."

The warlord breathed out in hard chuffs—his way of laughing. "I made you a promise once, do you remember? To bring you to my duke, blinded, castrated, and in chains. I make you another promise as well: before long, you will be proud to grovel and whine for me."

A woman touched him.

He sprang like a panther from the rim of the basin, tore the towel from Makhawis's hands, whipped it around her throat, yanked her off her feet. Her weight swung from his grip. Her hair lashed his wrists, harsh as nettles. The back of her head thumped against the frescoed wall. This he saw from a vast distance: hands, cloth, flailing hair, painted round eyes.

Then her voice came, as calm and distant as thunder across the steppes: "Please stop."

He felt the words's vibrations through his fingers, up the bones of his arms, to his skull.

He stopped. In a moment, he would begin to shake. Then he would have no control at all.

"Please let me go."

He loosed his fingers one by one, as if drawing hooks from her flesh. It took all his attention to do this, shuddering so that his teeth clacked.

Makhawis retreated along the wall but did not flee. Only a woman who had never been hurt in her life could be this stupid.

As she sidled away, she whispered, "Whatever that was, it's over."

The light was yellow in the eddying steam. She stood pressed to the corner as if the spirits of stone and plaster—or anything at all—could protect her. As if the couple mating on the wall directly above her were more than a mindless obscenity. As if the women who gathered swiftly between them could provide any protection whatever.

A predator would strike, then look for a sign of weakening before striking again. He watched her that way now, between the other women, as if they were no more than ornamentation. The towel was still around her throat. She raised one hand to it. In that gesture, he saw her awareness that he still might kill her, here and now. She was both afraid and ready.

Then she tilted her head back and looked directly at him, and the predator faltered. He saw himself as she must: a skinny, naked old murderer lost in a woman's bathroom—pitiful, lethal, absurd.

Nothing is ever over.

His rage collapsed into itself. He wanted to speak, to lie, to tell her it was not him that she should fear. But the sound that came out of him was not words, was nothing human. He howled like an animal blinded. His body foundered and sank to the floor. And the woman, the fool woman, tucked up her skirts and joined him.

She dragged his claws from his face, clasped his head to her breast, and then she was singing—*singing*! "Sleep, my child, my arms will mind you. Neither Death nor the Kinsman find you . . ."

Like a child, he clutched her skirt. Just the texture of the cloth was overwhelming, and her scent—olive wood, roses, woman—thrust the breath out of him. From that sensory chaos rose the silent, unbearable image of Juchii.

— | |

*And it is this moment, when this catastrophic reversal
is taking place, when the old cycle is vanquished and
the new not yet begun . . . the demonic forces gain this
ascendancy.*[xiii]

—*Juliet Du Boulay*

Dymas, Aristodemus, Xanos, and the whole damos council
escorted Akhaïdes to the river at dawn.

Temenus's shaman was there: a black-haired Herakleid
woman taller than any of them, enormously fat, rank with magic,
and tinkling from scores of tiny bells sewn to the hem of her skirt.
With her stood a small girl, her apprentice, holding a donkey that
carried a pack frame loaded with metaphysical gear. Temenus was
there, with Kresphontes at his side and a crowd of Herakleids
behind them. Elawon arrived last and stood apart, wrapped in his
shawl, shrunken to an anxious stoop.

Akhaïdes placed himself where the Shaman indicated:
barefoot, ankle deep in icy water. He wore an old shirt—patched
and stained, short in the arms, but clean—and frayed linen leg
wraps.

Xanos had tried to explain these clothes, but Akhaïdes hadn't
understood then and couldn't remember now. Xanos and
Aristodemus together had overrun his fumbling efforts to dress,
doing it for him while Elawon had crouched unhelpfully in the
farthest corner. Dymas had waited in the entrance, the council
shuffling and yawning outside and the neighbors peering around
their door frames and murmuring to one another.

Then they had brought him here.

The Shaman took the spear from the armorer's hands and strode down into the water to face Akhaïdes, all her bells jingling. Her oiled black hair lay over her shoulder in a braided rope as thick as her wrist. Her sharp black eyes, cushioned in fat, studied him unhurriedly.

"You," she said finally, in the tone that Menetor, the priest, had used, though in a different language. "I know what you are, and who." She turned heavily toward Temenus, jingling. "Well?"

"Just the spear, Magissa," Temenus answered calmly. "Make it accurate."

The Shaman regarded him for a moment. Then she turned back to Akhaïdes. "Why are you here?"

He had no idea how to answer except to say, "Divine my brother."

"That is my next job today." She breathed out like a wineskin being pressed flat. "And as for you, let's not disappoint them, shall we?"

She passed the spear to him. He had forgotten how heavy it was, even held across his chest with both hands. Then she raised her face and hands to the sky and began to chant. Her voice rose like a birdcall, high and swooping. The sound of it jerked Akhaïdes back as nothing yet had, back through years, until these steep forest hills became the rocks and barrens of Arcadia, and a tall, blue-eyed boy in other castoffs lay hidden, spying on a rite that would never be sung for him: the formal passage to manhood. The fleeting image that twinged in the core of his spine. He shivered.

The Shaman paused and said, "Beware the moon. Above all, beware the Serpent. It sees all that you do." Her eyes sharpened. "It sees and judges. It's waiting for you."

"There?" He glanced up the river.

"Not there." She placed a closed fist on her breast. "Here."

Then she touched the same fist to the center of Akhaïdes' chest, reaching over the spear to do it. "Here."

He lowered his eye, and she began again to chant.

In the water around his feet, he felt the minute tappings of curious minnows against his ankles. He raised his gaze and saw an array of changing shapes that solidified into Herakleids: Aristodemus simply watching; Kresphontes reliably dour; Temenus with hooded eyes; Hippotes with head cocked, appraising; behind them lesser relatives, sober and sleepy, shuffling and murmuring. Satnios and Meydon, Makhawis's sons, stood apart from the older men. Satnios's eyes glittered with interest.

There was the damos council, old men whispering and scratching themselves. Beside Xanos stood a one-handed Dorian, whose expression gave Akhaïdes a moment's pause.

The Shaman sang on. Her words were slurred, the ancient dialect hard to follow. Akhaïdes looked up the river, braided and shallow even in winter, sliding between dark escarpments like a carpet through an open doorway, the rooms behind lit with clear white mist. Swallows circled and dipped over the water.

The Shaman's apprentice stood holding a group of plain clay figures on a wooden tray. The Shaman took a bird figure from the tray. "Your father, the crane, stands unmoving for hours until his goal is accomplished. He is patience. Your mother, the boar"—she lifted another—"cannot be turned aside if she does not choose to turn. She is tenacity. You need both for this trial. May they serve you well."

She paused for a moment and murmured, "That doesn't seem right. Surely not a crane." She looked at Akhaïdes for a moment, her head tilted, then set the figures inside a bronze bowl. From a basket, she drew a small, muscular snake and, holding it by head and tail, turned to Temenus, but it was Kresphontes who stepped forward, took a dagger from the apprentice, and sliced the snake's underside from vent to head. The animal tried to writhe, but the

Shaman held it firmly outstretched as its blood dribbled over her fist and down into the bowl. Then she dropped the still writhing creature back into the basket.

She said, "The snake is a great hunter. Orion is the immortal human power of the hunt. They both will serve you, hunter. This is the blood gift that binds them."

She offered the bowl to the six parts of the earth, then used her thumb to daub blood on the backs of Akhaïdes' hands and on the head of the spear. Her bells chinked faintly.

Temenus's eyes were closed, though not with concentration. He looked whitely ill. As Akhaïdes watched, Kresphontes returned to his brother's side and stealthily took his hand—the first sign of fraternal sympathy Akhaïdes had ever seen from him.

Looking at the king in his fleeting debility, Akhaïdes felt his memory stir. But like the stirrings Temenus had said he felt when they first met, it led him nowhere.

Nowhere except to Makhawis and how she had restrained him with those strong, tranquil arms and calmed him with her voice, had plaited his hair. Seated on a stool, holding him between her knees as if he were a child, as if knowing that the primal rhythm of her hands would soothe him more than any words could. She had bound his eye with a linen fillet, wrapped a soft blanket around him, and held him in her arms. All the slaves had been weeping, and they had taken him home.

Even now he could smell her scent on the immaculately plaited tail of his hair.

Temenus was already recovering: breathing deeply, opening his eyes. Kresphontes stood firmly by his side, hands behind his back in such transparent protective innocence that Akhaïdes felt a pang of something he could not identify.

Then the Shaman said to Akhaïdes, "Champion of powers, friend of hunters, beloved of ancestors, go." With a grimace—

perhaps at the formulaic utterance required of her—she added, "Do what you are made to do."

Akhaïdes came out of the water. Xanos held out hands wrapped in leaves to take the spear. Dorians did not concern themselves with pollution. Still, to deliberately take in his hands something an outlaw had held must be significant, even for a Dorian. Akhaïdes set the spear carefully into Xanos's leaf-gloved grasp.

Temenus himself came forward to open the shirt Akhaïdes wore and lift it over his head.

As the shirt rose, so, idly at first, did all the eyes on the riverbank. Then the men all stared, suddenly wide awake, at his wholly alien body.

From elbows to collarbone and down to his waist, Akhaïdes was tattooed, over and over in great, wild pictures of red and black: lions, birds, and chimeras twined together, a spread of wings across his shoulders, a herd of horses racing up one arm, a chain of crenellated walls descending the other. Men fighting and falling. Elephants, elk, camels, a dragon.

Only because he stood so close did Akhaïdes feel Temenus's sharp contraction of surprise. Then the king's eyes moved side to side, as calmly as if he were reading. He asked softly, "Is there a lion?"

"Not yet."

Temenus flashed a luminous smile. "That's the right answer, and thank you."

Temenus set the old shirt aside in the apprentice's hands and unfolded a new one. Akhaïdes slid his arms into the sleeves. The clean fabric, as thick as tent cloth, dropped down to conceal him. Temenus laced the front and tied it.

The king was too close. His scent filled Akhaïdes' head, and his fingers brushed Akhaïdes' skin again and again like a sweep of nettles. Then Temenus stood back a step. Akhaïdes knelt in the stones and pressed his hands together, palm to palm. Temenus reached to hold them between his own. Long though Akhaïdes' hands were, they nearly disappeared inside the king's warm grasp.

The Shaman bent sideways, wringing the tail of her skirt, her hands muffling the bells's voices. Glancing at her, at the round forearms, the slim wrists and ankles, the intelligence of the deep-set eyes, Akhaïdes wondered if she had ever seen an elephant. Then he lowered his head obediently, away from the woman's glare and the heat of the king's hands.

Finally, Temenus lifted him up. He took the spear from Xanos and gave it to Akhaïdes. Then he took Akhaïdes' head in his hands, drew it down, and kissed his forehead over the shaft of the spear, claiming this task as his own responsibility.

Drawing back just enough to look into Akhaïdes' eye, he said, "This is great work you have taken on." He still held Akhaïdes' head in his fingertips. "Show me, show everyone, how a promise is properly handled." He stepped away, his fingers trailing down Akhaïdes' shoulders, his arms, the backs of his hands, finally releasing him.

Akhaïdes had left his belt wrapped around the axe, laid on the neatly folded blanket in which Makhawis had sheltered him, on the dirt floor of the hut by the sea—the only magic an outlaw could use to ask for a safe return. Now Xanos stepped up to hand over the Chou dagger. Akhaïdes shifted the spear to one hand, took the dagger, and slid the naked blade into a fold of the leg wraps, on the outside of his thigh.

Xanos said, "You're going into Phocian and Lokrian territory. Any of them would eat a stranger without bothering to cook him first."

"Keep the horse for me."

The lawagetas almost laughed. "Every time I talk to you . . ." He snorted, resigned. "It will stay in my king's goat pen. I'll mind it myself. Does it bite?"

"And Elawon."

"*He* bites? Oh, sorry. Of course. What else?"

"Nothing."

Then Xanos did laugh. "You say that now!" He touched his forehead—an unexpected, undeserved generosity—and backed away.

There was Elawon, suddenly in view. He looked blankly tense, as if he understood none of this. Akhaïdes knew that Elawon would not forget last night, when the king's sister's slaves had brought Akhaïdes home, hidden in their midst, or an hour ago, when Aristodemus, Xanos, and the council had approached their door— not to expel Akhaïdes from Nafpaktos, but to collect him for this ceremony. No, Elawon would not forget, and he would never forgive.

Akhaïdes set the spear aside and sat on a rock to pull his boots on. The tops had been expertly mended, new soles of cured leather stitched over the old ones, new laces fixed. Only their shape remained, like a man's body once the spirit had gone away. A skilled slave must have worked all night to do this. He tied the laces and rested for a moment.

Makhawis was done. The Shaman, Temenus, Kresphontes, Xanos—done. Even Elawon had done his part. The rest is *for me to do. And not fail. Not fail.* Not a single one of them even imagined that he had never done anything like this before.

He rose. The Shaman's apprentice stood holding a woven packsack, a leather skin of water, and his coat. The water was a thoughtful gift since he could not drink anywhere others might drink after him. He did not know who had given it, but a glance at Aristodemus told him. He touched his forehead to the king's brother, then shrugged the coat on, shouldered the bottle and the sack, settled the spear in his hand, and walked away from all of them, up the river and along the gravel shore. Even here, even now, leaving still had the power to lift him toward gladness.

In Nafpaktos, dogs were barking, but here along the river was a fresh, unborn stillness. In the grass, tendrils of mist writhed like steam, like smoke. There, he thought with absolute clarity, there where the river turned back between mountains, the lion waited, elemental, serene, without judgment or mercy. Its regard would be unlike any other's. He would see only a hunter reflected in its eyes.

* * *

In Temenus's private chamber with the pillow-cluttered platform along one wall, Makhawis took the cup that her slave, Deione, offered. The page who had fetched her tiptoed out, Deione went behind the screen, and Makhawis was alone with her brother.

The room was bright with sunlight, and the cup in her hands was warm, but her fingers were cold.

Sitting on the platform, legs comfortably outstretched, Temenus said, "I waited last night. I even sent for you. But my page couldn't find you and you never came. I had to deal with the outlaw this morning, knowing nothing about him. You even let his appearance catch me by surprise. Those—what are they—those *pictures.* But I've trapped you at last."

He softened this with a smile. "Usually, you sit beside me and we talk together easily. Usually, you can't wait to tell me what you've learned. But this time? What's the secret?" Through the smile, his voice had an uncommon edge.

She drank the warm posset without tasting it. When she lowered the cup, he was still waiting, eyes bright.

She raised one hand to the high neck of her dress. The back of her head was still tender where it had hit the wall. "There isn't any secret," she told him calmly. "Your outlaw couldn't be duller."

He tilted his head back and hooded his eyes.

"I apologize for not coming last night, but I fell asleep. How was he this morning?"

"Dull. Flat. No one there."

"And that's him. It was like washing a dog, or a rug. He thanked me for the bath, was not interested in lying with me or anyone, and my women took him home."

"You talked about . . ."

"He had nothing to say." She swallowed.

Temenus shifted on his seat, drummed his fingers on the platform. "So what about what Delphi told me?"

"You were right before. It must be the younger one. What's his name? Elawon. I'll have him bathed for you if you like."

She stood and he sat, each watching the other carefully.

"Or," she added, "someone you haven't met yet. Someone you'll meet today. Tomorrow."

He tightened his lips and touched them with the tip of his tongue. "Yet something takes me back to that dream you saw, before I went to Delphi. Do you remember?"

A wind through dark trees. Cold hands.

"I remember." She swallowed again. "But it doesn't have to mean anyone. Especially not him."

"I could give him more time to show what he is. If he comes back from the lion."

Or you could lay yourself down on the sacrifice stone of a madman's obsessions. That thought shook her so much that she fumbled the cup, nearly dropping it.

"I thought so," Temenus said quietly. "There's still something you haven't told. Who are you protecting: me . . . or him?"

The sound of his voice as he wept. Some word in another language, repeated over and over as if in worship, or like a confession under torture.

She answered coolly, "Neither of us. But send your little Arcadian to me. Then, if he is the key the priest talked about, give him a better place to live than the one my women described. Not in this house if that outlaw . . . will live with him." She turned and called, "Deione."

The young woman came from behind the screen. Makhawis handed her the cup, still nearly full, and gave her a glance so harsh with warning that Deione instantly dropped her eyes and started for the door.

Behind her, Temenus said, "The outlaw is many things, but he is not dull. I don't want to think you might be lying to me."

She did not stop, did not answer.

"Makhawis."

For the first time in her life, she left a room without her brother's permission, and without telling him good-bye.

* * *

Akhaïdes did not start from the height where he had first discovered it, and he did not start from its last kill. If it had ever been hunted before, that was what it would expect and be ready for. He would have to come to it from a direction and in a way that it would not imagine. The less it understood him, the less he behaved like any hunters it might have known before, the less it would fear him, and the less likely it would be to simply leave this country for a while. And the closer it would let him come before taking alarm.

He followed the river all day, seeking sign. Cover was sparse at first, the brush eaten back by goats, then the bared branches broken off for firewood, leaving twisted skeletons sprouting strange green fingers up their sides. The lower branches of trees had also been stripped away as high as men could reach. If he met it here, he would have no escape upward.

He moved between cliffs, crossing and recrossing the cold,

braided water, searching up each steep, narrow ravine, all of them running with snowmelt, for the place a cautious beast might drink. Examining each clump of grass for a telltale nest of bones cupping the roots. He often touched the trees, rocks, the ends of the grasses, but they told him nothing.

By sunset, he was beyond the range of Nafpaktos's flocks and men, back in the safety and peril of the forest. The river's walls had opened out a little, admitting more light but still almost unscalable. He had seen traces of deer, badgers, rabbits, foxes, mice, and, more rarely, wolves and Lokrians—the feral people of the forest. He had crossed one path that must belong to Phocians. It was wider than those the Lokrians used, and it led up the side of a ridge at a low angle, easy to climb. The nearest tower lay east, out of sight, but long after crossing the Phocian path he still smelled smoke and garbage. He ate bread from the sack, drank from the water skin, and slept that night in a tree, with the coat to keep him warm, under the moon's closing eye.

The spirit of wood held dreams away, so it was not a dream when three men no taller than children appeared to stand beneath his tree. One laid a hand against the trunk, raised his face to starlight, and called softly, "What do you hunt, Hunter?"

He answered, "Lion, little father."

"The earth knows where it is."

"The earth will not speak to me."

"It always speaks. But you listen to those ones now."

Akhaïdes understood. He said, "I know your sign."

"We saw on that float thing, out on water, you saw us where none of those ones saw."

The three heads bent together for a moment. Then the man called up to him, "Hunt easy, so. That lion is no friend of ours. Lokrians do not mind."

"You have my gratitude, little father."

"And later, when you hunt those who silence your hearing the earth, remember the Lokrians." They vanished with not even the movement of one single leaf to mark their passing.

Akhaïdes slept.

* * *

The cool hand on Elawon's forehead felt wonderful. Then he remembered that he was in Nafpaktos and there was no one here to touch him in that way. He dragged his caked eyes open.

The Shaman's face was so near, it took a moment to focus on her. She said, "There you are," as if she were the one who had placed him here, flat on his back on his bed of stinking seaweed. But he had crawled here himself as soon as Akhaïdes left. What day was it?

"Have you eaten or drunk anything?"

He couldn't remember. His head hurt too much to think so hard.

A man's voice—Xanos?—asked, "Will he live?"

"You'd better do what you can to ensure it. It would be a poor gift to give your hunter—to come back successful and find his brother gone to his dead."

At that, Elawon should touch a fist to his forehead, to repel such thoughts. But he couldn't find his hands. He realized that the rattling he thought was inside his head was actually the sound of the Shaman's bells.

"*Your hunter*," the Shaman had said. So the man here was Temenus himself. *It takes my dying to get his attention now,* Elawon thought bitterly.

Temenus asked, "Will he come back successful?"

And Elawon felt a stab of resentment that even now the subject was Akhaïdes instead of himself.

The Shaman said, "This is what I see. This man will drink this potion. My apprentice will heat it and give it to him every hour of this day and the night."

"And he will survive."

"He will."

Elawon heard Temenus exhale heavily. Relief or impatience?

The Shaman asked, "Why is there no door here? Why is there no fire?" She climbed to her feet, her bells sounding. Elawon saw her gaze pointedly around the hut, then at Temenus, who had the grace to look embarrassed.

The potion was heavy with the taste of bitter greens, garlic, and willow. Was that a touch of nepenthe as well? It eased Elawon's throat immediately. The clogged channels inside his head began to open. He could breathe.

"So now what do I do?" Temenus asked.

"What you do so poorly," the Shaman answered. "Wait."

* * *

Sometime after noon the next day, Akhaïdes stopped to sit on a boulder embedded in a soft backwash. He rested the spear against the side of the stone, and his arms on one upraised knee. The other leg dangled. The sun embraced him through the shirt and coat. He leaned his head back, the light on his face.

He had heard that the Shang hunted lions. Ten mounted warriors for a single beast, and they still lost men sometimes. A lion, which would never climb a tree, they said, would not hesitate to climb a frantically shying horse, to rip the rider from its back. His own Bajgani had claimed to love and respect lions, although many years had passed since they last saw one, and they could not describe one. He himself had only touched and traded the dry skins of lions long dead.

Nearly fifty years ago, Echemus had told stories that included lions. As Akhaïdes hunted through his memory for them, he stumbled upon something older still: nothing about lions, not even a true memory, but only a moment's image. A man in a gilded leather helmet lifted him up in both hands, kissed him, then set him down, and turned and went away. Akhaïdes still could smell bronze, leather, and sweat. He still could feel the soft prickle of the beard, the hard, dry lips against his face. There was a lion in that somehow. He could not see it, just felt that it was there.

This image never came to him the way dreams did. It was just a picture, peaceful and strange, rising into memory at intervals of years. Echemus had told him it was he himself, on an earlier visit, that Ephialtes remembered. Only lately had Akhaïdes realized, looking into still water when he drank or prayed, that the face under the helmet was much like his own. This memory, then, could have been a foretelling of himself, perhaps even an augury.

Some said that auguries were only possibilities, that it was taking them for truth that made trouble. Hyllus, for example, had thought he knew what Delphi meant, and so had gone to his dead with Echemus's arrow in his throat. If Akhaïdes' vision of a man in rich warrior's dress were an augury, seeking the truth in it would have brought only trouble. Temenus's drive to understand his own augury could do that, too.

Echemus had liked him. Echemus had taught him. Echemus was now more than forty years with his dead.

Echemus. A kiss from a stranger. What, why, how, he didn't know, nor should he. He looked down and saw that the earth would still speak to him after all. There, where the shadow of his head touched the ground, was a single great paw print in the sand.

* * *

He followed the lion for days without seeing it. It was huge, its pug marks bigger than Akhaïdes' open hand. And it sprayed, so it was male—trebly dangerous because it had no females to hunt for it, and because, if Dymas was right, it was the only lion left in this part of the world. Men often fought hardest when it mattered least. And although animals should know better, it was the same with them.

By the afternoon of the fourth day, the lion knew both that Akhaïdes existed and that he was following. It circled away from Nafpaktos, following its usual trails but staying clear of human settlements. It left an account of growing uneasiness for Akhaïdes to read. It rested frequently but spent each stop sitting or lying upright instead of prone. It slept for shorter periods and chose, among its regular sleeping places, those that gave more cover than comfort.

It stalked, unsuccessfully, a family of marmots. Marmots were poor meat and hard to catch. Although the lion caught none, it tore open the burrow to the depth that Akhaïdes' arm could reach. It was either very hungry or already annoyed by its inability to understand what he wanted.

Akhaïdes kept the spear in his hands at all times, and he traveled with an acute awareness of his depth blindness and his sightless side. Any shadow of a rock, any bush, any fallen log might conceal death. He was in the lion's country now. Sign was everywhere: multiple layers of spray-coated tree trunks and rocks. He had invaded its private garden, its den, its web. It knew every leaf of the country through which he dumbly followed.

He slept in trees—a few hours only of the deepest, dream-free sleep. The rest of the night, he watched the swiftly dwindling moon. The lack of sleep did not distract him but rather served to concentrate his attention. He thought only of the lion, knowing that this, more than anything but fate or luck, might preserve his life.

The bread he carried was tough as leather. They had given him only bread, assuming he would also kill to eat, but he dared not. Eating only bread weakened his scent, made him smell less predatory. Being respectfully quiet would keep the lion quiet. Should he kill here, it would understand his purpose at once and would have to avenge the insult. So he ate only bread and the things he could easily find: berries dried on the vine, baby ferns, grubs, the seeds and roots he knew, that he had tried to encourage Elawon to forage for them in Nafpaktos.

To thin his scent further, he cleaned himself often, stripping off his clothes and hanging them in the icy air while he rubbed his body with leaves. Once the lion circled back to inspect one of these places: the tracks paced impatiently around the bush as if trying to read the meaning of a foreign tongue. Finally, the lion had ripped the bush out of the ground, shredded it, and urinated on it. This, less than half a day after Akhaïdes was there.

One night, a cold rain began at dusk and fell until dawn. Akhaïdes heard the lion's voice for the first time, low and tentative, then building to a furious chant, a sound so elemental it was almost below the threshold of hearing, like a rising earthquake or faraway thunder. It grunted for hours while Akhaïdes hung in a tree, barely breathing, knowing how little it mattered that he prayed, yet praying all the same. No power hereabouts was likely to favor such as him over the lion.

The lion traveled all the next morning, then, in the warmth of noon, curled up under a knot of berry vines and slept a few fitful hours. Akhaïdes found the vines crushed more rudely than the creature's usual fastidiousness allowed.

While he watched, a single leaf sprang straight on its stem. He twitched as if it had leaped at him. Then he reached into the nest. It was not warm to the touch, but not cold. With enough care and inner stillness, he could measure the size of the beast by the heat it had given to the ground. It had been gone an hour, no more. Here it had slept. Here it had raised its head, sensing Akhaïdes' approach. Here it had stared back down its own track for a moment, nostrils gulping scent, maybe calculating even as Akhaïdes now calculated. Here it had decided to rise and go on.

Small clumps of hair had snagged in the brambles. Akhaïdes gathered it gently. It was mane hair, coarse and golden, and he stood distracted, holding it, until a soft sound behind him brought him instantly and violently alert. He dived sideways and rolled to his feet with the spear ready. A deer bounded up the ravine in wild alarm. Akhaïdes crouched there, the spear across his chest, his heart hammering, too tense even to curse himself for allowing the distraction that could have killed him.

If a deer was there, a lion was not. He followed that thought. The lion hadn't eaten for days. He followed the deer.

* * *

All afternoon, he herded the deer along the lion's trail. He did not press it hard enough to make it flee again, but neither did he let it bed down as it would no doubt prefer during the light of day. He just eased it gently and steadily forward, keeping enough of its attention on himself that it would not notice the freshness of the predator's track that it followed.

Just at dusk, the deer stepped into a crescent of meadow beside a shallow lake. The open space was filled with tall grass, where a lion could rest and watch its trail unseen. Akhaïdes edged sideways, to a pile of fallen masonry—a long-abandoned house at the limit of the open ground.

Creeping between heaps of stone, he rose behind a still-upright section of wall and peered around it. The deer stepped, paused, stepped again and paused, big ears constantly turning. There was no other sign of life, not even a bird. But it was too early for birds to be sleeping. They should be here now, at sunset, drinking, circling, calling.

His breath was too fast, too shallow. He forced air in deeper, held it longer, while the deer turned, looking all the way around. As its gaze passed him, beyond it he saw the slightest shiver in a clump of tall rushes. There was not a breath of wind. He sank down to a cautious squat, set the packsack and water skin aside, and slipped off the coat. Holding the spear in one hand, he laid the other open palm against the bare earth, steadying his heartbeat and asking its help.

He crawled into the meadow, flat to the ground, trailing the coat behind him. He could see the deer's head between the grass stems that leaned silently aside. It bent its neck to nibble something.

Then he felt the lion's contraction and rush in his own body. The deer's head shot up, it sprang toward Akhaïdes, and he saw in its face a perfect foreknowledge of death. It made a high, arcing leap, and the lion filled the sky and snatched it down.

There was the briefest struggle, a scream and bleat, a thudding of frantic hooves, a long gurgling moan. The grass waved and convulsed, then stopped. Then the lion rose.

Akhaïdes had been right. It looked no more like a cat than a pig looked like an elephant.

He had been prepared for its immensity, though not for its actual presence, the power that poured off it. Its great, blocky head looked even more massive from the thick, tawny ruff that framed its face and bulked out over its shoulders and chest. Its face—the heavy bones and broad nose—reminded him of Hippotes.

The lion snarled, twisting its neck around without releasing its hold on the deer's throat. It did not see Akhaïdes and surely had no idea he was so close, but the warning could be meant for no one else. The sound was low and liquid, visceral as a lover's moan.

The image of only seconds before still filled Akhaïdes' mind. That sudden vision across the sky, the reaching arms, the great paws . . .

The lion sank into the grass, beyond his sight, and he heard a nuzzling growl.

He gathered his feet under him and stood. Stepping deliberately, feeling through the pliant soles the soft soil, the hard strings of roots. The scent of grass drowned in the stink of blood.

Its back was to him. It was crouched down, holding the deer carcass to the ground with its paws as it tugged open the belly.

Akhaïdes stopped. He moved the hand that held the coat sideways, away from his body. The lion turned its head and saw him.

Looking at him over its shoulder, it did not move at once. The golden eyes were calm. The moist nostrils worked, and the ears rotated toward him. Then it got casually to its feet, turning to see him better. It stood over the deer. Its nostrils flexed again, and he saw it recognize him and understand. He let the coat fall open from his hand.

The lion tentatively raised one paw, curving it inward. It looked away, then back, as if seeking information—what they should do now, together? Akhaïdes spread his feet, bent his knees. The lion took a short step forward and stopped.

"Come," Akhaïdes said.

The lion thrust its ears back into its mane, trotted three steps, and charged.

Akhaïdes flung the coat over its head. It gave a startled bellow, then backed up in a rush. As the coat slid off, Akhaïdes jammed the butt of the spear into the ground.

The lion sprang. Akhaïdes leaned his weight back on the shaft but, in his depth blindness, misjudged everything. The spearhead missed the open mouth and vanished into mane, inside one shoulder. The lion hit it with a shocked grunt, like hitting a wall. Its eyes leaped wide, and its forelegs clapped together. The spear's shaft arched as the beast's weight drove the point deeper. Akhaïdes lunged away. The lion came shambling after him, all teeth. Blood poured down its foreleg. The protruding shaft swept toward Akhaïdes' legs, and he fell backward over the deer carcass.

And the lion was on him. He rolled sideways, and a paw came down to stop him. He got to his dagger before the great arms closed around him. Claws opened like fingers against his back.

The golden eyes, frank and implacable, came at his face, blocked only by the spear's shaft. In these last moments of his life, Akhaïdes jammed the dagger into the lion's body somewhere, but could not move his arm to rip. So he pulled and stabbed again and again. Hot saliva flooded his face, but the lion could not bite him— the shaft was in the way.

Akhaïdes clung to the great, shaggy neck with one arm and stabbed with the other. They rolled over together. Their weight wrested the dagger's stone blade from his hand. Fangs raked at the shaft, so near his face.

Then the lion was heaving itself to its feet. Akhaïdes wrapped his legs around its midsection, both arms around its neck, fingers buried in the mane, and held on. Hard against the bloody chest, he felt the heart's furious clamor. It rolled again, but he rode it, the strength of his horseman's legs keeping him tight. It couldn't rip him away with its arms as a man might, and he clung too close for the hind paws to rake him off. And it couldn't reach past the embedded shaft to bite him. It screamed in frustration. The fangs snapped at him, left and right around the spear, as if through cage bars. Its breath stank and scorched.

Suddenly, a bloody cataract flooded Akhaïdes' face, and he felt the animal's power catch and falter. He kicked free, clawed over the ground to pull away, and rolled to his knees, palming blood from his eye.

The lion flailed on the ground, biting at the spear that still protruded from its chest. Then it lay still, flat on its belly on the swiftly blackening dirt, gnawing the wooden shaft in silence, through a steady pulse of blood.

Akhaïdes sat down on the ground. The lion looked at him. The golden eyes were calm again. Akhaïdes spread his hands, palms up, fingers open: *I'm sorry.*

It splayed its paws, heaved upward, pulled its hind legs under. Then the front legs collapsed and the spear snapped. It rolled slowly onto its side.

Akhaïdes waited, but it did not move. He staggered up, went to it, looked down.

It was not breathing. The eyes were open, bland as a dog's. He knelt. He had swallowed much of its rich, potent blood already, and now he cupped more in his palm and licked it up.

"Preserve me," he whispered. "You are now my brother."

For the first time in claustrophobic days, he looked up and around. It was almost dark, and he did not know where on earth he might be. In that moment of uncertainty, he saw the last thread of the moon tremble and vanish into itself. This was the moment when its spirit broke free, loosed from the bonds of its great, plodding body and the track it must follow. No longer a fish in a bowl, a donkey at a mill, a rabbit in a burrow, it spread vast, invisible wings and flew howling up the sky. In response, the ground bent away from Akhaïdes, pitching sharply down on all sides. Then, drawn by the moon's sudden wild freedom, the sky itself groaned, lifted, and sprang away like a heavy bird taking flight, shedding stars like sparks of snow.

Akhaïdes snatched grass in each hand and held on. Stars darted at him—before his face, behind his elbows. Straight above, too, but if he moved to look, he would lose his balance and fall forever. Then even the earth was not there, the grass fraying in his grip. The surface under him clenched and shuddered as the moon heaved through unbeing, through the cataclysmic change. He flung up his arms to hide his face.

Then he felt—he did not have to see—the gust of spirit hunch out of the lion's body, then stretch as if throwing off too tight a wrapping. The head surged up, cleanly molded, then grew, distended, and tore into strands. Fierce mist poured around Akhaïdes. Then, drawing away, it dissipated and was gone.

Something under his knee stung. A random, meaningless stone. He uncovered his face warily, saw grass, soil, rocks—all the real things holding him to the earth. He saw the lion's flattened, empty bulk. Blunt hills surrounded him, layered thickly and clad in ordinary trees.

He drank in the deep, sweet scents of pine and sun-warmed dust. He raised his eye to twilit sky bland as an overturned dish, gentle stars keeping scrupulously to their places, a slim, quiet moon reborn.

He got to his feet. He had held himself so tight for so long that his bones crackled with relief. When he looked up again, he saw Orion, the hunter of hunters, striding across the sky. Had he helped? Hindered? Akhaïdes did not know.

He found the dagger in the mangled grass. The end of the blade was snapped off, and the tang ripped through the grip. The coat was clean and unbloodied. Leaving it where it lay, he crouched again, pressed both open hands to the earth, and prayed for a long time in Arcadian, then in Bajgana, then in Arcadian again: *Thank you, forgive me, don't punish me, don't punish him. I am sorry.* He kissed the soil between his spread fingers. Then, under a clean night sky, he lay with the maned neck for a pillow, until the sun returned.

* * *

In the predawn, he used the stub of the knife to finish opening the deer's belly. He gathered grass, twigs, and larger deadwood and cooked the liver. His stomach rebelled at the rich taste, but he forced himself to eat it. Then he went to work.

He had no experience at skinning, and the broken knife made it more difficult still. The edge of the spear blade was not suited to such a task, and to flay an animal with the weapon that killed it was an insult that only a stoat or a sheep-killing dog might deserve.

It was a full day before he finished with both the lion and the deer. The air was warm, the sky cloudy but bright. Wasps descended on everything but the blade itself. Where did they come from in the middle of winter? Born, like ordinary bees, from the blood of the slain? His own arms seemed to have grown a thick, humming coat. He rolled the lion's skin around the two halves of the spear, the deer's skin around that, then tied the bundle with the leather thongs that had closed the packsack. By the time he was done, the treetops all around him were full of crows, foxes loitered in the bushes, and the whine of the wasps sounded like burning inside his skull.

He stirred the coals of the fire, added wood, and cooked the deer's heart. Some men despised deer for their wariness. But he remembered how this one had soared against the sky, doing what it had to do, right up until the last instant of its life. He waved the scent of the cooking upward, a gift to Orion, then ate the heart itself with admiration and gratitude.

He needed water. His head was beginning to throb, and his eye felt shrunken and dry. The water skin was empty, and this shallow lake, even though slimy and full of insects, was still forbidden. He needed fresh water all his own.

He put out the fire and laid the coat over the rolled skins. Then, hoisting the bundle to one shoulder, and the packsack and water skin to the other, he examined the sun and the angle of the shadows and walked south, on a thready trail between the two nearest hills.

Here, too, was lion sign. This pass had been part of its world—

the road it had used, perhaps, to hunt the Dorians's goats. How long would it be before deer and even goats might wander here in ignorant fearlessness? How long before these lands forgot lions?

He found a leaf-choked limestone basin fed by a dribble of snowmelt, burning cold, with no outlet but the porous rock itself and the bushes that overhung it. Here he pulled the shirt off and rinsed it again and again until it wrung clear. Then he scrubbed his face and drank. The water numbed his skin and made his jaw muscles ache. He rinsed the fillet and used it to swab his throbbing eye, stood to shrug the shirt back on, then knelt and drank again.

As he was drinking, he felt movement behind him. He wheeled, and the lion stood watching him with calm, golden eyes.

It was as naked and bloody as a thing aborted. The sun gleamed on the slick bare flesh of its shoulders and broad, earless skull. It twisted its head and snarled, the sound low, liquid, intimate. The water spilled out of Akhaïdes' mouth and ran over his chin, down his upraised forearms and into his sleeves.

The lion swung its bare, tail, slapping branches. Leaves clung to its pink, marbled flanks, and lymph dribbled down the blunted forelegs. The hole in the chest no longer bled.

Akhaïdes pressed his fingertips against the ground and rose. He fumbled the skins, coat, pack, and water skin into his arms and sidled around the pool. The lion did not move, but when he started away, it quietly followed him.

* * *

It did not hunt and it did not drink. When Akhaïdes climbed a tree at dusk, it lay down at the base, head up, quiet, patient, faithful as a dog. That night, the Erinyes came down in a clamor of screaming and flapping. But when the lion stood up, they veered sharply away, soared, circled, and finally roosted, calm as owls, on high distant limbs, preening their leathery wings and murmuring, but approaching no nearer.

* * *

The first person he saw was a young herdsman. The boy bolted off his rock, scattering goats in all directions. His dogs raced to defend him, then faltered and stopped. Their ears drooped, and their tails crept down, between their legs. The boy backed away from Akhaïdes, then whirled and sprinted down the tumbled field into a belt of trees, the dogs tight at his heels. The goats watched them go, eyed Akhaïdes briefly, then went back to their browsing, so he knew without looking that the lion had left him.

Half an hour later, he was descending between terraced farm patches, where men stood in crumbled soil, leaning on hoes and shading their eyes to watch him pass. Then they shouldered their implements and followed.

He reached the river before men came out from Nafpaktos, but when they came, they came in numbers—every man in the city, it seemed. Like the shadows of birds, they spread out over the flats.

Akhaïdes stopped, dropped the bundle from his shoulder, and leaned it against his knee. They surrounded him, their smell rank, their noise intolerable. He did not understand their language, did not know their faces, could read nothing in them. One of them moved a hand toward him, and he snarled at it. The hand quickly retreated.

Then they all waited, jostling and yammering but coming no closer. The dagger slid into his hand—even broken, it could be useful. They saw and quieted a little.

Then came a face that he did know: long, angular, and clever. The gray horse thrust its head at him. All his wariness flushed away as the horse walked into his embrace and pressed its bristly muzzle to his face. It snuffled at his hair, then sighed deeply and set to lipping his hands.

Now he recognized Xanos—the Dorian, he remembered, the lawagetas. Xanos's face was wary and cool, but it was he who held the horse's lead, he alone who seemed to understand Akhaïdes' bafflement. He glanced deliberately downward, leading Akhaïdes' attention to the bundled skins.

Akhaïdes pushed the horse's head away, knelt, and picked the tie open. Freed, the skins unrolled by themselves, the brown-gray of deer slowly giving way to the brown-gold of the lion's haunches, back, and shoulders. Laid across the hide were the two halves of the spear. He leaned to push the roll the rest of the way open.

The mane was as he remembered. The horse leaned down to snuffle at it, then snorted loudly and raised its head to look away.

Someone murmured, absurdly, "He did it," as if he might have come back had he failed.

Akhaïdes picked up the broken spear, stood, and examined men's faces. Since the armorer was a Herakleid, it was to Aristodemus, the clan chief, that Akhaïdes offered the spearhead on its splintered shank. Aristodemus bent to fill his hands with protective grass, then, smiling, took the gift. Akhaïdes turned to Dymas, the Dorian king whose arguments had made the task possible, and offered the broken shaft. Dymas took it in his one hand and said, "Well done, Hunter," in a voice that simply meant what it said.

Then Temenus stepped forth from among ordinary men, with his brother Kresphontes at his elbow. Akhaïdes went down on both knees, gathered the lion's skin in his arms, and offered it to the king.

Temenus laid both hands on it, directly before Akhaïdes' face. His hands were clean, the nails trimmed, the backs dusted with fine dark hair. The hands smelled of lemons, leather, and Temenus's own particular scent. They wore no rings.

Kresphontes said, "The king accepts this prize for his people."

Two thin, dark, shaven-headed men in black tunics came to lift the skin from Akhaïdes' arms. They were tanners, safe from the contagions of both death and outlaw. They had to wait for Temenus to move his hands. As he did, he told them, "When you finish your work, don't take it to the Shaman. Spread it directly on my chair in the megaron."

Akhaïdes had forgotten the sound of Temenus's voice.

"It will still be polluted, Wanax," a tanner said.

"That's correct. No one but me will be able to touch it." Temenus paused. "I knew when it died. I know its name."

The tanners gathered the skin—their hands were bleached nearly white, but the nails black—then bowed their heads and carried it away.

Then Temenus stood silent again, so Kresphontes had to say, "The hunter is entitled to the other skin, and to a meed of honor."

Akhaïdes cleared his throat. "I told you I won't take a reward."

"But you'll take a gift from the king," Kresphontes said. "You have to."

Akhaïdes looked around and found Elawon. Except for the anxiety in his face, he seemed well, his illness cured. Akhaïdes said to him, "Your hair was lighter."

Kresphontes said, "What?"

Akhaïdes looked up into Temenus's face again: the opaque eyes, the blemished skin, the taut, vigilant mouth. "A house," he said. "Give my brother a house in the first row."

Kresphontes snapped, "No!" but Temenus turned on him, and he flexed his jaw and added nothing more.

"A house is available," Aristodemus said. "No one has lived there." He caught several men's eyes in the mass around them, then added, "The damos approves."

"Then it is given," Temenus said.

Kresphontes raised a hand to rub over his face but had to

continue, "And what will you ask for yourself?"

Akhaïdes still looked at Aristodemus. "My lord, please give my brother an occupation. Responsibilities."

"I'll find worthy work for him. Yes."

From the corner of his eye, Akhaïdes saw Elawon straighten.

Kresphontes asked fretfully, "Is that your meed? Is that all you want?"

Akhaïdes finally realized what Kresphontes feared: that he would ask for absolution. Kresphontes was calculating what it would cost; Aristodemus was simply waiting for the king to decide. And the king himself . . .

Akhaïdes leaned and kissed Temenus's shoes. The rumbling of the men around them fell to silence. The shoes were old and plain, curled at the toes, restitched at the seams, the laces mended. They tasted of oil-cured leather and dust. A poor man's shoes. Temenus's.

Temenus sank down on his heel and laid a hand on Akhaïdes' hair. "Why are you doing this?" he said. He looked up and around, then back. "What *are* you? I have to know."

He shifted his hands, as Akhaïdes had known he would, putting one on each of Akhaïdes' shoulders. Their warmth flowed down his spine and along his frigid limbs.

Akhaïdes whispered, "I don't want a gift from you."

Above them, Kresphontes murmured intensely, "My lord Wanax . . ."

Temenus, ignoring his brother, said to Akhaïdes, "Never mind. In time, I'll know all about you. And I'll know what you want from me."

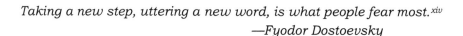

Taking a new step, uttering a new word, is what people fear most.[xiv]
—*Fyodor Dostoevsky*

At the same hour that Akhaïdes returned to Nafpaktos with a lion's skin on his shoulder, Tisamenus Oresteides and his Companions returned to Orestes' city.

The paved road, with fig and pomegranate trees at either side, led between cultivated fields bright with young wheat. Then, as the land began to rise, the road wound through a village, then another, of tiny whitewashed houses, their long shared facades broken only by low doors and deep windows. The faces peering through these openings, and the people who stood aside to watch Tisamenus pass, showed neither welcome nor disdain. They simply looked at him and at the line of chariots and carts behind his, then turned back to whatever they were doing.

Above the second village, on the right, stood a tract of ground no larger than a goat pen, overgrown with weeds and brambles as high as a chariot's wheel. Above this waste rose the twenty sharpened stakes on which Orestes had impaled the rebels who killed his family, except for Tisamenus and himself, fifteen years ago. Tisamenus vividly remembered riding up from the port on a hay cart, his small legs dangling, past the twitching, moaning fruit of Orestes' vengeance. He remembered his own fierce pride in his father's power, and how the rebels's exquisite suffering had helped, a little, to ease his grief.

It was here that the dog left him, bounding out of the chariot to race after a hare, into the fallow brush. Then the road curved around a hillock to the left and here was their welcome: three score men from the palace, lining the road, waiting dutifully. No one called out or cheered, but then Tisamenus heard a voice he knew. Philaios Taleides, a Mycenaean Companion, his best, oldest friend, limped and elbowed his way through the silent throng. Although Philaios was not as tall as most men, they drew aside when they saw who it was. Eyes brimming with pleasure, he leaned heavily on a walking stick as he hurried to greet his blood brother.

The driver stopped the ponies, and Tisamenus bent over the rail to grasp his friend's hand and press his bare cheek with his own. The warmth of the grasp moved Tisamenus as it always did. He held Philaios's shoulder with his other arm for a moment, then drew back. "Come," he said. "Ride with me."

"I shouldn't. This is *your* triumph."

"It's no triumph at all. Please, ride with me."

Awkward with his stick but with many hands to help him, Philaios stepped up into the chariot. The driver moved aside—a little grudgingly, Tisamenus thought, but he did move. The ponies started off again, hooves slipping a little at first, haunches working.

Philaios held the crossbar with one hand and draped the other arm over Tisamenus's shoulders. Since they were the same height, Philaios could smile directly into Tisamenus's face. Dark eyes aglow, mouth relaxed, fragrant, as always, with the cardamom he still used all this time after his wedding. With a jolt, Tisamenus remembered how well Philaios knew him and loved him. How could he ever have forgotten?

The men along the roadside were smiling now, calling Philaios's name, reaching out to touch the ponies and the chariot, which they never did when Tisamenus rode alone. Yet Philaios was shaking his head modestly, holding his old friend closer, indicating who was the important one here—certainly not himself—even as the sound of his own name began to precede them.

"No triumph?" Philaios asked in Tisamenus's ear. "How not?"

"I lost the best gift. I couldn't stop Thymoetes' siege. And I let him insult me."

"Thymoetes?" Philaios pulled away to stare at him. "Why would he do that?"

"I met Temenus Herakleides. He insulted me, too."

"You met him at Delphi? And did the oracle say anything?"

"It gave me a message for the High King."

"Anything just for you yourself?"

Tisamenus started to say yes, but the driver glanced at him quickly, his face severe as always. A warning?

"So tell me," Philaios said, guessing correctly on his own.

"Later."

"That reminds me. I've arranged a party for you, to celebrate your homecoming." Philaios laughed fondly. "Sustenance, comfort, entertainment."

"Wherever it is, I hope it's warm."

"You can count on that. You must have been so cold, for so long. This is a terrible time to be traveling. I myself can't even go out to my demesne."

Tisamenus gave him a wry grin. "You never go there anyway."

"Because it's either too cold or too hot to travel—or it's raining. And what good would it do for me to go? You know I'm no farmer." Philaios laughed again, easily. "And I need to be here for you. I was so worried that you might return and I would still be bedridden and couldn't come to see you."

"I would have gone to you."

"I was so sorry not to be able to travel with you. It must have been . . . Thymoetes *insulted* you? Your wife's father dared do that? I can't believe it. You'll tell me all about it."

"Yes. Yes, I will."

"The old men and their plotting. Do you want me to talk to

your father for you?"

"Would you, please?"

* * *

It was here in this narrow lane, under overhanging walls with no room to turn and nowhere to hide, that Tisamenus could most easily be killed. He had left the chariot at the foot of the ramp and let Philaios go a little ahead, allowing more room for the swinging leg and the stick, and now he strode, with only his driver, up to the gate. He felt the driver's unease. That dour broken-nosed man, whom he had known all his life and so rarely spoke with, certainly would not be spared in any javelin shower meant for his master. Above the gateway, the great stone lionesses stared, their gilded eyes remote, as each step upward found the two of them, Tisamenus and the driver, still alive.

One leaf of the gate stood open, and he could see the court beyond it, packed with swaying, shuffling bodies. These were all the palace workers and residents who, rather than walk down to meet him, had waited here to see how he fared. They had just now greeted Philaios with enthusiasm, even though every one of them had surely seen him already today. And now they turned back to regard Tisamenus, all of them quiet now, as if they were waiting to sniff him over for dirt, for blood. For weakness. He put on his most confident face and strode into the palace of his fathers.

* * *

Kanatpa's father was Thymoetes, king of Athens; her husband was Tisamenus Oresteides. She was 17 years old. Judged beautiful by most who saw her, she had the thick black hair of her father's family, and the diminutive elegance of her mother's. In the four years of her marriage, she had borne no child. Still, her husband had not discarded her, so she waited as any wife would, surrounded by her women, in the High King's bathroom, with a basin of water ready to wash her husband's feet whenever he might come here.

She could not bathe his body properly: the drains of Mycenae did not function, and even here, so high in the citadel, the stink that came up from the High King's derelict bathing tub was so strong that she had finally asked a woman to block it with a bowlful of stones. The room was warm, at least—the stove still worked—and as clean as it would ever be.

They reheated the water three times before he came. Then he came alone. No escort, no announcement preceding him, no flourish at all—like an ordinary man. The door swung inward, and there he was, slim and golden in the light from the overhead well.

He came in. Stopped. Said, "Wife. Good day."

She swallowed the lump in her throat and kept her eyes on the floor. "Good day, my lord husband," she whispered. "Welcome home."

"Are there clean clothes for me?"

"There are. And a bath for your feet, if you please."

He crossed the room with that familiar stride, every place he stepped precious beyond gold. He sat down, then leaned his head against the back of the chair and closed his beautiful eyes while women hurried to take off his shoes, unwrap his legs, and lift his feet into the basin.

One woman held a cloth to wash his face; another scrubbed his hands. But it was Kanatpa alone, the thick, perfect flag of her hair over one shoulder, who took up the implements to clean her husband's feet. It was not proper, in this room, in this company, to touch him above the ankles. It was her women, not her, who would remove his clothes and replace them with the new things that she, by herself, had spun, woven, and stitched for him. While they undressed him and then dressed him again, Kanatpa would kneel here with eyes downcast. The women of Mycenae, she knew, admired her modesty and reserve.

She caressed his toes, his heels, his high and perfect insteps, with cloth, pumice, and water, then with warm oil and her own small hands. She trimmed and buffed his toenails, never looking up into his face.

Her women murmured to one another, "There will be a baby now." But if Tisamenus noticed the tears that cooled the water and thinned the oil, he did not remark.

* * *

Philaios strode along the muddy stone floor, climbed three steps, then turned into a corridor floored with wood that had once been polished but was now spongy and gray. A thick, rough-edged rug was all that marked the entrance to the High King's private chamber—it and the two men in matching leather armor, holding spears whose points nearly touched the cobwebbed ceiling.

"Good afternoon," Philaios said to them both.

"The baron Hawmai is inside," one told him.

Philaios smiled. "All the more reason for me to be there, as well." He laid his free hand on the man's shoulder, setting it so that the rings on his fingers caught the light.

The man returned the smile, then moved to pull the latch and press the door open. Philaios glanced into the man's eyes for just an instant as he passed, and felt a jolt of interest. This one could be useful later. Philaios would remember him.

Now he was inside the tiny, dark antechamber. A slave scrambled to open the inner door to light, warmth, carpets, wall hangings, and sickroom stench.

In a glance, Philaios took in the High King's tall pallet,

Hawmai on a stool, slaves here and there. Hawmai looked surprised to see him, and the old man on the pallet turned his head.

Philaios bowed deeply, then knelt and touched his forehead to the floor. "My lord Wanax," he said. "I beg your pardon."

"Who's that?" The voice was scratchy and high, querulous even in those two syllables, but alert.

Philaios raised his head. "It is only I, my lord Wanax. Only Philaios Taleides. I apologize for this disruption. I'll leave right now," he said without moving.

Often, once the High King started his head moving, it would continue for a while on its own. It did so now, the dappled bare pate bobbing over spiky collarbones and rich blankets as Orestes rasped, "No, stay. I want you to hear what Hawmai is telling me."

Philaios backed onto his heels, then rose as gracefully as he could on the stiff leg and the stick. A slave set a stool next to Hawmai's. Philaios approached, touched his forehead respectfully at Hawmai, who smiled back at him, and sat.

"My lawagetas tells me that my son performed poorly. What do you know?"

Philaios brushed his hair back from his forehead. "He fears you will be disappointed."

"He lost my gift to that outlaw."

"Outlaw?" Philaios glanced at Hawmai. "Oxylus?"

Hawmai started to answer, but Orestes interrupted. "My own doctor's gone to look after that one. What perversion: keeps a wife that won't get pregnant, picks up roadside trash." Orestes drew in a breath, his skeletal chest rising into even greater relief. "I wish *you* were my son. At least you have some sense."

As often happened, Philaios had no idea what Orestes was talking about. He glanced again at Hawmai.

"Tisamenus took in a second outlaw that he found in Arne. It fought Oxylus, beat him, and stole the Regent's gift for the High

King."

"No! And where is he now?"

"The outlaw? Gone away with Elawon Hyadeides, who I always thought had some sense."

"Why would Elawon do that?"

"They were born as brothers."

Philaios's eyebrows rose. "Elawon, brother to an outlaw? I can hardly believe that."

"And now our wanax's own doctor is tending Oxylus. Tisamenus sent for him even before he was all the way back to Mycenae."

"Our doctor tending an outlaw? But the doctor's needed here!"

"That is exactly what the High King was saying," Hawmai observed.

Philaios took the hint. He turned back to the pallet and touched his forehead. "I ask your forgiveness, Wanax."

"Wish you were my son," Orestes repeated. "But no beard, either. Married?"

"Yes, Wanax. Several months now." They had had this conversation before.

"And you're still wearing cardamom for so long. *Hunh.* Yours won't get pregnant, either? Beat her. If that doesn't work, send her to her dead and get another. No divorce. Women go around telling lies afterward. Make a son, and I'll adopt you."

Hawmai said, "I'm sure that Tisamenus's wife—"

"Her father's a man. My foster son. He should have taught her better, but too much incest in that family already. It's why my son keeps her and his pets: dogs, outlaws, women." The High King paused. "I don't want to see him," he added more clearly. "If he has the nerve to come here, send him away."

Hawmai began carefully, "Well . . ."

Philaios settled back to hear what else the old men would say.

* * *

The Nafpaktos house had been inserted between the Dodonians's patchwork mansion and the Aetolian king's rambling residence, sharing a wall with each but wearing its own fresh-plastered facade and having its own door and window. Just past the Aetolians's house, the ground fell into a steep, narrow sinkhole with mud at the bottom, then rose immediately to support the Carians's tall, blue-washed tenement. Xanos's house lay somewhere in that direction, behind a gravel forecourt. Directly across the path stood a compound of storehouses and animal pens.

No one ever said for whom the house had been built, but it had never been occupied. It was small compared with its neighbors, but enormously big for Elawon: two rooms high enough to stand in, stone built and smoothly plastered. Like the king's palace, these houses backed against steeply rising ground. Above the street stood a porch with steps up one side, but the floor was of flags set directly in earth. The house was wedge-shaped—widest across the front, with a waist-high work platform along one side of the front room. One step up was the back room, then a narrow exit door with a high threshold to keep out water. Beyond that, a stepped, ~~crooked~~ passage led up past a cooking shed to a clutter of smaller houses and lanes above.

The wooden doors and rafters still wept pitch, thick and sweet-smelling as honey. The leather hinges added a tannic sharpness, and there was also the lemon scent of fresh plaster. Mice had already taken up residence, and peered warily down from the rafters. A small snake, bronze-spotted with a yellow throat, already lived under the porch. Wasps zoomed in and out the open doorway, where Elawon stood and laughed aloud with pleasure.

When the Shaman came with the small girl apprentice and the donkey in tow, she found Akhaïdes sitting on the ground at the foot of the steps, the deerskin folded beside him, the gray horse standing over him. She unloaded a lamp and some other things from the donkey, jingled her way up the steps, and turned and summoned Akhaïdes inside. Then she sent Elawon out and closed the door.

"Magissa, please," Akhaïdes said to her. "I shouldn't be here."

"Stand over there," she told him. "Now raise your arms like this."

He obeyed. With the door shut and the window hole admitting the only light, the cold gloom was soothing. He closed his eye to hear her better as she moved from corner to corner in an intricate pattern, singing a chant in time with the bells she wore. As she passed near him, the singing and chiming stopped. He opened his eye.

"You should never be alone," she said. "You were good at it once, but not now. What a load of trouble you are!"

He regarded her steadily, giving her nothing.

"Nafpaktos admires you today. But someday I might be the only friend you have. Remember. And remember that the Serpent remembers you."

He lowered his arms.

She added, "Be careful of the king."

"He is . . . imprudent."

"He would use you to your capacity, which is greater than either of you knows. Don't punish him for your failings. Don't punish yourself for his."

She lit an incense lamp and lifted it, smoking, toward the six corners of the world, then glanced at him. She said, "The Lokrians were right."

"What?"

"The little people you spoke with—they were correct. Everything in this world is a trade, a bargain, a covenant. You chose to give yourself to fate in one way rather than another. Fate will return what it owes you for that. You know this is true."

"I know it."

"Then live with what you dealt for, and be as content as you can be."

Akhaïdes raised his arms again in the suppliant's pose.

"Aristodemus gave me a gift to do this for you," the Shaman said. She lowered her hands and shook one out. "I really need a lamp that's not so heavy."

She began to chant again. Akhaïdes recognized the Old Mycenaean language, but he could not understand it. When the Shaman finished, she turned back to him.

"Now you can initiate conversation with your brother, but with no one else. Now you can live in his house without polluting him."

He lowered his arms. "I can't live here."

"You got this house for him, not for yourself, but it's you who has Nafpaktos's respect, so he does, too. And didn't the priest of Delphi tell you something that keeps you here? Didn't you know you're a hostage still?"

"Hostages have value that others are willing to trade for." He swallowed. "How can I live here?"

"Quietly, I hope. Modestly. Respectfully. Like the hostage you aren't."

"But there's something I have to do."

"You have business in Arcadia. Is that why you came back? The only reason?"

He looked away.

"But that road is closed to you. And where else would you go? Just wander off into uselessness, after coming so far."

He stood still, listening.

She added carefully, "Will burying your brothers make you believe that your son is safely with the dead? It doesn't work that way."

His head whipped toward her, but she held the lamp like a shield between them. He stood frozen, his heart thundering.

"No one suspects. Only I." Then she added, "Breathe."

He sucked in air. "What else do you know?"

"What I can guess. What the incautious tell me, or as near as tell me. What is drawn on the faces I see. What the air around a man can whisper when all else is still. What these mice and the young snake under your porch know. What the Serpent itself knows, sometimes." She paused. "I never talk out of turn. I only listen and watch and do what I have to do—like you."

He tested how he felt. Fragile. Precarious. Brittle. As if his body were glass or dry leaves. As if his spirit were a membrane so thin that a touch could dissolve it from the center outward. Both murderous and mortal—all shadows of the way he had felt when Makhawis, out of ignorance, set the world askew. But the Shaman had done it deliberately, just to see what would happen next.

He straightened his back and lowered his shoulders, feigning composure. "We'll never talk of this again."

"That will be fine. Remember, except for the house and furniture and conversation with your brother, all the rules against you still hold."

"Why is this house different from the other?"

"The shelter by the sea? That didn't belong to anyone and never had. That's why the damos—why Kresphontes—arranged for you to be there. And I have to admit, I admire the speed of his thinking when he did that. A favor wrapped in an insult. Even so, I'll have to purify it so it can be used again, even for animals."

She put her empty hand on her hip and turned a slow circle, scanning the room. "But this house is Elawon's. And here you'll have all the things needed for living: furniture, bedding, utensils. You'll have to be careful of all of them."

Akhaïdes looked around the fresh, empty space.

"Things will come," she said. "Although the house is his, those will be yours."

"I don't want them."

"That won't keep them away. I'll explain to your slave how to handle them, clean them—all that. It's complicated, but it's important that she make no mistakes."

"I don't have a slave."

"Temenus will give you one. He can't let you live unattended when he means to honor you. If you're lucky, she will be one Makhawis has trained. Temenus's wife's slaves are worthless, but his sister's are excellent, and they never gossip—unfortunately for me and my reputation for omniscience."

Akhaïdes walked past her, then paused at the door.

"Yes," she said. "Now you may touch it."

He unhooked the loop and pushed the door open.

Elawon was sitting on the edge of the porch. He half-turned and smiled at Akhaïdes—an act so unexpected that it alone would have stopped him.

Then he looked farther. Beyond the gray horse and the Shaman's donkey, dozing together by the steps, the path was full of people: scores of men and boys, all standing or squatting, leaning against the opposite fence, talking, waiting for something. The talking faded away as one and then another saw him there.

He felt the Shaman's heavy tread behind him; heard the whispering chink of her bells. She murmured, "The admiration I warned you about. You must give them this."

He walked out. Everyone went silent, expectant. He stepped aside and pressed his back and his open hands to the wall. The Shaman paced to the edge of the platform, next to Elawon, and raised her arms, her sleeves falling down to her shoulders.

"You are lucky people today," she called. "Your hunter returned, and Fortune came with him. One hunter joined its dead, and one was created. The hunting lion is gone forever. This other hunter was gone five days. Let five be the gifts you give him, and five be the days you honor him and honor the hunter he defeated."

Five days, Akhaïdes thought blankly. The wall was rough against his back. There was nowhere to go.

"Speak your gratitude."

All the people called out together. Dogs shied away, the gray horse snorted, and even the donkey raised its head to gaze myopically around. Akhaïdes pressed more tightly against the wall.

The Shaman called, "Do not forget your debt, and your praise, and your honor. Outlaw though he is, this hunter earned them." She lowered her arms. The sleeves slid down over her dimpled hands. She turned and saw how Akhaïdes stood.

To him alone, she said, "You brought this to yourself. Don't waste it."

"I understand."

"Do you? If not, it's a pity."

Akhaïdes bowed to her and touched both hands to his forehead. "Pity has nothing to do with me."

* * *

Gifts arrived steadily all day. Families, lineages, villages, and tribes united to send bags of beans and barley, cheeses, jars of salted fruit and olives, a table, stools, two leather-webbed bedsteads, dried vegetables, drawn ducks and geese, blankets, rugs, baskets, jars, pots. Children brought nuts, colored leaves, and the dulled wings of last year's butterflies. Their previous neighbors from the beach sent a group of unpollutable boys carrying Akhaïdes' axe and belt, which they had oiled and polished; his coat, which he had thought mislaid in the melee of his arrival; and the beautiful woolen blanket that Makhawis had wrapped him in and that, as a result, was now polluted beyond use by anyone else. Their old neighbors had also sent, for caution's sake, an additional gift of sweet fruit cakes, and bread stuffed with cheese and nuts. They were taking no chances: hero or not, the madman they knew must still be fed.

From Xanos came five jars of mead and an invitation to keep the packsack and water skin as well. Dymas gave half ownership of five goats. Kresphontes sent five glazed bowls and matching cups. Aristodemus sent five bronze implements, including a beautiful Hurrian-style bit. Temenus gave, besides the house, a long hooded coat of wolf skins, and, as the Shaman had promised, a slave. Deione arrived with a veritable dowry of tools, foodstuffs, herbs, and preserves that took two boys with barrows to deliver. No one missed the fact that the king had given three gifts, so owed two more.

Elawon ate cakes and gloated over the incoming treasures. "I knew it!" he crowed. "I knew we'd have a house in the first row!"

A page stepped into the open doorway, located Elawon with a glance, and said, "My lord Aristodemus is asking for you."

Elawon pulled his shoes on, combed his hair with his fingers, and hurried out.

Deione put her things in the back room, looked over the goats and gave her approval, then started arranging goods as the Shaman had instructed her. Meanwhile, Akhaïdes tied the gray horse in the cooking stall and gave it barley in a leather bucket. Then he crept down the passage to stand in the main room, among the heaps of wares.

Deione, bustling through on some errand, stepped warily around him, then stopped and came back. She asked, "Master, would you like to sleep?"

Relieved, he said, "Yes, please."

"Do you know how to use a pallet?"

He looked at her. She was short and plump, perhaps 30 years old, with round cheeks and a kind mouth. She wore her hair tight on her neck and tucked sensibly behind her ears. She did not wince to look at him, though her face showed caution. It occurred to him that she probably saw her being given to him as punishment. Perhaps she was right. She probably believed that he did not want her, and in that, she was definitely right. Yet they were bound together, like chariot ponies, by the king's will.

She had asked him a question: whether he knew how to sleep on furniture. He did not. He had slept on bare ground, in caves and holes, on rocks and cliffs, on silk, sable, and cashmere, on horseback and camelback, even in trees. But he had never slept on a contrivance like this.

Deione was waiting for an answer. He said, "No."

Sweeping a pallet clear of goods, she rolled a pillow for his head. She would have helped him undress, but he flinched away so violently that she could only watch him pull off the shirt and unwrap his legs. She blinked but did not otherwise react to his body's extravagant decorations. She just folded the shirt and leg wraps while he lowered himself onto the creaking platform. She covered him with Makhawis's blanket—that much, he allowed—then put the axe and belt, still rolled together, on the floor under the head of the pallet.

While kneeling so close, she said softly, "A message from the Wanassa."

She must mean Makhawis. He half closed his eye in assent.

"She says to tell you that she told no one."

"Not the king?"

"No one."

"She has how many women?"

"They don't talk out of turn. Never."

"The Shaman said that." He closed his eye completely, believing her, and shutting off further conversation.

If he showed any willingness to continue, she would now ask,

"What is it?" but there would be no answer to that question that someone like her should hear, or understand. He lay perfectly still, barely breathing, and finally she rose and turned, and left him alone.

* * *

After unwrapping Makhawis's special gift to her, Deione realized that she should have done this first of all, for it made clear that her new work was no punishment.

It was a small but beautifully carved stone figure of a crowned woman sitting on a chair, with oversize hands open on her lap. The Lady of the House, the keeper of order and domestic harmony. Deione brushed the figure respectfully with the hem of her dress, set it on the end of the work platform nearest the door, and laid a pinch of dried violet in its lap.

"Protect us all," she whispered. "Help me to make this a peaceful home."

The only way out is in.[xv]
— *Junot Diaz*

Temenus leaned back in his chair in the clerks' room and said quietly, "So let me be sure that I understand. Your king promised me masts and oars for ten ships. Now you say he won't give them to me. And why is that?"

The Aetolian's eyebrows were almost white, and they moved constantly as he spoke. "We have lost more land to the Dorians, Wanax. They treat with him, then do as they please. We all are squeezed down to the coast, and very uncomfortable."

Temenus half closed his eyes. "They have pushed you out of your forest?"

"Not yet," the Aetolian allowed. "But—"

"So?"

The man hesitated, then burst out, "They're your friends! How can we trust you when we can't trust *them*?" The eyebrows jerked and danced.

Temenus was not disturbed. "Isn't that like saying, 'How can I pet a dog when a cat once bit me?' And not a year ago, they were your friends, too, when you quarreled with the Ithacans."

The Aetolian glanced away.

Temenus added more gently, "A year before that, you and I were friends."

The man twitched, startled, as if he had believed the rumor that Temenus had so many partners he sometimes forgot them.

Then the brows pulled down hard.

Temenus asked, "Where shall I go for masts and oars, if not to your king? Would he rather I got them from the Ithacans? Or does he want me here in Nafpaktos forever, with the Dorians and the Tribes all around me, our population steadily growing? I would prefer to expand into the Peloponnesos, but if I can't get there . . ."

The Aetolian stirred uncomfortably. Across the room, the clerk Koretoros stood watching impassively.

Temenus said, "Do you know, there still are those who do as they promise? My Hunter is one like that—and with something more difficult than cutting a few trees. Keeping promises has not yet gone wholly out of fashion."

The Aetolian looked away dully, apparently unruffled at being compared to an outlaw.

So Temenus leaned to open his shoes. Lifting his feet out of them, he hooked his fingers into them, then stood up, barefoot, with the shoe hanging.

"My lord,' he said, "here I am with my shoes in my hand. My life, my future, and yours depend on your king's keeping his promise to me. Will he do it, or will he not?"

The Aetolian stepped back, eyebrows high, finally nonplussed.

"Or shall I go to the Dorians and tell them what you just told me? You believe they treat badly with you now. What if they actually wanted to harm you? You might care for that conduct even less. Or shall I send all the Aetolians in Nafpaktos and their dependents back to your king, to try to eat from the lands he has left to him? How soon would you come back to me, I wonder, with a different message?"

Temenus set the shoes carefully side by side on the table and stood looking at them thoughtfully.

The Aetolian finally ventured, "Wanax?"

"It is interesting, isn't it," Temenus said, "that even something like that—cured hide with no fat on it, old, worn, in bad repair—

could look edible after a while."

"Some say that you're unlucky. A lion in your flocks, an outlaw in your city—"

"The lion is gone, to the outlaw's credit."

The eyebrows rammed together. "An outlaw here at all. And an oracle you don't understand—"

"Shoes," Temenus said. "Imagine."

The Aetolian gave up. "Wanax, I'll do as you want."

Temenus turned back to him. "No, my lord. You'll do as you promised, as you agreed already, and as you and I remember. Go and convince your king so."

The Aetolian bobbed his head and made a motion toward his forehead with one hand—the best Temenus could expect. Then he turned and fled. Koretoros closed the door behind him and turned back to his work, not meeting Temenus's eyes.

Temenus sat down beside his shoes. If this was what humility was like, he hated it. The outlaw—*his* outlaw—had kissed those shoes, had used gut-wrenching humility to get what he wanted, and that had worked. But it couldn't have felt like this. He laid a forefinger on one shoe, behind the turned-up toe, perhaps where Akhaïdes' mouth had touched, perhaps not.

Already, the other clerks were scratching at the door. They would have seen the Aetolian's face. They would come in pretending to be pleased and impressed. They would come in secretly disappointed, since the Aetolian no doubt had bribed them but would not bribe them again. All for a few trees that still might never appear.

The tanners had not mentioned when the lion's skin would be ready. It would be days and days before Temenus could bury his face in the mane and breathe a simple, wild scent again.

He shod himself again, and Koretoros let the others in.

* * *

The rest of the day was better.

He went to see the woodworkers, the clan of men expert in doors and lintels, steps, shutters, and furniture. After their initial alarm at Temenus's unexpected appearance, they conceded with some interest that yes, they might build chariots, though none of them had actually seen one. Temenus described how chariots worked, and what he remembered of the design. One of the men drew sketch after sketch on the ground, changing and correcting them as Temenus talked.

Fir, pine, cypress: they discussed the kinds of wood they would need for each part. They knew—their eyes turned a little furtive here—where to find the best withy. Flax, not wire, they said, would bind the joints best. Wire was killingly expensive and would eat through wood; leather would harden when it got wet, and would eventually break. Flax would stretch but could be tightened.

Temenus took the leader of the woodworkers to talk with the spinners—not the fine workers, such as Makhawis and her women, but the women who made string and the heavy thread that was woven into fabric for bakers and tentmakers. He kept at it until each understood what the others needed, and each agreed to a complex set of exchanges that Koretoros recorded, probably inaccurately.

Then the four of them—woodworker, spinner, clerk, and king—went to see the armorer. They stood in the entrance to his workshops. The spinner, being a woman, could go no closer to the fires. There they talked about fittings for the chariots. The armorer had seen chariots and had studied them. He had an unquenchable curiosity for mechanisms, and not even the newest puzzled him for long. The metal pieces for a chariot, though. Ah . . . He stroked his long braided beard, calculating swiftly, and gave Temenus a weight of bronze that made the king's heart trip. Even the clerk had a coughing fit.

Temenus returned to the palace and wrote a message to Dymas. The Dorian king lived in the same building, of course, in the best guest room. Even so, Temenus guided a clerk in ciphering a letter that began with a respectful greeting, then listed all the promises Dymas and his brother had made since the past equinox: five hundred hard hands of bronze, use of three fields that Dorian sheep were still grazing, access to a certain road between the lakes, half the water from a certain spring, a hundred seasoned fighting men and their families instead of the steady influx of unskilled refugees. He described his need for a chariot troop and the material to equip it: wood, flax, metal. He mentioned the ponies that Dymas had said were not being used. He finished with a courteous but not abject closing, then sent his page off with the pithleaf in his hand. Dymas would not answer, but when the page returned, the clerks would store the leaf so they could—perhaps—find it again when Temenus needed it.

He ate bread dipped in wine, then napped through the warmth of the afternoon on the cushioned platform in his private room. With the first breath of cooler evening air, he called in his wife. The sex was purely functional, tedious, and quickly over.

When he returned to the public rooms, a messenger was waiting. Temenus accepted a letter from the Carian king complaining of Hippotes' assault on that king's nephew. The letter made no mention of the amends Temenus had made. It only explained, in obscurely ornate language, that the king's nephew was recalled home due to the lack of respect shown him in Nafpaktos.

After reading the letter and listening to the messenger's recitation, Temenus considered the messenger himself: perhaps 30 years old, tall and spare, with the dark coloring and prominent nose of all Carians. He seemed perfectly ordinary, but Temenus knew the Carian king, knew how cagily he played. The messenger's hands were clean, the nails trimmed and buffed. He did not smell of a winter's grime, and his clothing seemed too deliberately plain, too clean, too new.

In front of the clerks, Temenus gave the messenger a written apology and made sure he memorized it correctly. He also gave three gifts for the Carian king, from his own treasury: a serpentine carving of a fish, a necklace of silver beads, and an ivory fan with only one broken rib. Then he walked the messenger to the palace entrance and released him with a touch on the arm that made the man twitch and look away.

That twitch was interesting. Clearly, the messenger had been warned to beware of Temenus, yet no one would bother warning an ordinary man to avoid attracting a king's attention.

As an experiment, Temenus told him quietly, "Come back when you can."

The man—still not looking at him—answered, "I will, my lord."

"After the message is delivered. Don't come back as a messenger. Just come back."

"Yes, my lord."

Temenus left him there and walked away, feeling the man's eyes still on his back. Yes, my lord, indeed. If he returned—*when* he returned—Temenus would learn what he was, and who.

The door to his treasury—the only door in Nafpaktos with metal hinges and a clasp—still stood open. Temenus did not look at the few remaining items on the little closet's shelves. He did not look at the bundle that held the most important object he owned: the skin of the Nemean lion that Herakles himself had killed. He simply closed the door and sealed it, and went back to work.

At sunset he dined with his brothers, according to their habit. They sat side by side in Aristodemus's private chamber, a table laid before them, while women poured water over their hands, dried them, then brought the dishes in: fresh bread; baked lentils with meat, mint, and coriander; dried vegetables in yogurt.

"He's very good," Aristodemus said. He studied the basket of bread. "The Arcadian Elawon, I mean. While you were going around planning the end of the world, I showed him our records. He understood the method immediately."

"Will he serve?" Temenus asked.

Aristodemus picked up a round of bread. "He talked about something they do in the east. Every time they borrow, they do it at a fixed rate of repayment, and something extra for the borrowing."

Kresphontes said, "When we repay, we always repay more. It's only honorable to add to the gift."

"But the addition is fixed. The rate is long decided. And it's the same for everyone, over the same time period."

Kresphontes looked puzzled. "You mean, whoever borrows from anyone, the repayment is controlled by the damos?"

"By the king's law. And this is interesting: if repayment takes longer, the rate is the same but the total is more. The rate is figured for the amount, but also over time."

Aristodemus paused. "That's what Elawon said." He lifted his bread as if to bite it, then lowered his hand to rest it on his knee. "Elawon said that here in Nafpaktos, more is going out than coming in."

Temenus said, "It's the hungry time."

"More has gone out than come in for the entire year, every season."

Temenus pushed lentils onto his bread and took a bite. "Is there pilferage?"

"Of course there is," Kresphontes told him tartly. "There's always pilferage." He let down the long whip of his black hair, twisted it around the fluted rod, and thrust the rod back through the resulting knot. He touched his palms together reverently, kissed the bead of unfired clay—the lot his brothers had drawn for him long ago and that hung from a thong on his wrist—and reached for bread.

"True, there's always pilferage," Aristodemus conceded. "But it's difficult to figure out how much."

"I've said many times that we need guards." Kresphontes took a whole round of bread and bit the edge with his bright, straight teeth.

"Using guards doesn't work," Aristodemus told him, "unless you can trust them more than the populace. We don't have enough Herakleids for that, and even they can be unreliable. Look at our head clerk." He rested a moment, his bread still on his knee. "Elawon said we should seal the doors."

Kresphontes raised an eyebrow. "Seal a whole building, like a treasury?" He tore off a new bite and started to chew.

"He'll lock the doors with his own seal. Then he'll know in the morning if anyone went in." Aristodemus picked a few crumbs from the edge of his bread and ate them.

Kresphontes said, "Everyone will go in. No one will want to go first, but once the door is open, the place will be stripped to the walls. Our cousin Koretoros will probably be the one to break the seal."

"Use *my* seal," Temenus suggested.

"Everything has your seal on it," Kresphontes reminded him. "Everyone is used to seeing it. It doesn't slow thievery, except from your treasury. And even there, only because it's in a public hall. Yet it didn't save Mother's wedding jewelry." He dipped his bread in the yogurt.

"We executed some Phocians for that theft," Temenus reminded him.

"But we never found the treasure. And the Phocians still dislike us for it. I would have preferred to keep them at least as contented neighbors, if not as allies."

They ate in silence. Temenus watched Aristodemus choose

lentils one by one and put them between his lips. When he finally began to chew, Temenus relaxed.

Aristodemus said, "I'll ask the Hunter to seal the doors."

Temenus said guardedly, "He probably doesn't have a seal."

"The priest can devise one," Aristodemus said. "If he seals something with his own hand, only a Dorian would dare break it. And the Dorians here have no need to: their own kings supply them with better quality than they could ever steal from us. And I doubt they'd break it at someone else's request."

Aristodemus glanced at Kresphontes. "Talk to the priest. He favors you. He'll tell you how we can do that."

"No! That thing shouldn't even be here. It's dangerous as it is. If you start giving it privileges . . ." He stood up. "It'll be the ruin of us all. Find some other way to protect your olives."

"I found one. Seal the door."

"It'll kill our luck if it stays here." Kresphontes turned to Temenus. "You have to get rid of it! Give it the last gifts you owe it, and send it away."

Temenus looked at him. "Have you been complaining about him to other people? Why else would the Aetolians care?"

"You put it in a house right next to theirs. *That's* why they care."

Aristodemus said, "Sit down. Elawon could be a real steward for us at last. If we put the outlaw—the Hunter—out, how long would Elawon stay? Sit down, I said."

"So don't put it out. Kill it." Kresphontes sat down.

"They seem to care for each other very little," Temenus observed.

"Still," Aristodemus said, "I don't want to risk losing Elawon. If it makes you feel less fretful, Kresphontes, call him a hostage instead of an outlaw."

"There are two kinds of hostages: those we hold for ransom,

and those we hold for security. It is neither. It isn't worth anything."

Aristodemus smiled. "If there's a third kind, trust Temenus to think of it."

"I won't go to the priest. I won't help you keep that outlaw here."

"We have to do something about the pilferage," Aristodemus said mildly. "Even if we get a very good harvest, we'll have barely enough to last the year." He tore a hunk of bread and trailed it through the yogurt, then regarded it thoughtfully.

"As more refugees come, how long will our food last?" Temenus asked. "Eat, please."

Aristodemus ate the bread.

Kresphontes was tearing his bread into little triangles and stabbing them, like knives, into the yogurt, one by one.

"How long will our food last if refugees keep coming?" Aristodemus said, then ate some lentils for Temenus's benefit. "I can't tell. Elawon could."

Temenus said, "That's the heart of the Aetolians's complaint, and the reason they wouldn't give us the timber they owe. The Dorians herd their most troublesome populations in this direction. The Phocians and the mountains slow them down, but then they go into Aetolia and Caria. I wrote Dymas today to complain again."

"Keep a copy of the letter for the records," said Aristodemus.

"I plan to—and hope the clerks don't lose it."

"We have more mouths to feed here every day," Aristodemus said. "And most of them now are families whose land rights no longer exist."

Kresphontes came out of his sulk. "And most of them also without a single fighting man. They bring nothing with them, build shelters out of trash, and whine for food. We should drive them out."

"No," Aristodemus said. "We Herakleids have been refugees

just like them. Do you remember Athens, and the Phocian tower? I do. If it weren't for Makhawis's mother, we might have starved. I won't turn away people who have lost their luck."

"The Carians are leaving," Temenus said.

"Again?" Aristodemus asked. "*All* of them?"

Kresphontes answered, "Not enough of them. The chiefs will go but leave their poor behind. You watch. Without anyone to lead them, they'll make trouble. And wail for food they aren't entitled to."

"They're leaving with the man Hippotes bashed into the wall," Temenus said. "He shouldn't have done that. I'm tired of excusing him, And paying for him."

Kresphontes' eyes flickered. "He's bad tempered over Makhawis. You should have left him his wife."

"I need her free, to marry her to someone better."

"You've spoiled her for years."

It was an old argument that no longer held Temenus's interest. "Get Xanos to make sure the Carians's house stays empty, will you? They'll come back eventually."

"We owe every goat and sheep to someone or other," Aristodemus said. "I can calculate which debts to pay off and which can wait. Elawon will help with that."

Kresphontes cocked an eyebrow. "You'll trust an outsider to know so much?"

"An Arcadian won't owe loyalty to anyone here but us, for taking him in. And he didn't bring a huge family to steal for."

Temenus mused, "We use the tools that come to us."

Aristodemus and Kresphontes exchanged a glance.

"Some olive butts cracked in the cold," Aristodemus said. "The fruit is moldy. We'll wash them in vinegar and give them to the poor."

"We have fine greens because of all the rain," Temenus said

absently. Little crisp stuffed pies were the only thing his wife cooked, but she cooked them well.

"And the city smells even worse for the running of everyone's bowels," Kresphontes said. "Families have been building their own ovens again."

Aristodemus noted, "There are too few ovens. A hundred women have to bake their families's dinners in the middle of the night."

"They use fire pots all the time, and we don't stop them. But ovens use too much wood and are harder to find. Xanos broke up three just today."

"Were the men angry?" Temenus asked. He spooned yogurt and lentils on bread and ate it, cocking an eyebrow at Aristodemus, asking him to do the same.

Aristodemus pushed a few scraps of meat onto his bread. "Men don't pay much attention to cooking," he said. "It's women who quarrel over oven time, wood, water . . ."

Kresphontes added, "And over those invisible lines that are always changing between garden plots. Men fight over trees and animals."

"And women."

As if on cue, two women brought in stewed fruit with honey. Temenus watched that Aristodemus took a share.

Aristodemus asked, "What do you plan for the next allcall? Is there anything I should know in advance?"

"I'll announce Elawon's position as our steward, if you want."

"Yes. That will give me a few days to be sure that he'll serve well. Then, if it's heard in allcall, the clerks will complain less. What else?"

"We'll discuss the augury again, and probably still come to no conclusion."

"Wheels, wheat, women, and a leader with three eyes." Kresphontes would never bring himself to openly criticize an oracle, but even he looked discontented.

They ate.

* * *

Kresphontes tried to will himself to stay away. For once, his discipline failed him. He watched his wife tuck the smallest of their children to her breast. Then she gave her silent smile of consent, and he padded softly out of the room. He wandered for a few minutes down random turns and passages, until chance brought him where he knew it must: to the megaron.

By the fading light drifting down from the wells in the roof, he could see the unwanted children, Makhawis's pets, in a corner, snuggled in pillows and blankets, playing some finger game. A few turned their heads, saw that it was only him, and returned to their play.

He saw the long shadows of the pillars, the uneven floor stones, the thyraic tiles of animal figures set into the wall, the three chairs together. The center chair, a little taller, was Temenus's, the king's.

Kresphontes had never sat in that chair. He did not even know a word for how wrong it would be. And yet . . .

If he were ever to sit there, the proportions of the room would align themselves more perfectly. He, Kresphontes Herakleides, would not be a man waiting year after year for the throne of a city he had never seen, in a land he could only imagine, while his life flowed past. He would be a king, with family, allies, friends, and rivals a web in his hands. He would know how to interweave them until every man's will was his own will, in a vast machine driven by *his* desires.

Soon, only days from now, that chair would be altered forever. A lion's skin, Herakles' emblem, would drape it. Not for

Kresphontes, but for Temenus. A confirmation for Temenus, and none but Temenus could sit on it.

The children stirred, looking toward the entrance. He also turned.

Two short, thin men with shaven heads, wearing black tunics, carried a large bundle between them. Seeing Kresphontes, the tanners stopped. He waved them in and they came, more slowly.

"Pardon us, my lord," the older one said. "We just want to check the fit of this—if it will need a separate backing."

Kresphontes stepped aside. Their distinctive smell—spoiled meat and dog shit—followed them faintly as they walked past him to Temenus's chair, where they opened the felt and unfolded the lion's skin.

As if handling some ordinary thing—a fleece, a woolen pad, a pillow—they laid the skin over the seat, up the back, along the arms, talking quietly to each other.

Kresphontes backed away from them, started to turn, then stopped. "Is it salted?"

The older tanner looked up at him. "Yes, my lord. Scraped and salted, but we haven't started the bating yet."

"When will you?"

"Tomorrow."

"And then it will be ready. . ."

"In ten days or twelve, depending on the weather."

"Does . . . does the king know it's here?"

"Not that I know of, my lord."

Kresphontes glanced at the entrance, at the children quietly matching and hooking fingers, at the chair, at the skin, at the two men waiting for him to speak.

"Leave it."

"My lord?"

"Will it spoil if you leave it here just one night?"

"No, my lord. We salted it."

"Leave it, then. Come back for it in the morning."

They didn't answer him, but simply folded the felt cover and took it with them out of the megaron, as if what they left behind had no importance. No value.

Kresphontes stood there a few moments longer. But the lion, waiting for its true master, said nothing to him. He left without looking back.

* * *

Penthilus's rooms, Tisamenus knew, were the cleanest and the warmest in all Mycenae, and his people served the best food. Sustenance, Philaios had promised, and here it was: plentiful, fresh hot fare with strong and unexpected spices, clean water cooled with ice, heart of wine.

Comfort, Philaios had promised, and here it was: firepots burning, polished floors gleaming, warm couches and covers, friends. Philaios toasted Tisamenus's homecoming as if he had returned in triumph.

By the bottom of the first cup, Tisamenus himself was beginning to wonder whether the rebuff that the guards had given him at the door to his father's room was perhaps a compliment he somehow misunderstood. By the bottom of the second cup, the time he had spent standing outside that door—clean, fragrant, humble, respectful, wearing all new clothes—only to be sent away without explanation by none other than Hawmai, seemed almost paltry.

Entertainment, Philaios had promised, and here it was: three hermaphrodite whores dancing, singing, having sex with each other, then with themselves—a startling feat, though not impossible.

By the bottom of the third cup, Tisamenus wanted to talk

about Akhaïdes, the outlaw he had won and lost. He wanted to describe the contrast of this bright, warm room full of cheery debauchery with the grim sanctuary of Delphi. He wanted to describe Akhaïdes crouched against the wall at Arne, dripping with rain and a murdered man's blood; sitting next to the hound at Tisamenus's feet; giving his face to the sun; kneeling, pleading with the priest; pressing a dagger to his own throat; slashing through Oxylus's shield and armor, then crying out with such pain that just the memory of it was agonizing; staring into the dark with tears tracking his face; whispering, "Please do this."

But Tisamenus could generate no words to bring up such as Akhaïdes here, even though many of the guests were his own Companions and might know or even remember parts of the story. Even Sigewas Teller, drinking less than most others and watching everything, seemed too remote to speak to about something so complex.

By the time Tisamenus left the party, his weariness and tipsiness required that Philaios escort him. At Tisamenus's private chamber, guards held the door while Philaios steered him inside. Then they closed it softly.

The room was empty of slaves. Only the white hound lay on a rug in a corner, barely flicking an eye to them. Tisamenus's wife awoke, tossed the covers aside, and rose, her hair a dark cloud, her gown tangled around her. She came toward them over torn and dusty rugs, but Philaios glared at her, and she backed away and retreated to a deep armchair, where she curled up, head on her knees, in a pose familiar from long habit.

Philaios undressed Tisamenus, eased him onto the mattress, turned him onto his belly. On his knees, he straddled Tisamenus's hips to rub his naked back.

"You're tired," he murmured. "So tired."

Tisamenus mumbled something into the pillow.

Philaios leaned over him. "What is it?"

"I met such a strange man."

"I know. Temenus Herakleides."

"Oh. No. Not him."

Philaios smoothed Tisamenus's hair back and kissed his cheek. "Who, then? Who else was there?"

Tisamenus did not answer, and they didn't speak again.

* * *

In the first part of the night, Makhawis woke as suddenly as if someone had called her name. But the room was dark and still. All her slaves and children slept placidly.

A dream, perhaps, though she had no memory of it. She rolled over and gathered the blanket tighter under her chin.

She thought of the Carian chieftain Hippotes had struck for daring to say aloud that Hippotes was no longer her master. The Carian had accepted without grace Hippotes' apology and Temenus's compensation, then continued to sulk until Temenus asked her to bathe him, to soothe his feelings. She had been glad to do so, as much to expel the memory of her last attempt to bathe a man as to mollify the Carian. He was fine looking, with large dark eyes and smooth skin. Elegant, attentive, well equipped to please a woman—and totally unable to do so with any of the women who tried until they had to give up, mostly from simple boredom.

Makhawis had made Temenus laugh aloud at the story. It was one of her better performances, but it had only put her out of sorts. And Temenus, although he had laughed, had seemed to hold back in a way he never had before, just as she had held back from him about the night she had Akhaïdes bathed. She had flounced back to her own rooms, scolded her slaves, drunk a whole cup of wine, and fallen asleep still furious. But now she was awake again, and she knew why.

It had nothing to do with the Carian. It had to do with Akhaïdes. Her women had told her how he stole out of the mountains, not like a hunter returning triumphant, but like someone returning from a shameful tryst. How he presented the broken spear to Dymas and Aristodemus, how he knelt with the lion skin in his arms and kissed Temenus's shoes, how Temenus patted his head as if praising a good dog, how people cheered him.

One slave had also described how baffled he seemed. Feral as a badger, recognizing only the horse. *He would have recognized me,* she mused, then crushed the thought instantly as both untrue and deadly dangerous.

A madman, the slaves murmured. Yet Makhawis remembered how meticulously he had not touched her. He had grasped the towel, her skirt, but laid not a fingertip on her flesh. Even in deadly rage, he had retained a core that thought and kept thinking. And even in her fear, she had seen this and so had dared tell him to let her go. And he had let her go, so his monster had turned on him.

She could imagine no heavier burden than this: to be mad and to know it.

* * *

Aristodemus's wife touched the back of her hand to her husband's forehead. The tension in his face eased a little. His breathing was hoarse tonight, raspy and hesitant, but he had no fever.

As she drew her hand away, he opened his eyes. He touched his dry lips with his tongue and said, "Woman."

"Are you in pain?"

"It's of no account. Go to sleep."

She sat up and laid her palm on his face. "I will when I'm ready to."

"Rebellious wench," he murmured. "Can't think why I put up with you."

"Says the stubborn old man who won't admit when he's ill."

"If I weren't ill, you'd make me so with your fussing." But he smiled against her hand.

"Do you want Temenus?"

"*Tsk*. Don't disturb him for me."

"He would want to know."

"Save me from that man's hunger to know everything about everyone." He drew a grating breath. "He was the right choice, you know. Were you disappointed?"

"Never. Why would I want you to be king, if fate says otherwise?"

"He's a good king, with what he has. I wish he could have better."

"Temenus is a singular man for singular times." She tilted her head. "The way you fuss over them still, and both grown men."

"Grandfathers."

"Soon enough."

"I want to see my own grandchildren."

"And so you shall."

His thin, creased eyelids closed. "Shall I?" he murmured, and slept again.

There was nothing she could do then, except what she did: lie down beside him and keep him warm until morning.

* * *

Hippotes came late into the big room where the Herakleid bachelors slept. His heavy tread, even on an earthen floor, woke more than one cousin as he crossed among them. He rolled out his bedding, pulled off his shoes, shirt, and leg wraps, and composed himself to sleep.

Satnios, Makhawis's second son, was one of those awakened.

So near his older cousin, he could not miss the scent of wine, sweat, and sex. He felt a moment's worry, then realized that his mother's perfume, olivewood and roses, was not detectable: Hippotes had relieved himself with someone else.

Even so, the last thing Satnios heard as he slid back into sleep was a half-whispered growl, "Hawi."

* * *

The skin lay over Temenus's chair, glowing in the megaron's lamplight. He walked across the empty room, past the usual small children sleeping in one corner, and approached with wary respect.

The fur looked thick, almost like a rich fleece that he might dig his fingers into. The mane, which lay against the chair back, where his head would rest, was dense, undulating, golden and bronze. The face, crushed flat, would stand just above his own head. His heart thumped at the thought. The forelegs lay along the arms of the chair. He would sit on the lion's haunches, the hind legs below his own and the tail between them nearly touching the floor, his own virility tacitly implied.

It couldn't be tanned already. Why was it here? Who had known how much he wanted to see it now, tonight, to touch it, to be sure it was real, to be sure it was really his?

He could not see, as he drew near, any sign of a wound, and he wondered how it had died. The company of men, an allcall, was where such a story should be told, but Akhaïdes would not be allowed to tell it. Perhaps it would never be told.

Temenus laid his open palms on the fur and half-closed his eyes. As the warmth of it filled his hands, the scent filled his head. He realized that he had been expecting what he smelled before: lion, deer, and Akhaïdes. Now the scent was pure, raw lion.

He touched one flattened paw, then stroked up the foreleg, over the shoulder, down the back. Untanned, it was stiff and springy, almost like a live animal rising to his caress. On the right side he found, closed with tiny stitches, five or six slices through the skin. He found, as well, a meticulously repaired slash, no longer than a child's finger, just under the edge of the mane. These wounds seemed almost laughably trivial. He laid his fingers on them each in turn. There went the spear, but these? These had to be made by that primitive stone-bladed dagger the outlaw carried.

Akhaïdes favored his left hand, the armorer had said. If these were marks of his dagger, they must have been made while he and the lion were face to face. Akhaïdes had stood or lain in the lion's arms to kill it. Utterly impossible. Yet here was proof.

Temenus had allowed this hunt knowing that a mighty deed could come of it. Yet the reality was still beyond his mind's grasp. Even Herakles had performed no such feat. Stories were told about the Nemean lion's huge size and ferocity, but that skin—undersize, moth-ravaged, nearly hairless—lay in Temenus's treasury. After reverently opening it for the first time, he had never been able to look at it again. He had never shown it to anyone. And now an outlaw, the lowest of the low, had done for Herakles' heir a feat that Herakles himself had not.

Temenus turned and sat.

The back and haunches responded like a good horse's might, giving way and then rising again to receive him. He fitted his hands to the paws, one to one, until fingers and claws were interlaced. Another man's hands would not fit, but his were so big, the match was perfect.

He did not know whether Akhaïdes would come to another allcall. If he came, he would crouch by the door, as impenetrable as stone, as ghost, as reflection on water. Even if not silenced by his outlawry, even if questioned directly, he would find a way to avoid speaking of this deed.

The only reward he would accept for himself might be for

Temenus to pretend it had never happened. And in that moment, Temenus realized why Akhaïdes had kissed his shoes.

He rested his head back against the lion's mane and sat there, thinking nothing at all.

* * *

When Tisamenus woke deep in the night, at first he didn't know where he was. Then he saw the shapes of the curtains overhead, the dim barred light from the shutters, and Kanatpa in her chair.

As if he had spoken aloud, although he had not even moved, the dog woke, stretched front and rear, and came to him and licked his shoulder. He stroked its ears. Then Kanatpa raised her head and looked at him across the dark, quiet space. For a moment, he feared that she might speak, but she just lowered her head again. The dog wandered back to its rug, circled, and curled up again, and Tisamenus eased back into sleep.

He slept and dreamed. He was a bird, a hawk, perched on a step in Alecto's chamber at Delphi, then rising, skimming out into sunlight, cold wind streaming through his wingtips. When he looked down, the shadow on the ground was not a bird's, but a man's. And not his own.

He was a child, a young boy, clinging with blue hands to the snow-crusted mane of a pony that staggered through deep snow. Dark woods around him, and cliffs to either side, rang with the hunting calls of wolves and men. The hands that held him on the horse's back were not those of his own faithful lawagetas, not his driver's, and not Aranare's—each of whom had saved his life in those terrible times. The hands were long and fine, scarred and broken, strong as bronze yet gentle enough to hold a baby without chafing it or making it cry.

He was High King but he stood before the High Seat, weighed down by the ancient cape of Pelops, looking up to where the rungs and then the seat itself almost vanished in cloud. He could never climb so high. Then he saw the ladder and the hands that held it. *"Take what I give you."* The accent was still evident, but the grammar was perfect. *"Take what's yours."*

He was himself, waking again in Mycenae, in the high, curtained bed where he was born. As he opened his eyes, he saw, suspended as if by magic above him, his beautiful white hound, curled upright in agony, hanging by a cord around its throat, dripping drop after slow drop of urine onto the bed where Tisamenus had slept. But he was not sleeping now, not at all, and the dog was still there.

* * *

What is it? that good girl Deione had nearly asked. As if such stories could be told in words. And if she should see what he saw? What would she ask then?

When he closed his eye, they started again: pictures that no one in these lands would comprehend. Walls without houses, towns without walls, forests with no end, fields of grass so vast they were navigable only by the stars.

Here were men, women, and children that Deione could never recognize as such, because of the strangeness of their ways and their faces. Here was snow as deep as a horse was tall; rivers frozen all the way down, the fish suspended like jewels within them.

Here were ordinary animals as fantastical as any peryton or gryphon, whole chains of rainbows flooding the earth with ochre, amber, purple, and blue; grass-green skies and wine-red waters; gold and gems and human scalps swinging from a horse's bridle.

Here were thievery, fearlessness, deceit, and murder.

Here was a woman to blame only for patience, a boy to blame

only for loyalty, a girl to blame only for love, a man to blame for every crime imaginable.

Here were children laughing with delight into the face of the monster that had spawned them and would kill them.

What is it?

He would not tell her, not that good girl with her wary, innocent care.

But if she liked, here was a riddle for her: *When is a man not a man?*

When he is that child-spawning monster.

When he is raised by goats, educated by savagery, trained by virtue, awakened by incest, disciplined by rape, honed by murder, freed by human sacrifice.

When he can set the one thing he loves down in a cage of bloody human ribs and walk away from it and never feel the loss.

Then you tell me, you good girl: *What is it?*

He rose quietly enough to not disturb Elawon, who snored softly an arm's reach away. He dressed without a lamp, then moved noiselessly through the room where Deione slept, up the passage, and out into the dark. The horse woke silently, accepted the bridle, backed out of the kitchen stall and walked with him, its head at his elbow, through the sleeping streets of Nafpaktos, down to the sea.

The moon was still new, but it lit the restless surface of the water in smooth daubs and hollows. It touched the hills to the south, showing their summits but not the road to reach them.

That was not Arcadia, not yet. Along the sea, the land belonged to Elis and its people, strangers to him. He would have to cross that land and find passes through those hills.

Then, when at last he saw the earth climb and break and climb again to those heights he knew so well, his heart would find its true rhythm: a bush's rustle, a spring's gurgle and a stream's rattle, a hawk's keening and a fox's bark, a tortoise's hiss, the scrape of a rock among a million others as it turned and slid underfoot, the wind.

There would also be silence: the patience of a jagged cleft in a shelf of limestone, far too narrow, it would seem, to hide three bodies for so many years. And the circling of perytons above that place, long-winged and silent, casting the shadows of men.

Menetor, the priest of Delphi, had said, "You will never see the land where you were born again."

"How will you stop me?" he had asked.

"You will stop yourself."

I will not.

Every horse could swim, but some didn't know that and would drown. This one? It had leapt into the sea below Delphi, but only to immediately lunge out again. Here it would swim or not. And so would he.

Someone was coming, nearly trotting, careless of noise. And someone else. Three people: two heavy, one light. If he started right now, he might be away by the time they got here.

When Xanos was close enough, Akhaïdes asked, "Can sharks eat a horse?'

"Given time." The lawagetas sounded winded. Good.

The Shaman, also a little breathless, said, "There are other things there as well. See?"

He looked. About halfway across, the random flashing of the water changed to a wider, more purposeful glide and shine.

"Your Serpent," he said. "On her own business."

"*Your* Serpent."

"Nothing to do with me."

"What did she tell you?"

You believe you are ready. You are not ready. You believe you have finished. You have not even begun.

"That I can go back."

"To Arcadia."

"Delphi."

"It's not in that direction. When?"

If you would have what you want, you must give me everything: not this cheap humility, but body, mind, hope, fear, and all the hunger that fed you for so long. Come back when this is done. Until then, do not come again.

And yet, there was never only one response to any riddle. All he need do to create a second response was walk forward. Then let happen whatever would happen.

Xanos said, "The better Elawon does his work, the more people will hate him."

A small hand—Deione's—crept under the horse's chin from the other side, toward the rein.

Don't.

---

i Gardner, John. *Grendel.* Alfred A Knopf, 1971.

ii *Jeremiah 29:18*

iii Dylan, Bob. "Bringing it All Back Home" Columbia Records, 1965

iv Lawrence, D H. "Last Words to Miriam" 1921

vi Tugwell, Albert, translator *Albert and Thomas, Selected Writings.* Paulist Press, 1988

vii Epictetus

viii Adams, Douglas. *The Long Dark Tea-Time of the Soul.* Pocket Books; Reissue edition, 1991

ix Ozick, Cynthia. *A Cynthia Ozick Reader.* Indiana University Press, 1996

x Cioran, Emil. *On the Height of Despair.* U Chicago Press, 1996

xi Bacon, Francis. *Prefaces and Prologues.* P.F. Collier & Son, 1909–14

xii Creeley, Robert. "The Rain" *Selected Poems of Robert Creeley.* University of California Press, 1991

xiii Du Boulay, Juliet. *Cosmos, Life, and Liturgy in a Greek Orthodox Village.* Denise Harvey, 2009

xiv Dostoyevsky, Fyodor. *Crime and Punishment.* Random House, 1956

xv Diaz, Junot. *The Brief Wondrous Life of Oscar Wao.* Riverhead, 2006